the blood of a butterfly

the blood of a butterfly

Cover design by robert porter. @transomproject

ISBN: 979-8-9875107-0-4 (Paperback)
ISBN: 979-8-9875107-1-1 (Epub)

harlanmichaelgarrett@protonmail.com
thebloodofabutterfly.com
first edition

Acknowledgements

Can't thank my sisters & brothers enough for their selfless assistance and generous contributions.

Ash and her puppet, Agnes, Salvatore, Spoon, Merv, Noellee, Becky, Kane, Regina, Bingo, Miss Elizabeth, Greg at The Wheel, Mr Green, Cowgirl, Parise, Sophie Structure, Claire Copy, SusyQ proof, SusanP, JP, Snatch, Carlos, Cuz JG, Uni Jean, Mosaic Kitchen, Chelska's Hair, the tree on Mount Washington that turned into lungs, the red wig, an abandoned apothecary cabinet, radios, TVs, homemade brooms that still have seed pods, magic trinkets & the dew-drop bucket.

For my mother, Janice
My father, Ronald
And my baby sister, Annemarie

1

"Liam! Phone!"

A bit wobbly as he spins around, Liam heaves the unwieldy bolts of burlap fabric off his shoulder and lets them timber-thwap onto a battered worktable, sending a swirl of dust spiraling towards the impossibly high ceiling.

As he twists and shimmies his way through the buzzing warehouse, he briefly entertains the notion of clocking out and going home for the day.

"Okay." Wearing a mock grin as he casually walks up to the office. "Who's calling this time —hookers from outer space?"

The supervisor looks a little pale, holding up the phone. "Cops."

Running down the street at a somewhat steady pace now, holding his ribs and winded, he spots the classy neon pink "Bun Busters Burgers" sign–replete with a half-naked waitress looking over her shoulder, hands glued to her ample backside.

There is a massive police presence covering a large area around the restaurant: SWAT, helicopters, armored vehicles.

Weaving his way through the crowd, and unwittingly initiating some really bad bump-intos, Liam heads towards the towering cop standing guard at the barriers.

He pulls out various IDs and squints in the harsh sunlight. "Officer Anderson called me. I'm a counselor for Health Services."

As he's being escorted up to the drive-through lane, he spots Anderson —shiny bald, neck looking a little more like a tree trunk than he remembered. The grimace on his face says that Liam's presence is already annoying him. They'd met a couple of times at domestic disturbance calls over the years. Nothing like this circus.

"Liam."

"Officer. How long has he been in there?"

"A little over ninety minutes. He has maybe ten hostages. There's also an injured uniform inside who he overwhelmed at the front door. What's the story on this nut-job?"

"Wait, why did you drag me out here? Where are the Feds?"

"On their way. We've got a jumper uptown, and an armed robbery across the river. Apparently it's psycho-dickhead day all over the city."

"How did you connect him to me?"

Anderson interrupts his constant scanning of the scene long enough to let out a sigh. "He was careful not to give us a good look on the cameras at first, but when he started shoving everyone into the bathroom, we got enough for a match. Then he cut most of the power. You popped up on his bio. You his shrink?"

"Counselor. Mark is one of my consults."

"Okay. And?"

"He was in Special Ops, two tours, North Africa, heavy stuff." Liam's looking around, still absorbing all the activity. "Severe PTSD, agoraphobic. I'm surprised he made it this far from his house. Under normal circumstances, I wouldn't be divulging—"

"What was his status, last you checked?"

"Increasingly paranoid, depressed. A little angrier lately."

"Plannin' on doin' anything about that, were ya?"

"Hey, I'm not the only one who's been seeing him on a regular basis. We were all trying to get him to go inside for a stint. He's mostly just been melancholy, seems fairly stable at times."

"This situation looks stable to you, Liam?"

"Jesus, fuck you, Anderson. Last time I saw him he was down, and cranky, not acting out. Did you ask him what he wants?"

"Nah, we're all just pissin' in the wind out here, hopin' for a cool drink of lemonade..."

"Alright. And?"

"Nothin'. He only went in there to shake everything up. No quid pro quo in his head as far as I can tell. Just a big 'fuck you' to the world."

"Great."

Anderson leans in. "We need to know what the hell's goin' on inside that building. What kind of fire power, how many hostages, the condition of our uniform..."

"Whoa. You want me to go in there? Bullshit, man."

"Those people are terrified, and in the thick of it right about now –and you know it. You know him."

"So your plan is to add one more terrified person into the mix? No way. Forget it."

"There are families in there, for God's sake. Kids."

Liam quickly wonders why adults are generally considered more expendable than children. He's always found *kids* to be twice as vicious as any Green Beret he's ever counseled.

"I know what's at stake. You shouldn't be asking me to do this."

Anderson's eyes are on fire.

Liam deflates. "Fah-uck, fuck me."

The pair trudge through the sea of heavily armed squadrons as vehicles are juggled, and snipers on the nearby rooftops readjust their positions.

"Hi, asshole! Can I take your order?" The drive-through speaker continues to crackle and pop.

Liam stops dead in his tracks. "Mark? Mark, it's Liam."

"Happy Tuesday."

"Are you okay?" Silence. "Mark?"

"Yeah." He sounds a million miles away.

Officer Anderson nods like a show horse.

"Mark, would it be alright if I come in? I'd like to talk to you in person, if that's possible?"

Low laughter.

"Mark?"

"Sure, just walk through the front doors, so when I blow your fucking head off chunks of your skull will stick to the windows, you little bitch!"

Liam looks at the ground. "Mark, I'm sorry. We shouldn't be here now."

"Pah!"

"I am sorry. Please."

After what seems like forever, Mark's voice comes over the speaker. "Back door, by the dumpster, just you. I can see everything. Don't fuck me."

Liam barely gets out a "Thank you" as Anderson takes him by the shoulder and starts barking orders into his walkie: "Clear all bodies from the back door. Adhere to a perimeter of thirty feet. Once you've reset, no one breathes. Repeat, nobody has the green light unless you hear from me. We need to get the negotiator inside."

"I'm not a negotiator."

"You are now, Liam. Firepower, hostages, uniform. Got it?"

"Yeah, I got it. Three hundred of you out here and this shit is up to me."

"It's your buddy's fault that we don't have a choice at this point. Tell it to him."

As the last few officers settle in place at the rear of the building, the only sound is the steady whir of helicopter blades.

Liam's rubber-legged as he approaches the slime-covered door. It cracks open an inch. Heart kicking in his chest, he moves a little closer. In one swift motion, a massive arm reaches out of the darkness and yanks him in by the hair as the door slams shut.

2

Mark tosses Liam to the floor. "Don't move." He wedges a deep fryer into the doorframe, grease sloshing over the sides, all while holding an AK-47 inches from Liam's face.

Mark's eyes are blackened and recessed under his overgrown blond hair. He's built like a monster, and has apparently decided to tackle this particular operation completely naked. The ink on his flesh is glowing. No prison or homemade tats on this soldier. Every one top shelf –deep, black, shiny.

Lying on the sticky floor, it hits Liam that instead of burgers and french fries, the place reeks of steamy, wilted lettuce. The succulent aroma of Bun Busters. "Mark, I…" He starts to sit up.

"Stay down and get your fucking clothes off!"

"Okay, okay." Liam begins to awkwardly undress, and Mark fires a short burst into the wall right next to him, sending a pellet of plaster into his eye.

Screams erupt from the bathroom.

"As if your ass depends on it, *Lee-umm*."

From outside: "We got fire! We got fire!"

Anderson, steady through a megaphone, "What's going on in there? What's with the shots?"

Mark throws Liam a drive-through headset. "Tell 'em you're okay."

Liam shakes violently as he tries to adjust the headpiece. "We're okay. Everything's fine." Mark snatches the headset back and drags a freshly naked Liam, again by the hair, to the front of the restaurant.

Desperately clinging to Mark's wrist. "Fuck, man."

Mark heaves him into the corner. "Shut up."

Amid the scattered debris on the floor is a child's doll, a high-heeled shoe, french fries. A couple of the video screens behind the counter are scrolling static. The walls are shot to hell. There is a thin blood trail leading up to the women's bathroom, where some chairs are stacked up high in front of the door to broadcast the maneuvers of any potential mutineers.

"Face down, Liam."

Liam obeys.

Mark checks the few video monitors that still have a feed and slaps a fresh magazine into the rifle. At a table near the front entrance, he loads what looks like the officer's pistol with fresh rounds, smooth, like a machine.

"Mark?"

He walks the perimeter without getting too close to the tinted windows.

"Mark, what made you leave the house?"

"Nothing made me."

"How do you feel?"

"Fuck. I don't know." Eyebrows up. "Hungry." Walking over to the grill where a few burgers have been left to shrivel, he shoves a couple in his mouth. Chomping them up. "Pretty good shit."

"Can I sit up? Please?"

Through a mouthful of greasy meat, "Slow." Releveling the gun at Liam.

Liam's hand slips in some blood as he tries to prop his back up against the wall. "So, other than the cop?"

"They're all fine. They're taking care of his wound."

"You shot him?"

Burp. "He wasn't obeying commands."

"Can I tell them that everyone else is okay?" Mark is just staring into space, mindlessly eating another patty off the grill. "Mark?"

He tosses Liam the headset.

Deep breath. "All hostages okay. The officer is the only wounded, and he is…ssstable."

Anderson, again through the bullhorn: "How stable?"

With a gawky grin, staring at his reflection in a grease bucket by the back wall, Mark raises his hand and wiggles it. "Hand shot. Light bleeding. He's fucking fine."

Liam looks at the blood on the floor, then relays the news. "Hand shot. Minimal damage."

Anderson: "How many hostages?"

Wandering through the kitchen, Mark randomly turns knobs and hits buttons. "Twelve, including lefty."

Liam: "Twelve."

"You've got three minutes in there. Count on that." The megaphone squeals for emphasis.

"Mark, I'm sorry, this so sucks. My god, this—"

"Stop it." Pointing out the window, "This mess is their fault. All of it. Fuck…" He drifts away again, playing drums with the spatulas, tossing the gloves like frisbees.

"I guess I do know that on some… level and… so do they. They must. Half of those guys out there served. You know that, right?"

Wide smile, "They know exactly fucking nothing. And you can shut up now." Pointing the rifle.

Sobs from a little girl in the bathroom trickle into the room. "Please, God. Please, God. Please don't kill us." She's getting hysterical. There are muffled sounds of adults trying to calm her, but she gets even louder "Please, please, please!"

Mark yells, "Keep her quiet in there! Quiet!" The sobs and murmurs fade.

The variety of packaging and nuke trays are becoming an endless source of fascination. Short little laughs pop out of him, as if he's uncovering hidden secrets. "You ever eat any of this garbage?" Mark holds up a gnarly black french fry.

"I try not to, but yeah, it serves a purpose, I guess?"

"I never did, but I gotta tell ya…" He pops the crusty fry in his mouth. "I'm becoming a big fan, y'know? S'pose it can't be helped, this lust we have for crap. Dumb animals, seriously stupid critters, boy. Fast food, fast cars, fast tracks, fast whacks… shove 'em in the grinder, pull 'em out the side. In. Out. Done. God damn pretenders. Frauds. They hold all the cards, and they blow it –every fuckin' time. Idiots. Ka-booooom!"

From outside: "You've got one minute."

"Ha! See what I mean? We better move fast, Liam, or we're screwed!" Shaking his head, "What a pack of pussies. Little toy tanks n' shit. *You've got one minute.'* Oh, okay."

Liam stares at the floor. The little girl continues to cry quietly in the bathroom.

"Mark, why don't you let them go? You've got me and…"

"Fuck no, asshole." Scratching himself, Mark looks up at the ceiling. All the rigidity leaves his body. His voice is soft now. "Stupid… critters… animals…animals… " Then he snaps himself straight upright. "Ah!"

Liam jumps.

"Alright. Get up. We're goin' for a walk."

"Can I tell them we're coming out?"

"Tell 'em whatever you want. Up." He motions with the AK.

Liam grabs the headset and, with some effort, pulls himself up. "We're coming out."

Anderson, robotic through the megaphone: "Unarmed, hands in the air."

Mark grabs Liam by the back of the neck hard enough to jolt the headset out of his hands. Pushing him forward, they shuffle through the debris on the floor and make their way towards the front entrance.

Liam tries to look over his shoulder, as much as he can. "Mark, the gun?"

Mark peers out at the mass of uniforms and armament that surround the building. Still holding Liam by the scruff, he casually sets down the rifle. Liam audibly exhales.

"Jesus. SWAT teams. Whirly birds. What would these clowns do if they ever had a real problem? Christ, it's just me and my dick."

As the pair reach the entranceway, Mark silently lifts up the officer's pistol and puts it behind his back. Liam, still in front at arms-length, stares up at a helicopter while barely pushing open the door.

The two nude men tentatively step out into blinding sunlight.

"Hands! We need to see hands now!"

Liam abruptly raises his hands as Mark lets go of him and lifts one arm. Hyperventilating a bit. "We're almost home, Mark. Almost."

"Hands, we need to see hands!"

Liam turns to see Mark pulling the pistol out from behind his back. He points it up in the air, loosely waving it around and doing a bouncy jig, lifting his knees high, giggling uncontrollably.

"Gun, gun, gun!" Coming from the hordes of police: "Drop it! Drop it now!"

The snipers hear Anderson in their earpieces, quiet but urgent. "Rooftop six, move the hostage."

"Mark…" Liam spins to face the police. "No, no, no, it's okay, don't fire!"

In that instant, Liam is shot in the shoulder by a sniper and drops to the ground.

Multiple voices stream over the walkies. "Hostage is clear. Fire! Fire! Fire!"

An avalanche of bullets thunders down on Mark from all directions.

Liam curls into a fetal position, screaming. His hearing fades into a loud ringing that makes his eyes feel as if they're going to shatter.

Mark finally falls. Still holding the gun, his head smacks off the pavement a few feet away from Liam's face, blood plopping out of his mouth. His body is now a lifeless sandbag of smoking wounds that continues to absorb multiple rounds as he bleeds out in the relentless midday sun.

3

In a cave high up in the misty mountains, a lost soul huddles next to a small fire.

The wind picks up and a rolling carpet of fog outside begins to swirl, occasionally revealing an endless sprawl of evergreens below. The first few snowflakes quickly morph into a blinding squall. One delicious deep breath, and she rises. Moving with measured deliberation towards the rocky opening, she embraces the reality that she is quite exposed.

A sudden gust or turbulence could strip her of this shelter and immerse her in the tumult. Yet there she stands. On the edge of a blizzard. Arms extended. Barely touching the storm. No boundaries in this moment. Only wonder. Nothing will ever be the same in this river of time, in the middle of such strong current. Preservation is grounding. But inevitably, the radical cravings swim out of the darkness. Emerging from hidden depths where only moments ago it seemed no light would find them. Their feathery touches command the spirit, and point our reluctant noses towards the east. Towards home.

The shackles of duty have been shattered and cast aside. She is inextricably tangled in the purity of collision. Never too far from the fire, yet drinking in wave after wave of falling snow.

Abby's journal: 'vacation visions n' such', or, 'the day I decided to squat and piss on all that corporate bullshit.'

4

"Hey, no problem, just go right ahead and cut me off! If you fuck like you drive, I feel sorry for your old lady, pal!"

Even though the insults being hurled at other motorists are quite colorful, this cab driver generally has the personality of a stick. Abby had given up on any jolly banter ten blocks ago, but as he continues to rant at people out the driver's side window, she's decided that she wants that radio. A white Sony mini-transistor, precariously dangling from the rearview mirror. Looks like it's in great shape. Luscious sounds radiating from the tiny speaker. It needs a better home.

"Excuse me, is that your radio?"

"My cab, my radio."

"Right. Any chance you'd wanna sell?"

"No."

She pulls a twenty out of her pocket and puts it over his shoulder. With a disgusted look, the driver snatches the crinkled bill from her hand.

Leaning up over the seat, she untangles her prize from the mirror. "Thanks."

He, of course, says nothing. And at the next red light, bounces back and forth between examining the twenty and curling up his nose at her, as if she smells of raw sewage. "This is all screwed up now," trying to readjust the mirror.

Taking in her new neighborhood through the light rain, she's quite pleased. Lots of activity, but not a mob scene. The block is run down around the edges, which is fine with her. On final approach in the herk-n-jerk taxi, Abby can see that the Lexington Arms is undoubtedly a place that once was. At least it's not plastic.

After tipping more than she should have for such a crap ride, she ducks out into what is now a heavy downpour. "Damn it." Barely hoisting the first duffle-bag out of the trunk with a huff, she leans around the car. "Hey, can you please help me with this other one?"

The driver flicks his cigarette butt far out into the street and rolls up the window.

"Thanks a lot!"

A tall book-ish-looking man in a burgundy uniform trots out of the building. "Here we go, Miss. I'll get that." He hands her his umbrella and grabs the bags as they make a dash for the long awning that connects the lobby to the sidewalk. Coaxing her to stay in motion, "Bring her all the way in, young lady. The cover is no help in this soup, I'm afraid."

They cross the threshold and stomp their feet, shaking off the weather. Abby is taken by the classic deco feel of the place –little hexagonal tiles on the floor of the entranceway that make out a large 'L', accordion angles of faded black-and-white paint on the high walls, patinaed copper ceiling.

The large, friendly man gently sets down his load, and extends his hand. "Reg."

"Abby," with a sigh of relief.

He seems giddy to be wringing the water out of his silver beard. After that cab ride, he may as well be Santa Claus.

"Maintenance?"

"Yes."

"Ah, we've been hearing. Welcome to the Lex."

"Thanks."

"No idea where Batts is." He twists around.

"Is Mr Batts cool?"

Reg nods his head like "yes", then quite emphatically says "No."

"Aces."

"Here, I'll show you to your apartment…"

Batts waddles in from out of nowhere. "Go show yourself the sidewalk. Do your job." With the frame of a melting snowman, he looks to be a biscuit away from three hundred pounds. Winded, thin greasy hair, psychotically uneven stubble –the Anti-Santa Claus.

Reg mock salutes Batts with a middle finger. "Nice meeting you, Abby. Let me know if you need anything, K?"

"I will. Thanks, Reg."

"Okay, okay, hi honey. I'm Mr Batts," with more than a little forced sunshine. He shakes her hand and touches her shoulder, lingering a moment too long.

"Abby."

She hadn't noticed until the handshake that he's wearing white gloves. Doesn't quite match the rest of the pee-pa get-up, but she's happy to have a barrier between herself and this one.

"Hell of a day, huh? Fucking weather." He shuffles away, leaving her to struggle with the baggage. "This way, elevators are down."

She follows him up a narrow stairwell to the fourth floor, adrenaline pushing her all the way.

The ceiling in the long hallway is awash with soft light floating through the transom windows. These transoms were made in the classic style, glass tilting inward from the bottom, directly over the doors. Most look to have original parts, but it's quite a mix with the newer, shiny replacement bolts and levers sticking out like sore thumbs compared to the old brass.

"I like the transoms."

He tries to catch his breath, nose hairs in play. "Pain in the ass. We'll see how much you like 'em a month from now." He jams a key into apartment 414. "Okay, this is you. Oh, here, let me get those," grabbing the duffle bags and dragging them into the room.

"Thanks." Abby looks around at the small efficiency: stove and fridge, dresser, a decent desk, old radiator, a single bed that looks more like a cot. But it's clean, and at this point she really doesn't need much else. Good enough for now.

Batts tilts his head and sniffs the air a couple of times, seems involuntary. "You'll have longer shifts and shorter shifts, no set hours, one day off a week, one weekend off a month." He's shaking his hands at her T-Rex style as he ticks down the list. "You can work out the schedule with JT. She's the other handy. Well, I think she's a 'she', know what I mean? Bit of a bitch, but she's a worker. Does mostly light plumbing and electric, stuff that I don't have to call in a pro for. And just so you know, sweetie, I don't want to have to call in anybody, for anything, ever. The frikken building has to be falling down first. You got that?"

She nods, and walks around the room, running her fingers over the appliances, counters, chipped paint on the cabinets. His voice drifts in and out, sometimes just sounding like grunts. "You'll mostly be on rehab assignments, prep for new tenants, transom repair –long list of those. JT also handles some landscaping. You might have to help her with that, make supply runs. You'll be painting a few times a month…" He gives her stink-eye as she pulls up the blind on her only window. The view is of a brick wall that's close enough to touch. Fine. Perfect in some ways, actually. She needs to focus on her artwork.

In the current light, she can see her reflection in the window quite clearly, and her formerly reasonable hair has gone completely electric-shock afro. She's too tired to care at this point.

Batts's voice drifts back into focus: "I have three other buildings to look after, so you won't be seeing me much…"

She perks up. "Oh?"

"But if you need something, ask Reg. He knows my schedule better than I do. You're technically on call twenty-four/seven unless it's an off-day, but this place is pretty quiet –mostly elderly, a few students. Christ, some of these kumquats are shut-ins for all I know, I never see 'em. As long as they're paid up, I could give a shit. Where was I… oh yeah, most of the supplies are in the basement…"

"I have some of my own tools, too."

"Yah, okay. Well, you'll meet JT out front tomorrow, seven am –sharp."

Abby abruptly sneezes and Batts backs all the way to the doorframe. "If you need anything, anything at all, Abby," lower, softer tone, "you just let me know, huh?"

She sneezes again and he bails, slamming the door.

"Okay! Thank you!"

She harrumphs down on the squeaky bed and lies back. The cracks on the ceiling form faces that fade in and out of the dim light, sketchbook patterns that point to the transom above the door. After digging out a pack of cookies from one of the bags and munching a handful, she grabs the lonely wooden chair and drags it over to take a closer look.

Carefully climbing up, she sees that it's a little rough around the edges, but it appears to be fully functional. Her fingers glide over the frame, the chain; she gently taps the beveled glass.

A limber, hurried man appears around the corner in the hallway and Abby leans way back. Red-faced with his right arm in a sling, he settles in by a large window at the end of the hall, shoulders slumped, framed by pouring rain. Were his eyes blue? He shuffled by too fast to really see. Big nose, character, straight black hair. At first blush, she was thinking Mediterranean, but something is telling her that he's Irish.

After a silent climb-down, Abby decides to prioritize her inventory.

Alright, how many cookies do I have left? And where's the newest member of the broadcast family?

Fishing out the transistor she bought from the cabbie, she dials in a clear station. Salsa. Not bad. "We'll call you Pearl. Meet the fambly." One by one, Abby retrieves eight other little transistor radios out of the first bag, leaving it half-empty. She lines them up on the bed as if they're soldiers standing at attention. A militant rainbow of aural love.

5

The next morning is cold and grey in the city as Liam enters the Lexington Arms. His mind is flicking through a dozen things when he ducks into the stairwell and narrowly misses giving a full bodycheck to a striking young lady.

"Whoa, daddy!"

"Eesh, sorry, I was…" With a half-smile, he reaches out to shake her hand. "Liam."

"Abby."

"Maintenance?"

She taps her tool belt. "Yeah, you can go ahead and save that money for detective school."

"Right, well, welcome to the party."

"Thanks."

He starts up the steps. "If you need anything, don't hesitate. I'm in 404."

"414." Awkward moment as she stares at the sling on his arm.

"Nice meeting you, Abby." He takes the stairs two at a time.

"You, too." *Whatever you just said your name was three seconds ago. Damn it. How about memory school, Ab.*

Inside his apartment, Liam pulls down the blinds, takes off his sling, and flops on the bed. The phone rings, and before he can say hello—

"Liam?" He can tell she's been crying.

"Lisa. Hello."

"Is that all you have to say? Well? Is it?"

"Look, I'm sorry it didn't work out."

"For who, Liam? Didn't work out for who?"

"I'm not going through this again. I've found someone else."

"Sure you have. You never could lie worth a shit."

"I don't know what else to say. I'm sorry."

"Don't be. Because nothing is over. Nothing, you fucking creep!"

"Lisa, don't do this."

"I'll do whatever the fuck I want."

"I told you before, don't contact me again."

He hangs up and paces back and forth in the dim space.

Beanie's is technically a coffee shop, but still resembles the neighborhood diner it was for so many years —fashionably warped counter, squeaky stools. The tables are too small for anyone but children and waifs. Abby and JT squeeze into a booth by the huge front window.

JT takes off her spiked leather jacket and black wool hat, revealing a sleeveless black shirt that reads, *Lick Me*. Translucent skin. No make-up other than raccoon eyeliner. Ratty jet-black hair. And even though she has a compact frame, she looks tough enough to walk through the park alone at night, but smart enough not to.

Abby watches the baristas buzzing around behind the counter. "Batts sure is a creepy crawler."

"No shit."

"How do you deal with that?"

"I haven't always been great at it. My mind wanders; sometimes he catches me off-guard."

"Wait, he never—"

"No, he'd be dead. If he gets close just cough, sneeze, make it phlegmy. He's a germophobe."

"Ah. Explains the gloves."

JT's looking around, shifting in her seat. "Yeah, he's just missing the clown nose and a chainsaw. If that shit doesn't work, tell him you have a ragin' rag, he'll disappear for a week. Let's get the java to go. Wanna show you something cool in the alley."

In the very trashed, very tight alleyway, JT sparks a joint and hands it off. Abby, in turn, takes a deep hit. "Thanks. Been awhile for a wake n' bake."

"Always somethin' cookin' in my kitchen. So. I've got some of the grounds covered, fucking hedges. He brings in people to cut the grass. I work with the furnaces and AC. You'll have some light cleaning; he has a service for some of that stuff, too, like the floors, n' whatever, but it's hit and miss. You'll do rehab, prep for the newbies. I'm sure Batts already went over some of this. Technically I'm supposed to have the green roof, too."

"Green roof? On that building?"

"Well, it's more like a green experiment, a glorified gutter-garden. And with freezin' season comin', I'm not going to have time to mess with all that. Not sure why he's so obsessed with it. He's pretty much afraid to go up there. I think he mentions it to the younger tenants as a selling point. And I do dig it. But my chores in the basement double when the weather turns. Like overnight. So she is already in need of some lovin'. I can pick it back up in the spring, but right now, I've got to put in way too much time with the hundred-year-old furnaces –the ones that he's too fuckin' cheap to properly repair. If the pipes freeze, we're all in trouble."

"What grows up there in the winter?"

"Sometimes nothing, which would make your life fairly easy. But there are a couple little greenhouses that have managed to keep the hardy nubs and perennials at least spring-ready when the time comes. A few solar panel-space heaters that, well, mostly work. Rain barrels, we use some of that water in season for other landscaping around the building." Taking a pronounced breath, "You don't have to, but I was hoping you'd take it off my hands for the winter. In case he asks, I can say you're on it, et cetera. It's not a bad escape from lumpy tenants and Mister Jazz Hands. What say you?"

"Sure. I'm in."

"Cool." JT holds out the joint.

"No, I'm toasty. Have to pretend I care here in a minute."

"Soooo, what's your story, Abby?"

"Oh, nothing too exciting."

"Nice hair."

"Fuck you. It's humid as shit, man."

"Um, no it's not? And I was being serious, kitty-kat, damn. Can I touch it?"

Uh-oh. "Sure. I guess so."

JT reaches over and gently squeezes little puffs of Abby's voluminous afro, making her way around to the back of her head. "Very cool. Fun."

Wow, she has a nice touch. "Sometimes it mutates into frikken tentacle hair."

"Different ain't bad."

"Heredity."

"Usually how it works."

"Yeah, so… Dad was black; Mom is kind of a hodgepodge: Welsh, Nordic, some Native American in her…"

JT holds in a hit. "Pretty sweet. Some of my best friends are Native American, dude."

"Riiight, and my mom's hair, well, kind of presents as sci-fi ramen. So most days I feel like all of the possible combinations in the human genome are seeking some kind of cosmic revenge on the universe… through my scalp."

"You said, 'Dad *was* black'? What's he now, blue?"

"Not sure. He was long gone before I knew that some people had dads."

"Oof. Deadbeat?"

"Nope. Opposite. According to Mom, he was all in, the perfect guy in every way. But for some unknown reason, she turned on him. Hard. Bad…Ugly."

"Yikes."

"Sorry, I'm just, rambling…" Am I this buzzed already?

"No no, go, fire away. It's fine."

"Apparently, it was a shit show. Got to the point where she kept kicking the poor guy out for no good reason."

"Could have been post-partum."

"Hard to tell… She's always been very fair with me, though. I honestly don't know that I've ever seen her cop an attitude with anyone. Always bouncin' around, all holly-jolly. Not that she isn't formidable." Okay, I'm an idiot. Verdict is in –babbly-brook-babbles river-rock stony-stoned. Fuck. First day of work, and I'm higher than giraffe booty.

"Damn. Sorry to hear all that, Ab. Then, no contact since he left? Nothing?"

"No. I guess he never looked back. But, there is this, well, Annalise—"

"Wha, Annalise?"

"Yeah, that's my mom's name."

"Oh, cool. Love it. Proceed."

"Sooo, yeah. Annalise, Mom, is way out of the closet these days. Sticks with hyper-intellectual, superiority-complexed females. Maybe she felt that Dad was holding her back on that level. I don't know. I'm fishing in the Freud pond there, I guess. Just a theory."

JT is definitely screening her. "Understood. What about you?"

"Hetero mostly, I think."

"Ha! No shit, girl. I meant your pop, do you want to see him?"

"It's not a burning desire. How do you miss what you've never really had? Maybe we're both better off. What's your deal?"

Roaching the joint, "I'm a cougar chaser, baby. Took a gig in a grocery store once just to follow them around, up and down the aisles. All damn day. Hot Mommies. I was pickin' up extra shifts for that action."

Coffee shoots out of Abby's nose. "Fuck, I just spit that shit out of my nose."

"Jesus killer, here," JT pulls out some napkins, "you're a mess. So yeah, one of my favorite particulars was to get them to reach way up for items to help me price check… *I am so sorry to bug you, but my manager is killing me today. Could you grab one of those chamomile teas on the top shelf so I can verify the list price? I can't reach that high.*' And then –wham! All stretched out, tippy-toed in them high heels, skirts bunched up, like Thanksgiving dinner yo – biscuits, gravy, jello-mold jigglin' all around—"

"JT… JT, thanks for the stalker-vision, but I meant your family. What about your mom, dad, brothers, and sisters? Do you have any kids?"

"Oh! Sorry. Nope."

"No one? At all?"

"Zero."

"Okay. Nationality?"

"Someone told me Hunky-Slovak, or something, at one point. I think they just said it to shut me up."

"What does JT stand for?"

"Juicy Trouble. Jesus Tricks. Just Tools. Jaunting Tramp."

"They all sound like punk bands."

"I'll go with that." JT puts the roach in a little baggie and gives it to Abby. "Here. Late night snack."

"Oh, um, yeah. Thanks. I've got a small stash, but I love mixin' n' matchin'. Cool." Her eyes involuntarily cross for a second as the baggie, and the morning, become a bit fuzzy.

6

A few pigeons drift in and settle towards the opening of the alley near the main street. They zigzag their way towards the pair, not so inconspicuously, pecking along the way.

Abby rolls her head around and stretches her neck, her gaze landing on the new guests. She takes a couple of tentative steps their way, which stops their progression momentarily. Then she stomps towards them aggressively. Her words come out in rhythm with each step: "Move, little vermin. Go on."

They only half-listen.

JT is checking out some of the graffiti by an old rusty door and shaking her head as if the culprit was either wasting their time, or had made some sort of unacceptable error in their execution. "Sooo, Abby... last question... was it always your dream to be doing maintenance in a shit building in a shit part of the city?"

"Weeelll, I—"

"I mean, by the looks of those Barbie-plays-handy-girl tools that haven't been touched, and that delicate skin, I'm guessin' this is what the gentry would call a relatively new hobby?"

"Hey! These hands aren't so delicate. I hit the heavy bag on occasion. Ardy's Gym. Fuck that shit up. And I'm an artist."

"Hm. Ever sell anything?"

"Nope."

"Impressive."

"The only thing I really give a crap about is chasing ideas. But I can't draw to save my life..."

"Hasn't sold anything, can't draw... I'm tracking, proceed."

"So I work in lots of other mediums. I write, take pictures, like everybody else. 'To the exclusion of all others' isn't a phrase that exists in my world. I like bouncing around. I can focus, but I can't sit still. I'm working on something with little transistor radios right now. Not quite sure what they want to be yet, but it all beats the shit out of what I was doing in my old life."

"I'll take a wild guess that there was money attached to this so-called 'old life', though. Correct?"

"Some, but—"

"Then I don't understand. Why would you walk away from a cabbage patch for this?"

"I couldn't handle the stress anymore, the asshole factor. And I was an asshole for sticking around past my giving-a-shit point. My clients could smell it, my alacrity turning to sand. Some people thrive on that stuff, all the manufactured drama. 'Just play the game', my mom would say. Felt phony. I was putting in seventy hours a week. Sometimes eighty or more."

"How many hours are in a week?"

"Not much more than eighty."

"Ah."

"In the end, I've just traded one stress for another, though. The odd-job stuff is cool, but to your point, I'm broke as a joke. Debts. Mom is on my ass. I'm not going back, though. No way."

"Mom is on your ass, huh? Wait until you get an earful from Batts. You'll wish you were nose-deep in the books of some global conglomerate."

"When I hear someone say, 'conference call', I throw up a little bit in the back of my throat. Truly, I'll pass. What about you?"

"Here for now. Been four years. Batts is a dick, but I have a lot of autonomy. And I'm an artist in my own way, I suppose."

"Medium?"

JT is still sizing her up. There's a long pause as she looks around the alley, starry-eyed, half-smile. "I lighten the loads of wayward travelers."

"Thief?"

"Nothing obvious. The more obscure, the better."

"Example."

"Tool belt feel light there, Abriella?"

Abby reaches around, and the hammer and a couple of other things are missing. "You bitch!"

Exhibiting the moves of an exotic dancer, JT proudly produces several large items she'd lifted. Last out is a hefty steel file that she magically culls from her ripped-up work pants.

"When? How?"

"Wrong questions. 'Why?' is far more intriguing."

Abby's defeated. "Welcome to the jungle?"

"We may never really know. Normally I'd've let you sweat it out a bit, but I'm too stoned."

"Best keep your hands off my stuff, missy."

"You're not my type, hon."

They both give in to a laugh.

"I have to admit, I dig the building so far." Abby tries to act as if she knows where all the tools go back on the belt.

"Yeah, man. Some of the deco stuff is fun. Overall, it's cavernous, dark, dank. Sure, it has its glorious imperfections."

"Too bad Batts is such a…"

"Sweaty sack of scrotum puss? Sad hand of fate, Ab."

"Okay, I'm off to see the wizard. Means, *I gotta pee*."

"Clever."

"Thanks for the orientation."

"Yep."

Abby starts walking towards the end of the alley as JT leans against the brick wall and lights another tube.

Lining up behind a dumpster, Abby drops her pants slick fast, and urinates on the uphill part of a slight downhill slope, golden streams finding their paths of least resistance.

She gets herself together and trots away on the balls of her feet. A little swirly, she barks over her shoulder as she rounds the corner, "See you back there. I'm gonna go grab some gloves. Be good now."

JT lets out a huge hit. "Bullshit."

7

Paul's apartment faces south and gets great light compared to many of the sealed catacombs in the Lexington Arms. Other than the obstruction of a fire escape outside one of the larger windows, it sits up high enough to get some kind of a city view. There's a hulking, claw-foot bathtub that is situated more or less in the middle of the floor in the front room. He's dusting off a couple of small, old-school TVs when Liam knocks on the door.

"Hey, Paul, it's me."

Without missing a beat, Paul tosses the feather duster and crosses into the kitchen area. He fills a plant sprinkler with water; harsh streams sputter from the weathered faucet. "Enter at your own risk."

Liam comes in carrying a small bag of groceries, and notices right away that Paul looks a little pale. He had always sported something of a flat-top haircut, although lately, he's getting closer and closer to just shaving it down to the skin. Maybe he doesn't like that it's gone completely grey.

Plenty warm in the apartment, but Paul's wearing a long-sleeve turtleneck.

"So, what have I been missing in here? What shakes?"

Paul waters the quite healthy aloe plants by the far window. "Oh, that would be my soul, shuddering in the presence of your perpetually shrinking vocabulary."

"Well, it's still large enough to parlay with the grocers so they can help me dig up some of these bizarro eats, sir." Liam ditches his backpack and coat, then methodically empties the brown paper bag, staring at each item as if it were purely alien.

Paul, disinterested, sets down the sprinkler and retrieves a small-ish box. "Did you know homosexuality is found in all animal species, to one degree or another?"

Liam lowers his eyes and rolls his head. "That's because it's perfectly natural."

"But it is always in the minority, never the majority."

"You mean like agoraphobia?"

"Such a clever child. Agoraphobic tendencies aside…" He unpacks the box slowly and methodically. "… animals need to reproduce to endure in the long run."

"Parthenogenesis. How's that for vocabulary?"

"Oh good Christ, Liam."

"Virgin births. Also happens in a large spectrum of the animal kingdom."

"What? Insects? Lizards? Snakes? As usual, you are amusing, yet hollow and futile."

"Play nice, or I'll take back your jackfruit." He enumerates the groceries. "Jackfruit? Ceylon cinnamon? Thai chili? Crab meat? Hope your toilet's working."

"Unlike most of the rest of the building, it appears to be somewhat functional."

"Who eats this crap?"

"The dying and the destitute."

"Holy drama. How are you feeling?"

"Like an angry pile of excrement." Paul wriggles the small classic Magnavox TV out of the cardboard and plugs it in. "But, per your venerate advice, I've been quite the enterprising cave dweller."

"Another TV?" Liam tries not to nod as he counts them all.

Paul gestures around the room at the other sets. "My only true friends."

"Thanks a lot."

"I surf for remote signals late at night. I get the least amount of interference during those hours in which the rest of the world lazily slumbers, allowing for ceaseless exploration."

"Well, the antennas are big enough."

"Is that a sexual threat?" Wagging his finger. "How are you able to manage in the warehouse with one arm?"

"Just about done with this thing. Been almost three months. I usually don't wear it at work."

"How assiduous."

"Okay. I'll be back soon to check on you."

"Again, with the threats. Well…" He vigorously rubs his hands together then claps. "What do I owe you for the supposedly nutritious items?"

"Hit me next time." Liam bundles up. "Gotta hustle."

"Fair enough. But a thank you is in order. How about some aloe as a parting gift?"

"Still have some from that last batch you gave me. Good stuff."

"You know, you're always in a state of transit. You're never truly at peace, young man."

"Well, you seem to be at peace on the surface, but you don't even have a fuckin' chair in here? And when did you get rid of the bed? You sleepin' in the tub? Is that peaceful?"

Paul rotates the channel-changer dial on the TV as if he's trying to crack a safe. "My parents didn't have any chairs until they immigrated to the States. And they both lived into their nineties."

"C'mon, man, they had za-bu-tons, or tamamis, right?"

"Ta-TAH-mi, Liam. Goodness. They'd slice you up in Tokyo for such a sloppy insult."

"Okay, okay, mats. They had mats, or some shit. Seriously, what's ticking in that condescending ball of vitriol? Why the extreme minimalism?"

"Congratulations on the articulation… Aaand it is with such sweet sorrow that I must say, the last grains of sand have fallen, fair knight." Paul opens the door to shoo him out. "God's speed on your ignoble quests."

8

Batts creeps on JT as she ferociously trims the hedges. She turns to clip a high branch that's just out of reach, and with a small grunt, swings the blades down from fatigue, almost hitting him.

He spits out a laugh. "Damn, watch it!"

"You watch it. These things still suck, by the way. You said we'd get new ones."

"Use the electric."

"They're a little dainty and impractical for some of the stuff I need to do around here. These branches are almost frozen."

Batts sniffs. "No one wants to use the tools; everyone wants to complain. Well, this should be it for the season anyway. Next year, promise." He not-so-subtly checks her out.

"Hey." She snaps the shears inches from his face; he doesn't flinch.

Reg stumbles slightly on the massive welcome mat but smoothly opens the front door for a regal elderly lady who strolls down the sidewalk towards the street. Tightly dressed. Gloves, purse, shoes –a little over-the-top, but all working.

Batts props up his posture. "Good morning, Ms Conrad. Lovely day."

Her voice is weary. "Batts." Brighter: "Oh, hi, JT. I didn't see you there. How is that new girl doing? Is she all settled in? No attitude, I hope."

JT again hacks away at the hedges. "Abby? She's okay. She'll do, I think. How you holdin' up these days?"

"Right side of the daisies, I suppose. The shrubbery looks beautiful, dear. All ready for their long winter's nap." The grounds are generally browning. A landscaping crew is mechanically raking up leaves and debris. Ms Conrad slowly turns and walks away.

Batts: still rosy, "Have a wonderful day, Ms Conrad." She doggedly continues down the sidewalk. He turns back to the hedges, and JT is gone.

From the roof, Abby watches the well-dressed woman walk down the sidewalk as one of the landscapers comes up to Batts and starts chatting him up. Ten stories high, she can only hear the buzz of equipment and cars beeping in traffic, but judging by the body language, this guy is sucking up as hard as he can. Can't blame him for wanting to get paid.

The "green" roof is ragged, but more together than she'd anticipated. There are some actual gutter-garden plants growing around the far edges, mostly weeds, a few toxic puddles of anyone's guess, and two makeshift greenhouses –neither of which is much higher than a one-person pop-up tent. But they appear to be relatively solid. The smaller one has been meticulously constructed of wood and glass, while the larger is almost all plexi. Slightly opaque little caves. As she crawls inside the larger of the two, she's surprised at how warm and humid it is. Abby takes off her weathered gloves and touches everything. "Do you have to touch everything? Yes, everything! You, shut up. No, you, shut up!" Okay. Puzzles to solve.

A sweet scent of decay fills her nostrils as she notices that the herb garden is *dead*-dead. But there are a couple of ferns, a cactus, and some miniature conifers that are still hanging on. She traces her fingers along the one-inch PVC that's connected to a bent-up garden hose. All of which will just freeze and split open when the temperature really drops, so she'll have to put that stuff in storage sooner rather than later.

The light is trippy, bouncing through the dirty glass. Abby makes a mental note to snap some pictures up here when she gets a minute to breathe.

The wind picks up and slaps at the structure, causing it to lurch and rattle a little more than she's comfortable with. As she stumbles back out of the greenhouse, a massive TV antenna seems to magically appear in front of her.

How did I miss this monster? Am I walking around staring at my shoes?

She makes her way towards it but is distracted by a rustling in the alley below. The whole roof acts more like a trampoline that bounces her in random directions as she walks. It's mighty unnerving, so she slows her pace and tries to anticipate the wobbles.

Carefully leaning out over the edge, she can see that a young skinny girl with firehouse-red hair is methodically dumpster diving behind the building. Bag over her shoulder, determined, she exits one old shaky-looking receptacle –which starts to tilt as she crawls out of it– then hops right into the next one. Agile.

Just then, Liam pops out of the building and dumpster girl quickly sinks down into the trash. He doesn't notice her and continues around the corner, on a mission, backpack, big strides.

Abby waits for the fiesty nymph to resurface, but she never does. The wind howls.

Must have found something tasty down there. Oh well, gotta be warmer than it is up here.

Rummaging through some of the supplies in the basement that are "arranged" next to the giant furnaces, she grabs a decent-sized tarp, a rusty bucket, sponge, rags, putty-knives, and a couple of other things she needs to tackle the first paint job.

JT said she had cleaned and cleared the unit for the most part: "It's a little frikken painful in there, Ab…" And that she'd also left her plenty of paint and "somewhat decent" brushes and rollers. Abby had doubts about the color – eggshell? She thought that was too dark. But she kept that to herself. Keep your mouth shut, Ab. You just got here, kid. She was still allowed to say "kid", right?

She feels like a bit of a fraud. But at the same time, far better than she has in years. The landscaping and gas station gigs were deliberate, if not shaky steps away from the old life, but this is a leap. She's wanted a maintenance job in a tenement building for some time now, and today there is a palpable sense of satisfaction as she strolls down the hall. Most of these jobs require heating and cooling chops, some background running basic wiring, etc. –all things she has no experience with. And as far as she can tell, maintenance is usually a boys' club, as with most things in life, and probably the hereafter, too. She imagines that if some type of heaven really exists, it probably smells of stale beer and filthy sheets. Maybe she's lucky on some level that Batts is just perv enough to hire women. And JT solves the HVAC requirements. Amazing luck after almost skidding off the runway completely.

The transoms are singing today as she makes her way through the building. A yellow tabby is perched up on one, locked on Abby's every step. Cigarette smoke billows out from another where the TV is set at nursing-home volume, laugh tracks bouncing off the walls.

Down on the next floor, she can hear a young couple with a newborn, dancing the dance of fate and taking their first swings at baby talk. "Who's the big girl? Who's hungry? Yeees." The infant starts screaming and crying.

"Uh-oh, who's cranky pants? Aaarrre youuu cranky pants? Little Miss Cranky Pants?"

Damn, just feed her already. Ah, here we go, 114.

Batts waived the usual probation period and gave Abby a skeleton key for the building, not because he trusted her, but because he wanted her to "do the fucking job".

After fighting with the lock, she nudges the door open with her shoulder, dumps the supplies, and sets Pearl the transistor by the window. "Okay, baby, stay with me now. Gonna be a long day." She powers her up and dials in "Reggae Breakfast with Dapper Don" on WQMX –Q 108. Which is technically 107.9 FM, but that's a bit cumbersome, no? Top of the dial, bottom of the production barrel. Their approach seems to come from the school of "fire, ready, aim!" Always broadcasting overlapping promos, dead air, odd interruptions. The DJs frequently forget they're live. But it has charm. And they spin a good variety of tracks. Bob Marley's "Sun Is Shining" is coming in loud and clear at the moment. Lovely.

Abby silently thanks the building and offers the song to the gods. To the universe that brought her here. Yes, some of this is going to suck. And no, none of it will make her rich. But after all these fights, struggles, doubts and scrapes, lacerations to the ego, to the soul, and let's not forget the bank account –the Lexington Arms is the soft landing she's been looking for.

Fuck, I forgot about edge tape. To hell with that, I need to get started.

After throwing the tarp, she begins to slap the chipped paint from the walls and into the tattered bucket. The place is nicotine-stained and gross, but she'd prefer to start this way. She'll have to wash it down a couple of times until she gets most of this loose stuff off regardless.

In the corner near a window that's not quite sealed, there is a hole in the wall that will need to be patched. Pushing around the edges of it, a giant chunk of drywall comes off in her hand. "Oh fuck."

"Abby."

She jumps a mile and the bulbous piece bounces on the floor and breaks apart, dust floating in the air. "Mr Batts. Good morning." How long has he been standing there?

He tilts his head. "Everything going okay?"

"Yes. I've started on the roof, and I'm going to get this guy painted today."

"Well, let's hope that's not the list for the whole day, pumkin. A dozen transoms waiting to be fixed out there." He leans in a little too close and hands her a list. "Last thing I need is for one of those old monsters to fall on someone. And try not to fuck the whole place up for one coat of paint, huh?" A little shitty as he's walking out: "And, if you're scraping, use the tools."

Bending down to collect the drywall pieces, she registers the now-gaping hole in the wall.

Yikes, I hope I can patch that.

Looking closer, she notices a piece of paper, or cardboard, sticking out of the gap. She slowly jostles it free. It's a postcard, with an urban winter scene on the front. The picture is thick with falling snow. Whoever took the shot had to be sheltered, probably through an open window. Evening setting. Exposure time was most likely minimal, or the snow would be nothing but streaks. Not much light coming from those streetlights, so they either had a zillion-dollar lens or used a super-high ISO. Tough to tell how much it's been doctored. Charming scene, though. Lots of trees line the empty street, old lamp posts, brownstones, big sidewalk, and oodles of glorious snow. The back is blank, nothing filled in.

"I'm keepin' you."

A glittery mist spirals in the air outside the window. Getting colder every day now. Snow soon. Yes.

9

Abby is running out of steam. Through the open transom, she can hear the new-baby parents and the elderly lady chatting at the other end the hall, all doing their best to be bubbly bubble machines.

"Ms Conrad, you shouldn't have!"

"I'm sure you've been doing everything for your little one, and nothing for yourselves." There's a big smile in Ms Conrad's delivery. "It's just a pound cake, but a darn good one!"

"Jeez, what presentation! You're a saint. Thank you so much."

"Of course. Just remember, it won't do to have the two of you worn thin. It'll make you ornery. And trust me, kids –I know ornery. Now, where is that little rascal hiding?"

The radio had long ago died, but Abby just stayed in motion all day, Batts's voice firmly embedded in her skull.

The sun is setting, must be after four, five? There's no way she's getting to any transoms now. She is too spent, crippled. But the place looks incredible compared to the "before" version she walked into. A light eggshell actually works well in this building.

She throws the brushes and rollers into the tarp and makes a hobo-bindle out of it.

"Oooh, maybe…?" Pulling the now slightly mangled transom list from her pocket, she scans the apartment numbers.

OK, 114 isn't one of them, but I can take a quick look at it anyway, while I'm right here, before I collapse.

Up on the step stool, she can see that the old transom has some decent wear and tear. The lockbox is a little loose. She quickly resets that. And the hinge on the left is letting go on the window side. No problem. Nothing is too stripped, so it all tightens up nice and snug. She gets down and tests it out, pulling and twisting the long handle. Still seems a little sticky, but no wobbles. Back up. A little solvent in the joints, not too much. Back down. She tries it again. Perfect, well, not, quite… Glass cleaner. Up again. Mean fast clean. And that's it. Enough.

There's a break in the rain, so the warehouse supervisor tells Liam to go across town with two linen orders on rolling racks. Most of it is sheer, light material, so he isn't too worried about tipping them over. These mobile z-racks that the cloths hang on are always top-heavy though, no matter how you slice it.

He rolls them to the door, but before he leaves, he quickly digs through the charity bin filled with used and damaged fabrics that will either be donated or tossed out eventually.

There are two large strips of black poly that aren't too disgusting. Keepers. Burrowing around some more, he finds a delicate, shimmering white cloth. Reminds him of winter. Not a Donner Party/cannibal chow-down/slow-death winter. It's more along the lines of a Norman Rockwell/Frosty the Snowman/ happy-time winter. He throws them all in his backpack.

"Hey, you pickin' through the trash or makin' that run?" The floor manager, looking a bit flushed.

"I'm out."

It's getting dark already. And the temperature's falling fast. The wind hits him head-on as he navigates the packed sidewalks and intersections, dancing around frozen puddles, tourists, and the homeless. Liam often gives the homeless folks some of the snacks that he invariably keeps in his backpack, but today he's fresh out. Lots of new, hungry faces on the streets these days.

The racks are rattling along at a decent pace, even though he's favoring his right arm. At his age, he always seems to be favoring something. If it isn't a bullet wound from a sniper –it could be anything: his back, his knee, elbow, wrist… Most of his joints are wonky now. He can't remember the last time he felt a thousand percent.

With his head down, navigating through a vigorous protest in front of the Bratton Chemical building, he sees a gritty woman barking into a megaphone. Full-throated and aiming for the skies, as if she's casting her derision right at the boardrooms on the upper floors. "Forty-four tons of that toxic shit dumped into the East River last year alone! We can get cancer all by ourselves, you know!? But hey, thanks so much for the generous offer! Your unending efforts, in that category in particular, are duly noted!"

Liam smiles and nods as he inches along the edge of the crowd.

Okay. I get it. Bratton Chemical is essentially nothing more than a dispensary of molten goo. For sure. But, c'mon, what does she think that bullhorn is made from –recycled balsa wood?

Man, just get me through this. And, whoa poppa, what is that smell? Oh my. Hotdog time. Fuckin' straight.

He makes his way to the ratty little wiener stand across the street and wedges his rolling cargo of linens as close to the brick wall as he can. Rubbing his hands together, "Two please, natural casing, extra onions." The slight gentleman manning the "Pupp-a-GoGo" cart never looks up or says anything during the exchange. Boom and boom. Done. Liam chows down as if someone were going to take the steaming hotdogs away from him.

Through the thinning crowds, he sees Batts across the street, making his way towards the park. Can't miss him with those gloves, brushing people aside as if they're merely curtains of inconvenience, all standing in the way of his destination. At least he's consistent.

Liam hears a squeak, followed by a loud crash behind him. One of the racks has tipped over into the muddiest puddle on the sidewalk. All the cloths are wrapped in plastic, but they're trashed nonetheless.

Tilting the z-rack back up against the wall, Liam asks the hotdog vendor to watch it for five minutes so he can hustle the other order through the alley. He hands back the second dog to the still-stoic but now slightly confused weenie master –and takes off.

It was seven o'clock before everything got straightened out. He'd swapped the muddy linens back at the shop, then hurried across town and barely caught the slightly annoyed client at her showroom, just as she was leaving for the day. Hopefully no one at work noticed. At this point, he couldn't care less.

After jousting with the always challenging, more-rust-than-metal time clock, he drags himself to the elevator.

His theory is that Lofty Linens keeps this sweatshop hidden away on the fortieth floor of this crumbling building –probably officially listing it as storage or something– while they run another, smaller, semi-phony boutique a few blocks away to distract the authorities. All in order to duck the hefty fines for what he is certain are dozens of major health and safety violations. Just a theory.

He likes most of the people well enough, and it's a convenient second job, but the owners are pigs. No ventilation, no breaks, just runnin'. A few days a week is tolerable, but he can't imagine what the full-timers and lifers go through in here.

The lanky blind guy gets on the elevator with him. Every day this pile of sticks is stoic and lifeless, unless an attractive woman enters the scene. And then –wham! He comes alive like horny hellfire. How does he do it? How can he tell the difference between the men and the women, good-looking and maybe not so? The way their shoes click on the floor? But a lot of the men have dress shoes too, some sounding almost identical to the women's, as far as Liam can tell. Could this kat discern the aromas of their perfume, make-up, hair products, every time? Whatever the method, the results are undeniable.

The elevator stops and a beautiful young girl in a business suit gets on. And we're off –tapping his white cane on the floor, painfully goofy smile, color in his face. Instantly transforming into a screeching carnival barker. "Is that Terry, Terry Katz?"

"Yes, Steven, how are things today?" Her voice is even, gentle.

"Oh, pretty good. Leaving late again. Winter's coming, yes? Soon we'll be complaining about the snow."

"I'm sure."

"Are you heading out to Ardy's Ringside later?"

"Not tonight, I'm beat."

He holds up his cane like a master showman. "First drink's on me."

The rusty bell signals her floor. "Maybe next time," all kinds of smiling and flirtatious. "Have a good night, Steven."

"Same, Terry."

Long look over her shoulder as she departs. He absolutely charms the socks off these folks. But never says a word to anyone else. Seriously looks fuckin' miserable most of the time.

A few floors down, a ragged young man and a strung-out punk girl get on, gaunt and pouty. And now Steven's a statue. Marble. Liam could lean over and open-hand paintbrush his face at this point, full force, and Steven wouldn't budge.

When they get to the lobby, the wannabe anarchists stumble out, and the new office manager –an alluring femme fatale– shuffles in with a security guard.

Instantly, and towards her and her only, "Hi, my name's Steven. You're new?"

Blind, my ass.

They all get off in the basement parking garage. As he snakes around the pillars towards the exit, Liam can clearly hear the receptionist's voice bouncing off the concrete, all gooey: "Well, it was very nice meeting you, too, Steven. I'm sure we'll cross paths again at some point..."

Liam has always preferred to walk through the alleys. Lots of layers to them if you look closely. Along with a hodgepodge of questionable smells, true. Summer is far worse for those. But still, these claustrophobic canyons reveal secret worlds to him. The places most people avoid often create colorful atmospheres for themselves to ward off the echoes of loneliness.

As Liam gets near the Lex, the wind again hits in his face. "God damn." He pulls his shoulders up and shrinks into his coat. But the sky looks amazing with the clouds trucking on by, occasionally revealing faint stars. City lights bouncing all around. Under a fire escape, he takes a breather, watching his foggy breath rise in the light rain.

Something moves behind a dumpster, but he doesn't flinch. Too tired to care. He straightens up and starts walking the last block. Then from behind:

"Hi!"

He spins hard enough to stumble. "Lisa?"

"No, I'm a ghost, fancy pants."

"I have a Protection Order; you're not supposed to—"

"Public throughway. Read the law, Liam."

"Go fuck yourself, Lis. Disappear." He briskly walks away.

She stands in a superhero pose, defiant.

Looking over his shoulder as he rounds the corner. "See you never."

10

Rain pelts the tall windows as Paul stares at the nasty gobs of fleshy viscera jiggling on the edge of his straight razor. Little giggles sneak out of him, in between wheezing and holding his breath.

How did so much slimy testament end up on that blade? Signs of age are certainly attacking his body from all angles, and in spastic patterns. Random chub and hairs showing up in places previously unimagined.

But there's no way my Achilles tendon is 'fat'. Impossible.

Now, one doesn't want to cut too deeply in that vicinity, or you'll lose the ability to locomote. But the results should be compelling, nonetheless. So the blade was at a little bit of an angle, as he recalls. And he did cut down through his heel a bit. But still, he didn't think he'd scoop out this bloody sundae.

Leaning back in the empty tub, he lets the straight razor fall to the floor. Some of the pulsing grit pops off the blade and floats up past him, disappearing into the ceiling. "And where are you off to?"

The old TVs are humming, static on all of the screens. Squinting, he can barely make out a signal on one of them. Some sort of Western. A cowboy riding a horse, or fucking a cow? A tiny stream of blood puddles up around the drain as he allows his body to deflate. Exhale. "Okay… good."

When he wakes up, the glow from the TV's is the only light in the room. With his first movements, his heel not so gently peels off the bottom of the tub, a feisty little bit of dried blood hanging from it. Hobbled and jerky, he shuts off the TVs and opens the curtains, unconcerned that he's still butt naked.

Once everything is reasonably together, Paul polishes the shiny instrument of severity. She is a beauty. Any dignified barber or gangster would be in love with this little gem.

He drifts… If I were Yakuza, this would be one of my weapons of choice. Pearl handle, flush casing, crafted in the Japanese style of steel –with a nice balance of chromium and carbon, and just a touch of nickel in there to give it that intangible magic when one pulls it across the skin. Nickel makes them feel so... even? Deliberate? Intentional. Seemed like everyone had at least one of these sexy slicers in their house when I was a kid. Who doesn't love a good straight razor? Delicious.

Now, this is the somber part –putting it away. "Until we meet again." The assortment of blades and daggers inside the red velvet box is a reassuring sight as he nestles the friendly weapon back into its home, no less warmly than a seasoned nanny tucking an infant into a crib.

After placing the sacred vessel back up on the shelf in the closet, he drapes a shirt up and over it –as if that will make it utterly undetectable– and shuts the door. Turning around, he slides to the floor without letting go of the doorknob.

Paul sits there that way for a long while, arm up in the air, like an indifferent scarecrow, staring out the windows into a brooding and heartless night.

11

What is the color of a sound that has no anchor? Are the ions yearning to save my wretched soul, or would they prefer to dance alone? Waltzing through the sea and the shore, summits and sky, desert winds, the cliff walls that line the river valley, the little transistor in my hand.

Even your static is beautiful. Sprinkled with hypnosis. Infinite patterns.

Answers are always fleeting, like the perfect song on a clear station at the exact right moment. The channel inevitably fades, the signal turns fuzzy, and we must hunt anew. Sacrificing the old rhythms to the gods, traversing an endless expanse.

But this time, I won't be alone. There's a fiery army of angels rising now, boldly singing to the heavens. Ever diligent, and steadfast by my side.

Abby's journal: "Fambly settles in at the Lex."

12

Abby wakes up with her hair in her mouth, paint clothes sticking to her back, eyes almost focusing on the little clock in the corner. Eight forty-four pm. She was out for a couple hours anyway. Holy shower time.

Striding down the street towards Zoe's, the light misty rain feels good on her face. It's nearly ten o'clock; she hopes Zoe didn't close up early.

Twenty yards away, she can smell the Nag Champa, maybe some Gonesh sticks underneath. Never any crap incense burning in that temple. Like that garbage claiming it's patchouli-scented, or tea tree oil –usually bullshit. The first clue is that they come in a variety pack. Second is that they all smell the same. Those shysters think people won't notice? Slime buckets.

It loosely reminds her of a batch of great black hash that was going around twelve, fifteen years ago. Ten bucks for a gram, and it would last a week. Smoked like silk. The real deal. Then, after a few months, it dried up, couldn't find any on the streets. And all the sudden in its place this 'opium' started making the rounds, but it turned out to be grape incense. Pricks were selling *incense* to smoke. Okay, you're obviously taking your chances in that world. She might have been conned into purchasing a bag of "weed" that was actually "oregano" once… or twice… But passing off incense as opium? That shit is immoral.

She stands outside of Zoe's Occult & Mystic for a minute watching Zoe deftly handle a customer from behind the counter.

Always wearing a string of beads, usually quartz, and a muumuu of the brighter earth tones, flowing, easy. But even when she's light-hearted and laughing, her presence is a little intimidating. Large frame, deep voice. She'd said once –a dozen times, actually– that in her native Haitian Creole, "Zoe" means "hard to the bone". Abby certainly isn't ever going to test that.

The lingering patron finally departs, and lets the door shut right in front of Abby's face as she's trying to walk in. Gotta love assholes like that. She re-opens the door, and little chimes ring out, just as one of Zoe's cats bolts through her legs and runs down the sidewalk. "Oh no!"

Zoe laughs. "Abigale! As I live and breathe!"

"But the cat? I don't even know which one it was!"

"Oh please, that's just Rudy gonna get a little somethin' to eat. How about a hug? What has it been, eight months? A year?"

"Six weeks, Zo."

"You lie like a cheap rug. C'mere!"

Big rolling hugs, Zoe kisses her on the cheek.

"I'm in the neighborhood now. The Lexington Arms."

"Uh, that's on 5th, right?"

"No, it's on Lexington, Zo."

"Ah." Zoe's right back to work, looking at receipts, her reading glasses clinging to the end of her nose; she casually lights a smudge stick of sage.

"How are things going around here?"

Another customer scampers in and immediately starts assaulting Zoe with questions, so Abby nods and walks to the back of the store to let her take care of business.

Happy, peaceful, creepy, bizarre. Zoe's place has layers of atmosphere. When you pass through the entranceway, you've crossed a threshold into hallowed ground. The essential oils and angel books are expected, but the voodoo artifacts and half-dozen makeshift altars give the place spiritual theatrics, electrifying, thick.

Abby makes her way to the "give & take" box —a large cardboard shell filled with cut-up calendar pages, pictures ripped from magazines and books, wallpaper samples, cheap prints— all shoved in around the edges of organized. The sign reads, "*Give & take. But if you take, please donate. Prayers and well-wishes are wholly unacceptable. Cash only. $1 minimum.*" Digging through her purse, she pulls out the snow-scene postcard she'd found in the wall at the Lex. The surface is smooth, most of the luster still intact. She reaches way down and buries it in the middle of the stack of random pictures.

Zoe finishes up with the customer, a jittery kid in his early twenties. She seems a little leery but sells him a small bottle of something or other.

"Okay now, young man, be thoughtful, be well." He thanks her and leaves. "God damn kids. Can't afford food, but they're buyin' ingredients for potions. And they got stingray breath like the devil! Armpits smellin' of onions and glue. Jeesh. What were you doin' back there?"

"Making an offering to the gods."

"My girl."

The door opens, letting in a swirl of wind, and Abby can't believe her eyes. "Mom? What are you doing here?"

"Abby! Gah! Well, you're always talking about Zoe's and, I had a feeling, so we took a detour, and… my baby girl!"

They hug and her mom slop kisses her face a couple times.

Abby wipes them off. "Alright, damn, what is it with you people? Zoe – this is my mom, Annalise."

Annalise warmly shakes Zoe's hand. "Ah, nice to meet you, Zoe. We've heard so many good things. And this place!" Her sparkling eyes take in all the magic. "Wonderful."

"Thank you, Miss. Some girl you have here. I keep hopin' she'll work for me one day."

Annalise pulls her grayish braids back, barely getting a scrunchie around their wily ways. "That's a great idea! This place is so cool. Why not, Ab?"

"Oh, boy. I need two of you on my ass now? I just started the other gig. Let's all just take a breath."

Chrystal walks in; Abby's always surprised by how severe she looks with her chiseled make-up and chopped blond hair. "Yes, how is the new job going, Abby?"

"Hi, Chrystal. Fine, so far, I guess. Chrystal –Zoe."

Chrystal looks to Zoe with a half-smile. "Pleasure." Zoe nods. "Well, your mom was telling me all about it." Reaching out to hold Annalise's hand, "The whole thing sounds… earthy."

"I suppose that's accurate. At least I don't have to be around stuffy creepazoids anymore."

Chrystal always has some kind of fringe or tassels hanging from the brims of her hats. It's like looking at a shaky old lampshade stuck on a mannequin's body.

Annalise is effusive. "Abby was thinking of working here with Zoe."

Zoe: "Correct."

"Ugh. Look, I need to stay in motion for chunks of my day, spend more time outside; it's half the reason I left the fishbowl offices behind. You know how many times I was in a meeting, and I looked out the windows wishing with my whole heart and soul that I was outside?"

"No." Chrystal, slight tone: "Tell us."

"Many."

Mischievous grin from Zoe, "Those windows are in need of a good washin'. That front stoop could use a fresh coat of paint. That's outside, right?"

"See, hon. It's perfect!"

"Maaaybe, but not right now…"

"Okay, okay, okay." Annalise digs through her massive Givenchy tote. "So, on a lighter note, we got you a small housewarming gift."

"It's just an efficiency, Mom, but alright, I'm down."

Looking up. "Wait, but you don't have any of your things? Your furniture?"

"Mom—"

"How are you living? Are you sleeping on the floor?"

"Mom, I told you, the place is furnished."

"With what?" Chrystal tilts her head.

"Sticks."

"Well, at least you can make a fire when it gets cold." Chrystal drifts around the shop, taking in the variety of stations.

"Sorry, Ab, you're right. Furnished, fine, good. Ah, here it is." Out of her bag, Annalise proudly produces a mini-transistor radio with a little bow on it.

"1955, 56? Cherry-wood Zenith? With a swing-out stand? Holy fuck! Where did you find this?"

"It's from both of us. You like it?"

"Oh my. It's brilliant. Thanks, guys."

Chrystal half smiles and keeps gliding around the store. "Car will be back in a few, Ann."

"Right. Well, I'm so glad we caught you, hon. We're heading to New Orleans for a while."

"Oh, that's awesome. When?"

"Tomorrow," Chrystal chirps, without looking up from the candle displays.

"I meant to tell you, Ab, but it all came together pretty quickly, and—"

"No, no, that's no problem. I'm glad you guys are getting out of town. Change of scenery. Always a good thing."

The bulky black car pulls up to the curb. "There he is." Chrystal makes a beeline to the front of the store.

"Okay. Travel safe. I love you. Call me when you get there."

Annalise takes Abby by the shoulders, looking her over. Glowing. "Definitely. And I love you, too. Oooh, it was so good to see you." More hugs.

"You too, Mum."

Chrystal's already halfway out the door. "Take care, Abby. Let us know if you need anything. Nice meeting you, Zoe."

"Don't be strangers now." Zoe's still waving as the pair crosses the sidewalk arm-in-arm. "Your mother is a seer."

"Like a barn owl. The first couple of guys I dated ended up going into hiding. Nobody in the neighborhood messes with her."

"I bet. Okay, time to wrap this up. Shop's closed. Ardy's for a touch of the liquid spirits?"

"Oh, not tonight. I need to crash. Next time, for sure."

"Alright, child. Be watchful. Solstice comin'. That's no joke."

"Understood. Great seeing you, Zo."

Zoe playfully pushes Abby towards the door. "Yes, yes, out, little trouble girl. You're standin' in the way of all my mojo now, damn. Scoot!"

13

Despite his best efforts, Liam can't stop shivering as he chats with Reg out in front of the Lex.

In contrast to the brief periods of slightly chilly weather leading up to it, the first truly cold day of winter wreaks havoc on one's sense of dignity. Our trembling bones seem to cry out, "You goddamn lump of shit! We are gonna fucking die out here!" This soon-to-be-forgotten adjustment to the icy weather that the body and mind will make over the next few weeks has only just begun.

"Do you have any thermal underclothes on, young man? Are you ready for this nonsense? Going down to fifteen degrees tonight, ten tomorrow." Reg's eyes dance and sparkle; the falling temps don't seem to be fazing him.

"Oh yeah. I wear long-john skivvies when it gets below forty. I'm outside a lot for work."

"Well, on the other hand now, too many layers will cut off the hose…"

Liam stops shuffling his feet, looks up.

"Choke the rooter, peel the onions, you know–make you sterile. Nonetheless, you should be somewhat weatherproofed against the elements. Anyway… How's the shoulder?"

"Almost whole. I finally lost that sling."

"And how's the doctor?"

"My doctor? She's oblivious. Love her, though. I don't want anyone going berserk over this. Bullet was in and out. No real long-term damage. So she thinks."

"I meant you."

"I'm not a doctor, Reg."

"So then how's the patient? I know we just shoot the shit here and there, but you haven't said much about it."

"Yeah." Liam starts shuffling again. "Some of it is deep."

"Well, thank goodness he didn't kill anybody. And I know you feel some responsibility –anybody would. But you can't lift all the strays in this world."

"True. Fuck, man, he was really in orbit. Just… gone."

Reg brushes off his cap and nestles it back on his head. "And now he's dead, and it's all your fault."

"I gotta wear some of it. I knew he was in trouble; I knew he was getting worse."

"So did a lot of people, from what you indicated when you got back from the hospital."

"I was drugged up."

"Well, you should take more drugs then, 'cause you were making more sense. Just do the old doorman a small favor and look after you for a while. Holidays comin', so everything will be turning into satanic holy hell here in a minute. In the meantime, treat yourself. Have a drink, tear off a piece, piss in the snow."

"Hasn't really snowed yet."

"It'll be on us soon enough. C'mon, throw me a bone, for chrissakes." The veins in his forehead are popping a bit. Now he's cold.

"Sure, man, I'll keep one eye on my shoulder and the other on my soul. Thanks."

"Alright. Good. It'd be quite the letdown if you turned out to have the intellect of a speed bump in addition to being nauseatingly altruistic. Well, that's enough of this rubbish. Best be getting on your way, killer; gotta go have a piss me-self." Reg turns and stiffly walks towards the building.

"When the time comes, we'll piss in the snow together."

"No, we won't." Reg stops on a dime. "Wait, where are you going now? You never mentioned."

"To check in on a consult. Hopefully, no one gets shot."

14

The flash flood had come from nowhere. Nick was driving. The car rolled and tumbled like a discarded toy. He was knocked unconscious but made it through. Sophia —his one-in-a-zillion, once-in-a-lifetime love and wife of fourteen years— did not survive. And even though it was an indifferent fate that rained down on him that day, he blamed. He blamed God. He blamed the world. But mostly, and with unending zeal, he blamed himself. And for the first time in his life, he really wanted to die.

Out of nowhere, he started trashing mirrors and punching out windows, not only in his own house, but at stores, laundromats, gas stations. Local shop owners were on high alert.

At one point, Nick tried to bust up a bingo game in a church basement because he thought the sign in the parking lot was taunting him. A ninety-plus-year-old woman read him the riot act and tossed him out before he could do much damage, though. Silver hair and fiery eyes, if he was remembering correctly. Said something about slapping the taste out of his mouth if he didn't leave. "Don't mess with me, junior. I'll show you psycho, bite your damned ankles off! Out!" Nothing about calling the cops. She simply shoved his ass out the door, swinging her purse as if she were carving a path in the jungle with a machete. Connecting solidly, more than once, with the side of his stupefied face.

On other occasions during the course of his rampage, he wasn't so lucky, though, and got hauled in for disturbing the peace. And just to add to the fun he had a massive arsenal of firearms littered around his house. They had yet to play a starring role in one of his dramas, but at the time, he was definitely considering an upgrade.

His son barely managed to bring him back into the world of the living, bit by bit. It took a couple years to really settle him down. Eventually, he was able to convince his dad that he didn't need such an egregious stash of guns.

And Nick has made some progress in other areas, too. But now, in some ways, he is still more isolated than most of Liam's other consults. At least Paul will step out for a minute to cross the street and harass some poor unsuspecting schmuck. Nick won't leave the house at all these days, unless goaded.

Liam knocks. "Nick? You home?"

Nick eases open the door. "You're hilarious."

It appears as if he's been eating for two. Diving head-first into the culinary arts as of late, and apparently not letting anything go to waste. At least it's not booze or pills.

Two giant figurines, Wolverine and the Incredible Hulk, sit on top of a dusty TV. The walls and windows are covered with tons of black fabric. Very little sunlight creeping in around the edges of the place.

"I brought you some more black poly, but it looks like you're full up."

"Oh! Thanks. No, no, I do need some more." Nick takes the bundle of linens in his arms and gently lays them across the dining-room table.

"Little dark in here, hoss."

"What, like my soul?"

"I thought you were making tapestries with this stuff."

"I am. Tapestries, curtains…"

"Don't tapestries typically have designs, patterns… something on them?"

"Oh, they're there. You just have to squint. Easier to see in the light."

"What light?" Liam looks to the four corners of the room.

"Okay, you just got here and it's nag-time already? How about some coffee?" Nick's already walking to the kitchen.

"Ah, yes. Thanks."

"How is linen land?"

"Slow, considering the holidays are right around the corner. Fine with me, though. Lots of other things popping up."

"You mean you have even more shut-in whack-jobs like me to get supplies for?"

"Hey! I throw insults. You heave them back at me, but no self-deprecation until I've had my coffee." Liam eyes what he's sure is a loaded Glock 43, 9mm on the mantel above the unused fireplace.

"Wait a minute." Nick sticks his head out of the kitchen. "*Lots of other things popping up*? Female things?"

"No. Well..."

"Holy shit! Spill! Spill your friggin' guts! Let 'em tumble out all over the floor."

"Yeah, there's a girl, lady, in my building..."

"Hell yeah, there is." Nick bounces in with the coffee.

"And, I don't know."

"You don't know; you don't know. C'mon. Always over here, pokin' at me for hours. Cough it up. You owe me some dirt, buddy. Sorry to interrupt, I'm listening."

"So you are. She's new. Maintenance. Some of the stuff I've been through lately, though, man, I mean, anything with 'maintenance' attached to it smells like a disaster waiting in the wings."

"Blah. Is she hot? Tasty? Normal-ish?"

"Definitely. No idea. And I sure as hell hope so. I've only bumped into her a couple times, but—"

"Ha! The old bumps. I love it. But, but?"

"We'll see. She gives off good vibes. And... it's just that I'm a little drained in that department right now."

"You see Lisa at all these days?"

"I hope not to. Alright, let's get this together, yeah?" Liam pulls out his notebook.

"Oh shite," bolting back towards the kitchen. "Can I get you anything else? Biscotti? Pizzelle?"

"Today's the day, sir. Let's set a date. You promised."

Nick reappears with a tray of Amoretti cookies. "Fine." He munches nervously.

Nicolas Cardamone is an intimidating dude. Not quite six feet tall, but solid as a rock, even with the expanding waistline. Doesn't seem that he's leaning towards violence at all, as far as Liam can tell... not that he's trusting his own judgment a thousand percent these days. And, no doubt, Nick is certainly suffering badly from this phobia. But to see this grown man, whose forearms are made of steel, recoil so sheepishly at the thought of leaving his house is nothing short of surreal.

"Next week, the twenty-second, three-thirty. We'll walk down the block to that bench across from the park."

"And do what?"

"Sit. Make fun of people. Fart. Tell tall tales."

"Oh, I don't know."

"You don't know what? When was the last time you met your son for coffee? Or went out to get the mail?"

"Adam shipped out on deployment last week. So frikken worried. And what? I get the mail."

Liam walks to the window and heaves aside untold layers of hanging linens. Nick peers over his shoulder, stirring the coffee with a little spoon as if he's scrambling eggs. The tortured-looking mail is overflowing out of the box and into a container on the ground.

"When you get the new mail, do you swap it out with the old mail, so it always looks full?"

Nick sets down his mug and marches to the door. He cracks it open and takes a labored breath. Leaning way out, he sweeps his eyes left and right. As he starts to duck back in, Liam is right behind him.

"Or are there only certain days that you actually bring it all into the house?"

"Bastard." Stepping out onto the doormat that reads "GO AWAY!", he meanders out to the mailbox as if treading on hot coals, then ferociously scoops up bunches of envelopes –cramming them into the pockets of his robe, stuffing a few in his mouth, before trotting back to the house.

A neighbor yells over in mid-trot. "Nick! What's the word?"

He pulls the mail out from his clenched teeth. "Hi... okay..." Then, under his breath: "Fuck off..."

Liam holds out his hand. "Want me to take some of that? Not the slobber pile."

"Move, please. It's cold out here."

"How do you feel?"

"Oh, fuck you. I mean, please?"

"Nick. Part of the deal. What's in your head right now?"

"Get inside."

"Why?"

"Because I'm afraid I'll have an anxiety attack."

"Right. Okay. You're afraid you'll have one. But you're not having one right now. What else?"

"It's noisy out here. C'mon, I need to go in. Liam."

"Sure sure, in we go."

Back in the living room, Liam takes some mail from Nick as he pulls out more and more from every pocket. Then he reaches way down into his pants.

"Oh, you can keep that stack too, partner. You okay?"

Nick's red-faced. "I am going to do this. For my boy. I am."

"And for yourself. It's a nice day out there. And you just went to get your mail. *And* you said 'hi' to someone."

"Technically told him to 'fuck off'."

"Semantics. Still counts as a greeting in this town. Next week. Bench. Very mellow. Two old friends chatting. In the meantime, maybe you could try to get used to grabbing the mail, once in a while, yes?"

"Oh dear God, yes. Dr Jekyll and Mr Hyde me. Mail. Fine. Bench? I don't know."

"Please. It'll be fun. We'll wear invisible cloaks."

"*Invisibility* cloaks. If the cloaks were invisible, we wouldn't be able to find them."

"Says who?"

"Have you ever read even one comic book or graphic novel, in your entire life?"

"Um… I've heard great things? I think. See? We'll have lots to talk about. You can get me all up to speed on the Hulk and Wolf-boy and whatnot."

"Oh my. You may be a little long in the tooth to be brought all the way up to speed at this point, Captain. What are you anyways, sixty-two? Sixty-five?"

"Forty-four, sonny. Go easy now. I'm kinda vulnerable, man."

Nick deflates. "Amen."

15

Batts takes off his gloves for three things: bathroom time, sexy time, and pigeon time.

As he crosses the street in front of a cab that clearly has the right of way, he suddenly remembers that he'll have to remind JT, again, to install the motion sensor lights in the public restrooms in the lobby. Owners keep saying that it will save money.

Right. Just like the automatic faucets that never fucking work —waving my hands underneath them like I'm doing a goddamn card trick, while the water just spits on and off. Modern conveniences. Assholes.

Walking through the park with the occasional slight head twitch to sniff the air, he hears a couple laughing on the other side of the lake. He stops to listen, and is suddenly awash with memories of the convention in Toronto last year…

Man, oh man, that woman was so cool, so smooth. Whatever her name was.

And he knew in the first instant that he'd have to pay her, like any other customer. But he cared not a bit. Hell, even better. They both laughed and had ass-slappin' fun all the way through it. When she took her top off, the giant gold hoops dangling from her nipples threw him for a second. They'd been well hidden underneath that yummy angora sweater. And, yes, these monstrous rings semi-obstructing her goods were a little bit of a letdown, but he didn't let the gaudy window dressing get in the way of his overall shopping experience.

Impossible to tell, but he was really hoping she wasn't faking the orgasms. He wanted to take her over the top, and in his wantonly shallow mind, he'd done exactly that.

As the clock was ticking, she'd asked if there was anything else she could do for him. All warm and fuzzy, love in her eyes, however practiced. "Nah, let's just chill, baby." Curled up on his ample frame, she gently rubbed his massive belly, which, even flat on his back, hid large parts of the room from him. He breathed in her hair, and that delicious skin. Clean.

When the time was up, she slid out of bed and slowly gathered her things to leave. Matter-of-factly, she asked if it was okay to take some of the hotel's little shampoos and such. "Fuck yeah, girl, fire away." Moving around methodically, as if in the produce section of a granite-top grocery store, she proceeded to fill her substantial purse with everything that would fit: hand towels, TP, shampoo, soap, 'Do Not Disturb' sign, bottle opener, matches, ice-bucket-lid (the bucket itself was too big), rocks glasses, a small tray that held some of the aforementioned, and a gold shower-curtain ring that was floating by itself on the rod.

When she reached up over the tub to grab it, he could see her muffins peeking out of the back of her jeans, and he felt himself getting hard again. "I've recently developed a taste for large metal rings myself."

"Yes you have, lover." She skipped back over and rubbed her jangling boobs in his face one last time.

Giggling, "C'mon now, don't hurt me with those things."

"Hey! You do like 'em, yeah?" She looked down at her creations. "Be honest."

"I do now. Abso-fuckin-lutely, honey."

She put on her coat, then with some effort, heaved the giant bag onto her shoulder and brushed back her jet-black bobbed hair with one hand. "Thank you, Michael. Best time I've had in months, truly."

"Thank you, little lady. Be careful out there, okay?"

"You bet. See ya next time?"

"Next time."

Warm smile as she closed the door behind her, and Batts felt whole. It had been at least ten years, and it was so perfect. Their testament of leaking used condoms laid in a heap on the floor. He certainly wasn't going to touch them. That shit was for the maids.

After he took a steaming hot shower and scrubbed his body nearly raw, he picked up the pillow she'd been lying on as he walked by their action bed.

A pair of massive, blinding white socks. White gloves. White pillow. All making their way over to the untouched second bed, as if tiptoeing through a classic cartoon. He tossed the bedspread to the floor and heaved himself onto the mattress, burying his face so that the sides of her pillow hugged his ears. Feet wiggling involuntarily.

My god, that smell…

The park is calming for Batts, especially this time of year –fewer dogs chasing frisbees, fewer idiots chasing dogs, less noise. No matter how rotten the day, he morphs into a gentler version of himself when he crosses the threshold into this sanctuary. The sun is in retreat when he finally gets to the lonely bench where the jogging trail splits off from the lake. After wiping the seat with rags for a few minutes, he plunks down hard, breathing heavy, nose hairs whistling defiantly in the wind. He loosens his gloves in a freakish mini-striptease, one finger at a time, then carefully folds them.

And almost instantly, they arrive –the winged guardians of the city.

These days, he tries to make it out here at least once a week. And even though it's never on the same day, or at the same time, the pigeons still know. They can feel his benevolence before he arrives. "Fuck them other people feedin' you crap. No one delivers the good stuff like me, right?"

He reaches into his coat and starts throwing out the seed that he steals on the regular from one of the buildings that he runs across town. The tenants are always spilling it on the ground in the courtyard over there anyway. Makes the place a haven for rats. So under the guise of sanitation and safety, he helps himself. "Gotta keep it clean out here, y'know?" Every once in a while a smokin' hot lady from one of the upper floors will come out and assist him with the clean-up. All bending over n' shit. Damn. Double killa.

And if the residents do manage to keep it in the feeders, he knows where they store the larger bags in the basement. If he has to hoof it all the way down there, he typically rewards himself by swiping the more expensive brands –the mixtures that are concocted specifically for parrots. Who the fuck is buying parrots?…

Scout, his favorite and the leader of the pack, hasn't shown up yet. Pinto colored –white and brown, one eye gouged out from a fight. Well, that's how Batts imagined he'd lost it anyway.

A few moments later, the he-man pigeon that is Scout makes his grand entrance from underneath the bench and struts through the somewhat sticky wickets of Batts's legs to join his comrades in the feast. "You're late, you little fucker." He tosses out some more seed, then reaches down and pets Scout's head. "Who's Daddy's fighter? Who's the tough guy?"

A couple of birds are brave enough to fly up on the bench in an attempt to share the limited real estate with Batts. "Git, git down. Git off-a here," waving them away.

Scout gets a few more gentle strokes, but Batts doesn't dare try to pick him up. Even petting him with one finger is tough on the nerves; he pulls out some alcohol swabs and vigorously rubs his hands, wrists, forearms. Dumping out the rest of the seed, he once again goes through the alcohol swab routine, grinding it on his face and nose as well, then just pitches it in the grass. The pigeons dart after it at first, but quickly realize that it's a false flag. After a few minutes, the pecking crew begins to scatter as the sun makes its final peek through the bare branches of the trees.

Batts puts his gloves back on and gets up to leave just as some of the birds, led by Scout, take flight for home. There's a little directional confusion as they almost fly right into him. He waves his arms as if he's frantically taxiing a plane on the tarmac, belly-laughing. "Holy shit! You little pricks."

16

It takes a minute to shake off the cobwebs from the little dust broom that was hidden in the far corner of the basement, but it's quite the find. Her mom would call them "whisk brooms" –small handheld jobs of tightly bound straw. This one is a beauty. Chewed up perhaps, but a keeper. "Aaand mine." Abby brushes it across one of the old furnaces a few times, and some of the petrified straw snaps off and falls to the floor. "Uh-oh. Alright, we're going to take good care of you now."

Even though it had only been a few days, she really is liking the gig, getting into a rhythm, and learning the building bit by bit. But she's so beat up by the end of the day, she has zero energy left over for her latest art project with the radios, whatever that's going to be. The lack of at least some progress there is starting to loom over her now like an increasingly heavy cloud.

Curled up in bed with little Pearl, she listens to a late-night call-in show about the paranormal. The host is very professional, and completely respectful towards all the callers, no matter how far out there…

"Good evening, you're on the air."

"Hello. I really love your show. We are so… lucky to have you. Thanks for taking my call."

"Of course. And who am I speaking with?"

"Well, my earth name is Phillip Adelson, but my real name is Keldar, and I originate from the Duron Cluster."

"OK. Keldar from Duron. What's on your mind?"

The host himself would admit, on occasion, that some of the folks calling in may be looking for attention, or are in need of professional help –maybe four-hundred-hours-on-a-couch professional help? But he would phrase it more along the lines of, *"And it's possible that a few of these good people are a little lonely, or just need a venue to express themselves, but…"* In the end, he always let the callers talk it out, say their piece. And sure, he would gently challenge some of them at times. But he pretty much just listened to what they had to say. He never judged.

Tonight's show ends with a segment that's all about coffins hanging off the sides of cliffs. Apparently, it used to be a burial tradition in parts of Southeast Asia. Considered both dignified and practical, in the sense that they were very difficult for grave robbers or animals to get to once they're put in place. Some cultures feel that if their graves are disturbed, or their corpses violated, they would then be unable to make the journey to the other side. Or, as many of these callers believe, they would be cut off from moving on to another planet.

Sometimes these makeshift caskets rest on beams or projections jutting out from the cliff walls, or they're set in crevices in the steep sides of mountains. While others simply hang by thick hemp ropes.

As the show is wrapping up, Abby tries to imagine herself lying in one. Feeling the wind all around her, light seeping through the cracks as the coffin bumps against the sheer rocks in rhythm with the rising air. The ultimate vessel. The final cave. She drifts off.

Bolting upright at three am, she immediately trots towards the bathroom to get some relief. Along the way, something bites her heel. "Damn!" Loose straw from the whisk broom, not so subtly demanding her attention. Seems as if they're developing a bit of an attitude. "I saved your asses, you little shits!" Still very groggy, she tiptoes the rest of the way to the closet of a powder room, which may as well be an outhouse, as no heat whatsoever makes it into this frigid alcove of necessity.

On the way back to bed, she turns on the light and sees a dozen pieces of straw on the floor, all pointing toward the not-so-innocent-looking whisk broom that's leaning against the fridge. "Grouchy. We'll call you Grouchy. Mostly because, you fucking bite!" She gathers up the loose spindles and scoots under the covers. Tuning Pearl to the jazz channel she leans back, still holding the straw in her hand, like a torch. Louis Armstrong's version of "St James Infirmary" winds its way through the room.

The song was the most popular dirge of its era. Lyrics centered on the story of a large man who's somberly telling his saloon mates of seeing his dead wife at the infirmary. And it prompts him to espouse about his own funeral, borrowing from a time-honored tradition of how people would like their send-offs to look and feel. In one line of the tune, he says he wants six dice players – "craps shooters"– to be his pallbearers, because they are his kindred spirits. His brothers. Fambly.

She grabs her purse and retrieves the newest arrival of the transistor radio crew –Cherry. Opening the mini kickstand in the back, she props her up on the desk. Picking out a loose piece of straw, she pokes it in one of the small holes that cover the speaker. "Not deep enough. Who are you talking to? Shut up!" They'll have to be glued on there, don't want to hurt her.

An hour later, Cherry is almost ready for prime-time, flat on her back now, with a dozen angry spindles from the whiskbroom sticking straight up out of the speaker holes. A bastardized mohawk of brittle rigidity. Climbing up on the chair, Abby unravels some thin twine and carefully ties the now spiky radio to the curtain rod, letting it dangle halfway down the window.

Back in bed she pulls the blankets up to her eyes and watches Cherry do her dance, slowly spinning and tapping the glass. She imagines the pieces of straw projecting from the speaker are physical manifestations of the sound waves, the life energy, the soul.

The radio is both corpse and coffin in a floating still-frame that captures its essence –a constant giving, that is only ever repaid with tender care and affection.

This is who I am. This is what I did. The evil spirits will not steal my song. The animals will not desecrate my lifeblood.

I'm on my way.

Black had always been Liam's favorite color. He should probably tell Nick that at some point. When he was growing up, his mom would often scoff that he looked as if he was dressed for a funeral. In those days, Liam was thinking more along the lines of Johnny Cash, or Roy Orbison maybe. Regardless, black was best. It always worked. Cool and easy.

Fourteen black notebooks are spread out on his kitchen table. Single subject, college ruled. "Nick" is up first. Rubbing his eyes, he reads the last few entries, then makes some notes:

December 16th, GUN, probably loaded, sitting on mantle. Pretty sure it's one of the only firearms left in the house though, as his son, Adam, has convinced him to part with most of the others. Nick seems to be in good spirits generally, especially considering Adam just left on deployment. Mail now an issue. Refusing to go out for anything unless I push him. He presents as regulated with the meds as far as I can tell. Going to try to take him out for a short walk, and hopefully get him to spend time with me on a bench that sits about a half a block from his house, across from the park. Want to give him some space to get used to the idea before we try it. Have to weigh that against the build-up of anxiety around what will be a big event, but I don't want to push too hard, too fast. Acupuncture also seems to be playing a positive role. I believe it's called the "seven dragons" technique, increasingly used for PTSD. Tough to tell how much improvement is due to what specific part of treatment, but arrows pointing in the right direction as far as stress and depression, at least on visits. Feedback from Adam corroborates most of this, so hopefully Nick is realizing some relief...

Liam shuffles through the other notebooks, and one scoots off the table and lands on the floor. He can't quite bend down and reach it from the chair. The warehouse has been kicking his ass, and he's a little sore around the edges. Giving it the full dramatic pause, he considers whether or not to just leave it there.

Somehow getting up to grab another beer from the fridge is a breeze, though, and on the way back, he scoops up the notebook. Flipping it around, he sees the name: Mark. He just stares at the cover for a minute. Then he pages through to the last entry...

Still very traumatized from his last deployment to North Africa. Mark refuses any more therapy or counseling. Has repeatedly promised to continue his medication, but I think the odds are long that he will maintain without supervision/counseling/program. Something has changed. I'm concerned that he won't let me in the next time I stop by. Starting to think nothing short of an all-out intervention will help. Hope I'm wrong. He does seem level and well-adjusted at times, but recently —only in flashes. His mind tends to wander, and then everything goes dark...

Staring out the window, Liam gulps down the beer. "Shit."

The empty beer can hits the rim and just barely makes it into the trash on the other side of the room, and the little Advent Window set by his nightstand catches his eye. He was always fascinated with tiny boxes and compartments. Secret spaces.

Advent Windows are an old Christmas tradition in which children would keep track of how much time was left before the holiday. Each day, you're supposed to open one set of shutters on the front of what sort of looks like the facade of a dollhouse, and inside would be a holiday symbol or religious painting. The last little window being Christmas Day. His brother sent this set to him from Germany. It's a gorgeous oak with a deep, dark-stained finish. Almost black. Far nicer than the ones he remembered from his childhood.

He opens the set of thumb-sized shutters for "December 16th", and inside there's an ornate oil painting of an angelic young girl in a white cap and nightgown, holding a candle. Singing. Rosy cheeks. A picture of innocence. This micro-painting the size of a postage stamp, sits back almost a half-inch from the front edge of the small window. He notices that there's some dirt on the frame. Taking a breath, he blows on the dust, which promptly puffs back in his eyes. "Gah." Somewhat blindly, rubbing his eyebrows and blinking wide, he makes his way back to the fridge and retrieves another beer.

Collapsing in the chair at the table, he sees that "Paul" is next up in the stack of notebooks. "Jesus Christ. I don't know if I have the energy for you tonight, Paul."

Papers and empty cans swirl in the wind outside. Also sounds like some kids are playing with a ball out there. Kind of late for that crap, isn't it? It's never totally quiet here. Never.

Giving in to the task at hand, he starts with Paul and moves on through the others, all needing more attention than he can give, writing well into the evening and knocking down a few more beers along the way. At one point, he turns on the TV at a low volume just to have some background noise to cancel out the random annoyances drifting in from the alley.

17

"He's a bit flustered and twitchy for my blood."

"Liam?" JT rapid-fire forks scrambled eggs into her mouth, quick hit of coffee. "I'd fuck him if he had the right reproductive organs, yo. He's the only normal kid on the block."

Abby, believing she's being smooth about it, looks out the window from their usual booth at Beanie's. "What does he do? I mean, he's in and out of there like a hummingbird."

Attacking the toast on all sides. "Garment district, counselor, some shit."

"He's a counselor for fashionistas?"

"Two different jobs, I think. Jesus Ab, why would I care to know such details. And, c'mon, it makes a difference? You don't have to dive in the deep end. Just… use him for sex. I'm sure he'd be thrilled."

"Oh, I wouldn't do that."

"Yeeeah. Well, I myself have a weather-resistant libido. Rain or shine, kitty-kat."

"Ha! Thank God I'm not the only one." For some odd reason, the whole conversation is getting Abby a bit aroused.

JT burps. "Stop interrupting."

"You interrupt me all the time!"

"Shhh. Then again, if I did go that way, I'd probably sniff out more of a rigid, professional type."

"Professional type? JT? The too-cool-to-be-you master of mayhem."

"I know it's loony, but there really is something… something about the corporate uniform that tickles me below the belt. I mean, it's pathetic, right? Fucking neckties. Who decides that they all need to look like robots? It's all about control. And why is it that none of their clothes fit? Are they raiding their little brother's wardrobe? If they reached up to grab a handle on the subway, their sleeve would rip wide open. Some of their pant legs are so short

I can see leg hair and shin bones. We are not supposed to see leg hair and shin bones! But, God help me, for some twisted reason, I'd woof down all those happy trappings if I was straight. Every bit of it. One bite."

"So, no tendencies that way at all? Zero? Never had a crush on a guy in high school or anything?"

"Everyone has crushes on guys in high school. But I knew when I was in second grade what the deal was. I've always preferred them sticky, stinky, and stacked. My only go-to, I'm afraid."

"Wow. As you've somewhat mentioned."

Other than semi-regular exercise, Abby never really thinks much about her body. Her aunt had told her when she was in her teens to always have a favorite bra handy —one that didn't strangle and maim, as most did in those days— and wear it to bed. Not all the time, but often. That practice faded over the years, and she's not even sure if it ever did anything to help keep her package together, really, but when she goes to the gym (Fuck, I have to get to the gym...), she feels that maybe she is defying gravity a little compared to some of the other girls. That being said, she also knows that she isn't "stacked", and it's making her a little jealous of JT's ideal find in a lover. Strange how jealousy can just pop up, even though she has no interest in JT, or any other woman for that matter.

Well, okay, she was certainly willing to dip her toe in the pool way back when... She'd more than willingly gotten her lips locked with a luscious girl at a college party, during a suck-and-blow card game. And, sure, that didn't exactly suck, or blow, but it wasn't her particular bent either...

JT hasn't taken a breath. "Somethin' about frumpy old chicks, I can't stay away. Okay, let's bounce. I have a sneaky surprise for ya."

"Oh, I shouldn't today. Need to get started and stay focused. Batts is pretty much not talking to me."

"Nice!" JT's licking her fingertips.

"No. He's pissed. Looks at me sideways."

"He was born pissed, Ab. You're doin' plenny. C'mon, I really do have somethin' to show ya."

"Hold up a sec." Abby leans in. There are two small cross-hatched pipes at the end of the nylon thread around JT's neck. "Is that a cross on your necklace?" She reaches out to touch it.

JT leans back, trying to swallow her last mouthful of food. "Mmm, ungh..."

"Oh! Sillcock key. Right?"

She chokes a little and points at Abby like "bingo".

"Ah. Okay. Got it. Took a minute to sink in." Relieved that she actually remembered what that thing is called. A sillcock key, as she had been not-so-politely informed on her last landscaping job, is a tool for turning on outdoor water spigots that have no handle. Just slide the open end of the key onto the little nub, and twist, nice and slow...

JT looks down at her good luck charm, then back up. "Right. Sillcock. Good get. I've always called it a 'cross-key'. It does come in handy, also fits my uniform. Why didn't you eat?"

"Already ate twice. I eat all day long. And I'll eat again, soon-ish. Mostly cookies."

"Healthy."

"I try to mix it up, but I think high-fructose corn syrup makes up about forty percent of my caloric intake."

"Strange, momma. Alright. Let's go, missy."

Grease and salt in massive doses must make people speak at ridiculously high volumes, akin to sudden-onset alcohol deafness. At Beanie's, one also has to compete with the ambiance of crashing dishes, granted, but at some point, everyone gets stuck in overdrive, and there are no upper limits to the noise level.

JT barks over her shoulder on the way to the door, "Who was your hero when you were a kid?"

Abby has to think about that for a second. "Godzilla. It's my first memory of something I found interesting. She was the underdog most of the time."

"She?"

"Yeah."

"Godzilla is a 'she'?"

"She had a baby. Laid an egg in a cave, or some shit."

"Nooo. Maybe it's like a sea-horse deal, where the males carry the baby. Or hermaphrodite."

"Don't destroy the lifetime gender-moniker hung on my earliest childhood memory, man."

"Okay, okay, just thinkin' out loud."

"What about you? Who was JT's hero when she was a pup?"

JT slides sideways through the fire-hazard crowd at the front door.

"Wicked Witch of the West. Completely misunderstood, that dame. I'd put on green clown make-up and drag around broomsticks. Convinced a neighbor boy that he was a flying monkey. Got him to jump off his roof into a pile of leaves."

"Ouch!"

"Broken collarbone? He sure was makin' a lot of noise. Ambulance got there fast…"

18

The sun is making a special guest appearance today, so as they walk down the alley, JT puts on her uber-dark glasses before reaching into her jacket and pulling out a small gold dish, holding it up high like a trophy.

Abby feels the weight as JT proudly hands it to her. "What? What is this thing?"

"Guess."

"Monkey helmet?" She spins it around, touching the edges.

"Nope."

"IUD for a hippo?"

"What's a hippo?"

"Giant candle snuffer?"

"Close!" JT manages to light a joint while taking back her prize, twisting her head to blow the smoke away from Abby.

"I surrender."

"It's a holy water dish." She's beaming.

"O…kay…?"

"Heathen girl, jeez. When you walk into church, you're supposed to dip your fingers in the holy water dish and make the sign of the cross, like this." JT dabs some unseen liquid in the bowl and touches her forehead, chest, left shoulder, right shoulder. "This one was just about out of holy juice, so it made the perfect target."

"Nice… score?"

"God damn right, nice score."

"How did you pull it off?"

"Thanks for teeing that up for me, Abrianna. Normally I wouldn't spill any sanctified secrets, but this is way too good. So, the cathedral was packed." JT's eyes are amped up with a splash of evil. "The dish was on the wall by the doors in the back of the church. During a particularly loud part of 'Hallelujah' –that's a song– I pretended to fall right into it, *snap!*, and that mostly jarred it loose. The little beastie was still hangin' on, though. Then a couple of lurching, handsy do-gooders come over to make sure I'm alright. I think the noise woke them up. Now I'm trying to hold this thing against the wall with my butt while they keep saying shit like, 'Are you sure you're alright, honey? Maybe you should sit down.' And the whole time I think I'm gonna barf."

"Barf? You were really that nervous?"

"Nah. It's just that most of those lemmings smell like garlic. Not sure what that is. Trying to keep the vampires away? Anyhoo, had to hold my breath 'til I could shake'em and they went back to their pews. Oh, pews are rows of benches, meticulously designed by the forces of hell to induce back pain and hemorrhoids.

So, once they stopped swiveling their heads around with stupid looks on their faces, I went right back to it. Hands behind my back, jiggling and twisting this stubborn little bowl, trying not to make a lot of noise. Timing my moves with the singing and responses."

"Jesus."

"Indeed. Had to unthread a three-inch screw. My fingertips were raw. A couple pieces of plaster bounced out in front of my boots. At one point I almost dropped the whole thing…"

"Oh my."

"Then in one move I yanked her free, tucked 'er up in my pants and tiptoed towards the door. Trail of plaster dust trickling out as I sashayed along the rear of the church, sporting a massive panty bulge, and grinning so hard it hurt. As I slinked through the archway, one of the living dead turned around and smiled at me. Older, well-dressed, curvy… Okay, she was on the edge of delicious. We locked eyes, I winked at her, and I was free. It was so beautiful."

"Wow. Ballsy. Yet professional."

"T'was, kitten. Truly was."

"Wizard."

"Sorcerer is more like it. I can be almost invisible when I get in that zone, girl."

"No, I mean I gotta pee." Abby runs over to her favorite dumpster, scattering a flight of pigeons.

"They have bathrooms here, y'know?"

"Shhh."

"So, now the boring crap." JT talks through her exhale of dope smoke. "Today, I'm going to introduce you to the workroom, and I have to throw some other shit at ya. Like, more than a couple things."

"All good, fire away."

"K. Workroom's on the top floor. It was a nice apartment at one point, but it's in such bad shape now that we haven't been able to rent it for a while. We use it as a go-to when things are 'slow', which they never really fucking are, and try to address the repairs that are within our purview. Damn, wrong word, within our... scope?"

"Charge, I think."

"Tomato... potato. Either way, she's in bad shape. Every now and again, Batts will go on a rampage about how the unit is still not rentable. Upside is I store some stuff around the edges of the place. There's a workbench by the big windows, or you can just go up there for peaceful Zen moments when you need them. Or, when you don't want to freeze to death on the roof. Oh yeah, been meaning to ask, how is the roof?"

Abby aggressively kicks at the pigeons on the way back from the dumpster. JT is kind of getting on her nerves today. "Out of the way, damn. Um, roof, yes. Sure. I've pulled the hoses inside, cleaned the glass, pitched a couple of goners. Tested the solar heaters too. They're all good I think..."

"Okay, okay. That's fine. As long as you have something to tell that hump when he asks. Ready to scope out the magic of the workroom?" JT holds out the joint. "You sure on this?"

"Yeah, I'm good."

"Discipline. Impressive. Right, we better move."

19

Abby hadn't been inside any of the units on the top floor. There are only a handful of them up there, as much of that level is overrun with a nest of industrial hardware and vents that snake into jumbled pathways to nowhere. And there's obviously been no attempt to diminish their impact. It's as if someone dropped in a floor four feet too low, exposing all the pipes in the process. So what would normally be a penthouse area or sweet spot is kind of muddied by the endless flowering of logistical mutation.

As she and JT make their way into the workroom in 1014, Abby's enveloped by the childhood smell of Grandma's house. A special kind of musty that doesn't offend. Age. Timid corrosions.

There are black hash marks and deep grooves in the hardwood floor that look cool as hell but would probably be unacceptable for most potential tenants. The whole thing is starting to buckle. Her mother would say that it's "beyond the pale". That's why Batts won't pull the trigger on getting the unit together: a new floor is not a quick fix. And as beautiful as she is, the deck of this creaky ship is probably ready to be pulled up and tossed.

In every corner are mounds of random "supplies": tools, scrap wood, paint cans. One of the doorless closets is overflowing.

"I'd say for your to-do list in here, just start with organizing some of this stuff, like that closet of chaos. It's totally my bad that this is in such disarray, but it's turned into a bit of a catch-all, I'm afraid." JT looks around and drifts away somewhere in her head.

"No problem. What about these windows?" A couple are cracked; one has a latch that's hanging sideways. Abby walks over and runs her fingers along the frames. Loose paint chips pop up over her nails.

"Yes, good point. Eventually, whenever, a decent cleaning and maybe tighten some of those buggers up. They sing a little when the wind blows, a bit out of key."

"Got it."

"And whenever you find the time, leave some of the paint leftovers up here, and make this the next job on your paint-list as well. How are we on supplies?"

"Plenty of paint, but I need to go through the rest."

"That's cool. Good." Deep breath. "I'm sorry, lady, this is five lists in one. I'm just getting it all out. Add it onto your already hefty pile, as you see fit."

"I totally understand. Lots going on here." She makes a couple of notes in a small notebook that she keeps in her shirt pocket next to Pearl.

"How many transoms so far?"

"I've gotten through about a half-dozen. I think there's one that will need to be replaced eventually. The frame isn't secure, and there's a strange twist in the metal rim."

"Just sit on that thought for a while. If it's not going to fall out, give it a beat before you relay those types of things to the boss. Best to pick your moments with him. Save the potentially expensive items for when he's one-hundred-percent jolly."

"And, when might that be?"

"Mmm, Christmas Eve? See! You're in luck. Right around the corner. Now, today..." JT picks up the occasional item off the floor, looking at them as if she hasn't been up here in some time. "... I'll need to borrow you for maybe an hour to help me move some of the outdoor, summer furniture into the basement. Probably should have done that six weeks ago. And in other happy news –I'm going to start passing along your phone number, so I'm not the only one getting 'Please come wipe my asshole' calls. Being on-call sucks; that's all I can say about that. But it's the only real hassle we have to deal with other than Batts."

Abby takes more notes: *order JT decaf next time...*

"I know this all seems like a lot right now, but you're doin' great. I wish I could dole it out bit by bit, but I'll be stuck in the basement soon."

"'Stuck in the basement', with the furnaces."

"You win the prize. And I'm taking this weekend off. I swear that's the last thing."

"I feel like I'm being 'last-thinged' to death."

JT bark-laughs. "Sorry. I've got the electric tingles over here. You can have the weekend after this one-off, but I need a break, bad. Long overdue plans."

"Oh, what are you doing?"

"Me."

"Cool. I was going to hit Ardy's tonight. Want to swing in for a fast one before you… do yourself?"

"Nah. Cool place, but too happy. I prefer a little regret with my party. Thanks though. Okay, I'm *done* done, swear. What say you?"

"I'm in. Thanks for, well, thanks. I mean it."

"NP chickadee."

Abby walks over to the open closet and peers over the top edge of the scrap pile to see what's buried inside.

Looking out over the city, JT takes in the morning glow of the rooftops and grit. She exhales and decompresses. Dreamy voice: "Let's go move some shit."

They half-gallop down the steps. "Was there someone here before me? I mean to help you?"

"Sniffles used to hire the occasional temp-slash-stiff, but the owners pushed for another full-time hire, which I may or may not have made some noise about. He was cool with it in the end. Gives him more of a reason to jump up and down on my world, now that I have help –'There's no excuse for…', fill in the blank."

"Well, thanks again. I really need this gig."

"We'll see how you feel about it after this weekend."

"That's kinda what Batts said about the transoms."

"Really? Hate to think he's in my head even a little, let alone to the point of mimicry." JT stops and reaches down by her boot to pull out a mean-looking knife, maneuvering it to pick up a large pair of panties that are tangled in the stairwell railing. "Somebody's goin' commando…"

Outside, Reg is staring at the upper floors of the Lexington Arms. One of those quick glances that turns into contemplation. Tall buildings always seem like they're leaning, but today, with the backdrop of unbroken gloomy clouds rolling by, the towering Lex appears to be the ghost of a rickety drunk ready to tumble out into the street, with only the stubbornness of age holding her upright.

Liam shuffles down the sidewalk, pale, stiff.

"You look like shit today, Liam."

"Feeling that. And thanks for letting that fly with zero filter, man." He half kicks at the dead grass gnarled up around the edge of the street. "Reg, you like this place?"

"Sure, it's okay," still looking around at the facade.

"Doesn't seem, I don't know, sort of raw lately?"

"My guess is this old girl has always been a little raw. Maybe your lenses are fogged-up."

"Maybe. You okay with livin' here?"

Reg's voice drops to a whisper. "No offense, Liam, but I wouldn't live in a shithole like this if it was the last gruesome toilet in the whole damn city."

"What? You're always so… frikken chipper, and sellin' it, and… and you're always here!"

"I know you're young, but you've heard of a 'job', right?"

Abby and JT emerge from the building through a swirl of dead leaves.

There are two distinct winter seasons. The first is the almost imperceptible icing of everything. Trees hang onto their leaves way past the first frost. And when they finally let go in a strong wind, it seems odd to see the brown-yellow-green piles scattered about when it's so cold outside. But the second half of winter doesn't allow for such adornment. The leaves are buried in the frozen ground and decaying, getting ready to feed the same towers they fell from. Looking for cracks in the rock-solid soil like hands in the dark. Digging with patience fueled by determination, attempting to find anything resembling purchase. Who knows, there may be a hidden pathway somewhere down there that just might lead them home.

JT rolls up on Liam and Reg at the end of the walkway. She starts to skip high in the air as she gets closer and jumps right in between the two men. "Reggie Reg, what's the word?"

Liam takes an awkward step backwards, almost bumping into Abby.

She gently puts both hands on his back. Feels good. "Look out there, cowboy."

He spins around, startled. "Abby. We meet again."

"Seems like we can't do it without some kind of near collision."

"Yeah, at my age peripheral vision is more of a fading memory than an active sensory perception."

"At your age?"

"Forty-four. And, let me guess, you're… twenty-five?"

"C'mon, man."

"Twenty-eight?"

"Add ten."

"No shit?" He lets that hang there.

"Please, continue. I've developed a pretty high tolerance for compliments." The wind kicks up, and they both kind of shiver at the same time. "God, I hate this cold."

"Yeah, well, at least we haven't had any crazy snow yet."

"Oooh, I love the snow, though. Too bad it has to come from clouds."

"Doesn't like clouds, hates the cold, loves snow?"

Abby's head goes sideways. "Makes total sense to me. When it's not too cold, but snowing really hard, and the wind is moving the clouds along fast enough that the sun peeks out. That's my jam."

"Oh."

"Running for the exits, huh?"

"No, no. I'm intrigued. What about rain?"

"Guess."

"Hate it?"

"Indeed."

"Got it, cool…"

JT is finishing up with Reg. "Okay, man. Well, weather's turnin', baby. You sure you're managing out here?"

"Oh yes, young miss. It's technically still early in the season and I've already nabbed a new scarf, and these." Reg proudly holds up his hands that are a little too snugly wrapped in a pair of black leather driving gloves. "People abandon things all along this stretch." He sweeps his arms, conducting an invisible orchestra. "But at the end of the day I'm more prone to believe that these amenities jump ship of their own free will. The way I see it, they're escaping to a better life."

"Don't we have a 'lost & found box', or some such thing?"

"Yes we do, m'lady. It's called the trunk of me car."

"You do a girl proud, Reg." JT turns and walks a wide circle around Abby and Liam. "Hey, Liam."

"JT." He barely acknowledges.

"Okay, Ab, I'll be out back."

"No no, I'm ready." She turns to Liam. "See you."

He fumbles through his backpack and pulls out a card from the agency. "Yeah, yes, I hope so. My number's on the back. If you're bored, or wanna work on some dance moves, or anything."

"You dance?"

"No."

"Perfect." She tucks the card in her back pocket and follows JT around the corner of the building.

JT walks backwards in front of Abby with a smile so wide it looks as if her eyes are going to explode. "Uh huh!"

"Fuck you, JT."

20

She loves the way the world looks through the green tarp.

When jumping into a pool –or more likely a lake or pond– as a young girl, Lisa would often expel all the air from her lungs, gently, and just let herself sink, looking up at the rays of light cutting through the water as she descended. On one of those occasions, when she was maybe thirteen or fourteen years old, a good friend of hers, Jammin' Jill, decided it would be funny to hold her under after she'd "descended", and was trying to resurface for air.

Lisa was somewhat frail back then. Later on, in high school, she'd gotten discernably bulkier, mostly to keep the bullies at bay. She would get up before school and lift weights, run, hike the trails. By the end of sophomore year, she was no one to mess with. And even though she was tight with the "burn-out" crowd, she was far from burned-out.

But it was a quite petite Lisa who didn't even see Jill swimming over from the edge of the pool that day. The sun was smacking the surface of the water mercilessly. Even with sunglasses or colored goggles on, you still had to squint. The neighborhood kids were amped up, splashing around and screaming, but she had managed to slip away from the crowd and drift down, ten feet under and a million miles away. Embracing the luminous shafts. It was heaven.

By the time she kicked off the bottom, her lungs were already begging for air. Just as she was about to surface, Jill's hands landed firmly on her shoulders and pushed her back down –hard. There was a good bit of laughing and shouting above her as she panicked and tried to swim to the side of the pool. But Jill was too fast and met her, shoving her down again. And this time, she held her there. Lisa flailed at Jill's hands and body, but it was no use; she just couldn't make it past her. She involuntarily swallowed some water and really started to freak out.

When Jill finally moved aside and let her go, Lisa exploded up out of the water, far into the air as she recalls it, with her right hand raised high above her head.

Jill, wide-eyed, shrank away from her. "No, no, no!"

She dropped her forearm on Jill's shoulder with such force that she submerged her momentarily. Then continued to push her down –hard.

But Lisa was still trying to catch her breath and coughing, and Jill just swam away.

When everyone saw that she was gasping for air, they all changed their tune and apologized, including Jill. She felt horrible. Lisa came back to life relatively quickly, though, and they all ended up laughing.

"Jesus, Lis, I thought you were gonna kill me! Your arm was like a hammer!"

"Yeah, something took over there for a minute–when I couldn't breathe."

"Right. Sorry."

The tarp is flapping gently in the wind, but is firmly affixed to the corners of three ratty dumpsters that are hobbled together in an alley, providing a soft green glow for Lisa's new home. There are a few rips in the fabric that allow her to peek through at the clouds in the sky. The frayed outer edges remind her of palm fronds, or straw hats. A bit of the tropics to act as a counterweight to the shit-brown winter that has firmly gripped the city.

Her fiery-red hair is hanging in her face most of the time these days, so the crimson framing feels especially Christmassy against the beat-up green tarp in the background. A load of happy blood around a sad lake.

She was fortunate to find the spot, just two blocks from the Lex, where a certain dickhead may or may not live. And for whatever reason, the sea of homeless folks never seems to make it over this way. Her only regular visitors are junkies and pigeons. And she loves the pigeons. So much grit. And even though they usually stick together, she could tell that if push came to shove, they could damn well make it on their own.

One day, a drunk kid tried to take a leak a little too close to her makeshift hut, and she leapt out of the shadows, demon-growling. "GRAAAH!" The suddenly vibrant young man did that thing a deer does when it's truly startled –involuntarily leaping straight up into the air, almost suspended, before running away. As if a wave of bad had swatted his ass broadside, like a canoe oar slapping a barn door. *Pow!* Then he disappeared, a wisp of smoke. Gone.

"Where you goin spring chicken, huh?" she yelled behind him, hoping to God he'd gotten his meat chewed up in his zipper.

Food is easy. In some ways, she's eating better than she has in weeks. Now mostly nose-blind to the unseemly fragrances of her new world, the grub still smells delicious if she shoves it up in her face and inhales deeply –whole loaves of bread, almost untouched take-out meals, half of a pizza that was still warm, all perfectly fine.

Last week she'd found a set of extra-large baby crib covers and cushions still in the box. Makes for great bedding.

The homeless shelters allow for sleepovers on dangerously cold nights, and a morning shower, too, as long as you don't show up every day. Churches provide an occasional salty meal, and the college kids come around with toothbrushes and survival packs. Other than enduring the edges of frostbite and her slowly melting brain, she's having quite the adventure.

She'll be the first to admit that she may be seeing shadows, hearing soft voices in the wind. Like when a fan is running, and you're just about dozing, and in the guts of its frequencies, you begin to hear a conversation filtering in from another room. So you get up, walk over, and shut it off. Then nothing. What is that? No one really knows. Scientists only pretend to know. They're good at presentation, which is just a form of distraction. If a child can keep asking "why?", and at some point you can't answer them, then you don't know.

Also, admittedly, it's tough to tell if she's sleeping or awake sometimes. Only sometimes. She prefers a world without clocks, though. Always has. That trip she took by herself down south years ago... Yeah, that was perfect. She just partied and napped whenever the mood struck her. Natural rhythms. Her clock –not theirs. Certainly not his.

She starts to hear something strange, and it's getting closer. Nodding in sync with the sound, now unmistakable –the squawk of a truck's backup beeper. All at once, it gets much louder and pierces through the rustlings of the alley. *Beep-beep-beep.* The pigeons take flight en masse. "Oh fuck." She scrambles to her feet to grab the tarp as one of the dumpsters is already being lifted up off the ground. Yanking the cover free, she cowers against the wall, trying to coax in her bedding and meager belongings with her feet.

Curled up in a ball and looking through a hole in the tarp, she sees the huge mechanical arms flip the dumpster –or what was oh so recently her favorite wall!– up and over, sending trash and probably a lot of good food, tumbling into the back of the garbage truck. Lisa sits very still, hoping the driver doesn't see her, or give a shit.

Why does he still have that Goddamn beeper on! He's not even in reverse! Fuck head!

The steel prongs re-extend, bringing the dumpster back down to earth in a hurry, too fast for her to scramble out of the way. Flat against the wall, she holds her breath. With a crash hard enough to lift her off the ground, it solidly comes to rest. Through another slit in the tarp, she can barely make out the frozen maggots clinging to the rusty side of the ancient dumpster that now sits only a few inches from her face.

The noise of the truck fades and, in its place, she gradually hears birds. Just a few at first, then dozens. All types —finches, jays, crows, pigeons— making enough noise to drown out the city sounds. The feisty cackles echo through the brick canyons. She is surrounded.

Too shaken to get up and move around just yet, she catches her breath and slowly pulls the tarp down off her face. Craning her neck to look around the dumpsters and then up at the sky —there are no birds. Not one. Yet their cries are strident, and growing louder by the second.

"Christ, I hope that's real."

21

Paul walks around and turns on all the little TVs. They are running a wonderful mix of static today, and he adjusts the volume on each one so that the sound just lightly touches his ears.

Sauntering over to the closet, he opens the door and stares up at the pile of shirts covering his cut box that's perched on the back shelf. What was initially a nagging heat at the base of his neck now begins to intensify and bloom. Then all at once, his feet are cement. Unable to move in any direction, anxiety grips his whole body so firmly that it becomes difficult to breathe. He remains this way for an unforgiving eternity. Frozen.

Finally, his heart rate slows, and the air wheezes out of his lungs as if through a pinhole in a balloon. Looking down, he sees that he never let go of the doorknob. Taking a step back, he slams the door. Gazing out the window, he opens the door again, and –*SLAM.*

SLAM… SLAM… each time with more force. *SLAM, SLAM, SLAM…*

After so many vicious swings, his knuckles are bloody. The wooden frame is splintered and chipped, and the door itself is warped. He ramps up a scream –"aaaAAAH!" And with one final thrust, he falls to the floor, grunting and coughing.

A half hour later, he's still hunched over in a pile, when Liam knocks.

"Paul, you in there?"

Under his breath, "Diabolical." Then, louder, "A brief moment, sir!" Scrambling to his feet, he throws a sweater over the mangled closet door to hide some of the damage and hustles over to the bathroom. The pasty, gaunt man staring back at him in the mirror looks like death. He starts to wash the blood off his hands and then sputters to a stop, staring at the soap bubbles. Liam knocks again.

"You want me to come back later?"

"Just a minute!"

Paul squeezes one of his ravaged knuckles and dabs the blood onto his cheeks, then vigorously rubs in wide circular motions. Instant rouge. Ha!

He tiptoes over to the door, takes a breath, and swings it wide open.

Liam seems uncharacteristically light and bouncy.

"Well, you look effervescent. Arrive empty-handed, did we?" Paul is really starting to hate him.

"Yeah, I feel okay today. And, right, sorry, I haven't been out yet. Just stopped by to say 'hi'. How are things... well, things, man?" All the plants are gone, so now the apartment consists of the claw-foot tub in the middle of the main room, and the growing crowd of small TVs posing as a minefield of static. As far as Liam can tell, the rest of the place is completely empty.

"Oh, I've just been keeping up with the narrative and documentary television productions. Hobbies, as you've suggested. I used to think the late-night horror hosts were the worst. Disheveled, drunken frauds, unspooling the only ancient rights-free garbage they can get their hands on. But now you see before you a dedicated fan. Magic Morty the Midnight Mortician is probably the most gratifying. At least his costumes look as if they are coordinated by a reasonably talented stylist. I don't get many solid signals during the day. So it's generally the aforementioned night-owl surveillance." Trying to keep his voice level, tinkering with the nearest TV.

Paul seems okay for the most part, but he's definitely been cutting again. Liam can feel it. "Oh yeah, Magic Morty, I've seen that kat a few times. Well, not sure exactly when I'll be back, but I'll bring some righteous goods for the next visit. What'll it be?"

Paul pulls a twenty out of his pocket with his uninjured hand. "Surprise me. Nothing pedestrian. And nothing American either, please."

"Gotchya." Looking around, Liam is a little jealous of Paul's place. While he's worried that it's been slowly emptied over the last couple of months, it seems huge now, with the shadow of the fire escape playing the part of a giant sundial as it makes its way across the immaculate hardwood floor. "Alright. Enjoy the shows. I'm out." Liam turns to leave.

"Indeed. No sling?"

"All gone, finally. Paul, you okay?"

"Tip-top. And I appreciate your diligence. Truly, young man. God's speed."

"Sure, no problem. Maybe we can review some things next time. It's been a while."

"The anticipation engenders an effusive cornucopia of erstwhile emotions." As Liam walks out, Paul shuts the door gently behind him and very slowly twists the lock into place.

The carriage horses are tethered to rails near the side of the road, at the edge of the park. Cold rain is coming down light but steady, and all the drivers are across the street at a small pub, smoking cigars under the awning out front. They huddle around kerosene heat lamps, so they can stay toasty and dry. Unlike the horses, who are helplessly exposed.

Liam goes up to the bulky steeds, who intermittently try to shake off some of the rain, and one by one, gives them a little pat. "Hey, buddy, how we doin'? Yeah, cold today, huh?" A bus rumbles by and splashes a wave of muck halfway up their hind legs.

Fucking assholes, leaving these guys out here in this crap. When the temps fall below twenty degrees, they have to put the horses inside and cancel the carriage rides, but apparently, thirty-five degrees and raining is no problem. Bullshit. No shelter, no nothin'.

One of the drivers yells out from across the street: "Hey! Don't feed the horses!"

"I'm not feeding them!"

"Yeah? Well, don't kiss 'em either, asshole!" Exaggerated chuckles from the crowd. Batts is standing among them, puffing away on his cigar. Somehow the white gloves don't feel that out of place at a cigar bar. He recognizes Liam, and yet makes no attempt to put the brakes on the drivers who continue their taunts.

"Hey, keep it in your pants, lover!"

"See ya 'round, princess!"

Unfazed, Liam goes on his way.

As he makes his way up the road, his thoughts drift back to Paul.

I'll have to contact the agency about getting more help. Someone else to randomly swing by and check on him. But it needs to be stealthy. If Paul smells that it came from me, he'll pulverize whoever reaches out to get involved.

Liam ducks into a trippy-looking store and hears a greeting from above.

"Good afternoon, sir." Zoe had been making her way around the upper edges of the walls for an hour, both dusting and assessing.

"Oh, hello up there."

"Can I help you find anything today?"

"No thanks, just going to... look around. Smells good. I deliver to a few places near here. Wanted to stop in a million times, but they keep me runnin' on a pretty tight leash."

With bit of a forced smile. "Well, we'll have to get you off that leash at some point. Let me know if you have any questions now."

"Sure, thanks." He's worried that she may be a bit too much for that stool, but her movements are measured and graceful. She seems at ease up there.

One of the altars catches his eye. It's constructed with half-melted red candles, and a worn-out replication of the Virgin Mary printed on some type of foil –a deflated balloon maybe? Her hands are raised in an arc of radiating light, presiding over the fifteen or twenty little crosses that are strewn about the base.

Taking in the wide array of spiritual gear, he's particularly impressed with the variety of tapestries. Rubbing the edge of one between his fingers, he can feel that it's probably a cotton/poly blend. Practical. He grabs another that seems to be thin burlap, or hemp. No mass-produced knockoffs in here. "I have a friend who's really into these, but he leans towards darker colors. Do you have anything along those lines?"

Zoe shakes her head "no", and goes back behind the register, keeping an eye on him.

In the back of the store, he comes across the huge "give & take" box. Digging through some of the slightly weathered calendar pictures and samples, he finds a postcard. The back is blank. Looks old, or was processed to look like an aged photo. Great snow scene on the front. Perfect.

Back up front, he sets it on the counter. "How much for this little guy?"

"There's a sign back there, and a collection box next to the bin."

"Oh?" He kind of looks over his shoulder. "Sorry, I missed all that."

"S'okay. Minimum donation is one dollar."

"Alright." He fishes out a five and hands it to her.

"Thank you so much." She puts the bill in the register and closes the drawer. "Very generous of you." Her voice is light, eyes dancing.

It slowly sinks in that he's not getting back any change. "Yes, sure. Worth it. This is perfect... Great, well, thanks."

"Mm hm. Have a beautiful day."

The little chimes on the door sing out as Abby walks in.

"Hey, Liam, what shakes?"

"Abby... Oh, I was just... absorbing all this stuff. How cool is this place?"

"Hi, Zo."

Zoe is a little wide-eyed. "Uh huh."

"Yeah, it's brilliant." Abby bends down to pet Rudy the wily cat. "I've been coming here for years."

"She may be workin' here soon too." Zoe can't resist.

"Zoe!" Then, to Liam: "I'm not going to be working here, that is, any time soon." She glares at Zoe. "As much as I do love it."

"Well," Liam awkwardly tries to split his body language between them, "it's nice to be wanted."

Abby gets up on her tiptoes and tries to look in the bag. "Whadjya get?"

"Oh, just a little something for the apartment."

"Can I see?"

"Well, I—"

"Damn, give him some space." Zoe butting all the way in.

"Okay, but, I kinda wanna see."

Putting her hands on her hips. "Jeez, you're nosy!"

"I'm nosy because I wanna see?"

"No. You're nosy because I say so. Now let him be on his way."

Liam inches toward the door. "I'll hit you back at the Lex, and I'll show you there. Promise."

"Okay..."

"Call me, if JT ever gives you a break."

"Well, I have to call you now. I hate intrigue!"

They both laugh.

Zoe rolls her eyes. "I'm going to throw up all over my vagina."

Liam blushes. "Right. Cool. Thanks again, Zoe. See ya, Abby."

"Soon. Byyyeee." She's still eyeing the bag.

"Come back again." Zoe waves and watches Liam walk down the sidewalk. Another one of her cats –Proxy– barely jumps up on the counter and rubs all over Zoe's belly and breasts. She cuddles the cat, shakes her head. "So, now, you." Shifting her gaze towards Abby, "What's up with the white boy?"

109

22

In a dark corner of the deserted park, Chrystal's posterior is finally warming up a bit. When she'd plunked herself down on the bench she didn't care that her coat wasn't underneath her, or that her "lined dress" wasn't actually "lined" for shit.

These last couple days she can only look down. It isn't as if something were blocking her from looking up. She just doesn't feel like trying, at all. The world of "up" means happiness and discovery and laughter and touch. The world of "down" is safer right now.

You are so warm and round and smooth today. I'll take care of you. Ah, yes. There you are now. Push it. Pinch.

An "Oh!" pops out of her unexpectedly. Looking around, there's no one in sight. The park is empty and bleak. Under her coat, she continues to rub herself with stiff fingers through the little sheer pockets in her dress. Feels so good. She goes harder, digging, moaning a little. Quick head on a swivel. Her face is grimaced. "I'll fuck your... fuck me... fuck..." Her juices are warm and expanding. She's chafed herself bloody. And even though it stings, she still peaks and shutters, over and over again.

Gently stroking her inner thighs now, the feeling dissipates in waves. Her breathing gradually evens out. She creeks upright off the bench and, sucking in her gut, begins to cry. Every attempt to hold it back fails. A vibrating growl trembles out of her, low and long, until she finally gives in to the relentless pain, and lets the tears flow.

After a few minutes, she gets herself together and takes a couple quick, sharp breaths. Head down, walking across the grass through a patch of frozen leaves, she wanders over the hill into a ravine.

23

Abby strides up the walk to the Lex as JT is coming out of the building. "Where's Reg?"

"In the lobby poop palace. Him and Batts are having a contest today. How was the break?"

"Eventful. Went to Zoe's. Saw Liam there."

"I bet you did. So, remember, I have you on-call now too. I'm going to put up a calendar in the basement that will list our days off, weekends off, who's on-call –all that hype."

"Oh, nice. Thanks."

"I gotta run out for a bit, check your messages at some point, K?"

"Got it."

"And Ms Conrad says her transom's broken. I don't have her on the list yet, but you better at least stick your head in there at some point today. She doesn't quite grasp the concept that if she tortures Batts –she's ultimately torturing us. So the earlier we put out her fires, the better. Doable?"

"No problem."

The elevators are finally fixed, but Abby takes the steps up to ten to check out the workroom one more time before she starts back into her day. "Takes the steps" –as in jogs a few flights, walks the next dozen, then just shy of crawls the last few.

Gym. Tonight. Fucking jiggling n' shit. Ugh.

Sort of funky all along here. In her little notebook she writes *"sweep/mop stairwell"*.

Huffing and puffing, she takes in a little too much of the mealy aroma as she opens the workroom door. "Ouchie." Not so nostalgic anymore. It's muggy, too.

The larger of the doorless closets just may be the catch-all for JT's entire maintenance world. She tugs at a paint tarp that's twisted up with the mountain of junk in there, and eventually shakes it free. Some of the random items tumble out onto the warped floor.

There's something shiny hiding deep inside this closet of infinite recklessness. The light socket is empty, so she grabs her flashlight and, kicking some broken boards out of the way, creeps back into the unusually large space.

From under a pile of debris, she pulls out a gleaming silver… hmm… not sure… maybe an ice bucket? For champagne? It's a bit roughed up but has all the trappings of something that might have seen much better days. Pewter, genuine hammer marks for the indentations, hoop handle with a sliding wooden grip. Her hands are happy. Kind of tall and narrow for any kind of functional pail, but it's a real beauty. Thick. Heavy as shit. "Aaand, one more time, say it with me everyone –mine." She rinses it off and sets it by one of the singing windows. "We're gonna be friends, yes?" The wind picks up and the windows seem to answer for the bucket, in the affirmative.

Carrying a step stool as she makes her way through the second floor, Abby smells freshly baked cookies, and drifts into a mini-trance.

Okay, here it is, 214, Ms Conrad's hut.

The tabby is sitting up in the transom again, whiskers twitching. "Hi, you." As she reaches to knock on the door, Ms Conrad opens it while nonchalantly walking back into the living room. She whisks her arms into the sleeves of a perfectly fitted, double-breasted winter coat. Midnight blue, tapered, wool. Yep, she's rockin' that thing.

"Hello, young lady. Abby, is it?"

Abby removes her work boots and is taken by how beautifully the space is arranged. Regal furniture, set in groups and lines, not over-crowded. Nothing too frilly. A woman with a plan.

"Yes. Nice to officially—"

"Glad you're still here. Batts usually has them running for the exits before they can sweep a sidewalk or water a plant."

The cat curls around Abby's leg and she scratches his head. "Male, yes?"

"Indeed. Stewart, meet Abby. And please be a gentleman."

"How old?"

"Old enough to cost me a fortune. He's named after Stewart Granger, he was a— "

"Oh, I know all about him. Great actor. Good lookin' dude. *King Solomon's Mines, The Prisoner of Zenda.*"

Ms Conrad stops in her tracks. "I am very impressed."

"My mom is a big film buff."

"Well, he was a real man. None left for your generation, I'm afraid – they're all dead. I have to go out for my constitutional, but Stewart will give you no trouble. He won't run. Hasn't left this place in years unless he's going to see," with her hand at the side of her mouth, whispering, "the V-E-T." She flips through her purse. "I just made cookies…"

"Ah, so you're the culprit." She knows damn well there are cookies in that kitchen. "I smelled them walking up the hall."

"Please let me know how they came out. Far too early for me."

"Normally I'd do that phony 'oh no thanks' thing, but today I think I may just take you up on that."

"Never be phony, dear. And you bet your patootie you'll have a cookie or two, or three. I hear you're addicted, as such."

"Who told you?"

"Oh, I have my ways. And I insist. Have at it. Whatever remains will be for the Jensens. They just had a baby, you know."

"Yes, I've heard her in passing."

"Angelica. A little saint." Proudly: "I know just about everyone in the building. Try to make my rounds. Do reach out if you need any introductions. I'm sure it's not easy being the new face around here." Ms Conrad looks her up and down.

"Thanks. Everyone's been pretty cool so far."

"Well, as I said, we'll give you some credence just for dealing with Batts, to this point anyway. I try to mind my Christian heart. Must be some good in him somewhere. Please lock up when you're done. I'll feed the menace when I return."

"No problem. Oh, Ms Conrad, before you go, what's wrong with the transom?"

She very deliberately looks up at it, then back at Abby, "It doesn't work, dear."

"Gotchya. Okay, well have fun out there. Nice meeting you."

"You as well. And thank you in advance. Goodbye, Stewart, you behave now." One more time rummaging through the purse. "Ah, keys. Good." She marches down the hallway and Abby slowly shuts the door.

The apartment is immaculate. No dust. No funk. She opens her step stool and climbs up to take a look at the transom.

Stewart ninja's off a chair, then the coat rack, and lands right in Abby's face. Not hissing or mean, just staring at her. Purring. "Damn, dude, ease up." She gently places him back on top of the coat rack so he can get a good view. "Alright, let's get this thing humming."

It hits her that the cookies are probably still warm. Hopping down, she bolts into the kitchen as if someone were chasing her. Stewart does a double-twitch but stands firm. Abby moans through a mouthful of melty chocolate chip cookie. "Oh my God, so good."

The end of the work day grips Abby's body as she limps into her own apartment. In the fading afternoon light, the dust broom, or what's left of it, looks up at her from the floor in the kitchen. It's been picked clean, like a roasted chicken in the fridge at a keg party. "So, Grumpy, maybe you need a better home, too," propping him up against the breadbasket on top of the refrigerator.

She eyes up all the spiky radios, that now form a large cross hanging by the window, and pointedly asks Grumpy, "Whaddya think? Not sold yet? Hmm. I like 'em."

The light is soft but even, so she gets out the camera and snaps off a half-dozen shots of the monument to radio zip codes, the frozen cross, runway of caskets, the tooth song of the grump, the static cactus. The broom straws poking out of the speakers are making long shadows against the window frame. And they minimize the rainbow effect of all the different colored radios. Kind of level the playing field a bit.

Every transistor she owns has been recruited for the assignment, except Pearl. There is some real bonding going on with her. And she needs someone to hang out with at *work*-work, and other practicalities, too –like putting on some music in the middle of the night so she doesn't have a nervous breakdown. Bottom line is that she loves the way Pearl feels in her hand. She fits.

Speaking of… She pulls out Mother Pearl and dials in a station. Ah, Psychedelic Furs, "The Ghost in You". The song that never dies. Thanks, Miss.

She reaches up and turns on the bottom two "cross radios", while being careful not to break off any pieces of straw, then gets everyone on the same frequency. A little staticky, not a very strong signal tonight. But the layers sound good. And every once in a while the straw vibrates and hums along with the music. A quick glimpse into our connection with everything, via post new-wave psychepoppicabritticamommaca.

Alright, and now –gym.

Half a dozen people or so in Ardy's Gym this evening. Not too crowded, but not dead. Decent energy, good vibe. The balmy aroma of sweat and recycled air is a bitter price to pay upon entry, the initial severity of which emphasizes the fact that Abby hasn't been here in almost three weeks. But hitting the heavy bag will be glorious.

And as far as the clientele goes, Zoe would say, "No prizes, but not many cracker-jacks either." That not-so-subtle derision aside, it is refreshing not to be the only black kid in the county down here. She hasn't even seen anyone with a decent tan over at the Lex. Also, and not insignificantly, the guys at the gym treat her like a princess.

"Want me to hold that bag, Ab?"

"No, thanks, I'll just keep it loose." She continues to pound the cracked brown leather shell of the fifty-pound sack. "Where's Ardy?" She knows, though. It's past three o'clock.

Half of the gym answers, "Bar", as a kid with a broom points up, and shakes his head.

Far from soundproof, you can always hear the jukebox and the crowd upstairs while you're working out. Even if the gym is packed, or everyone is yelling at the sparring going on in the ring, there is a perpetual hum drifting down from Ardy's Ringside Bar. The angels of the night are always singing.

She continues to punch from the shoulder. Focused and ferocious.

Home. Quick shower. Slightly too tight (okay –death-claw grip) jeans, decent shoes, then right back out to the bar for a fast one.

24

Long before Ardy's Gym, or Ardy's Ringside Bar, a fifteen-year-old Artemus Perceval Raines had made his way to the northern cities from a small Tennessee town just on the other side of the Mississippi border. "Made his way", as in fled with a trusty satchel over his shoulder, traversing very carefully through some mean territories. He'd left his mother and sister behind, promising to either return with some money, or help them tunnel out, too. There were simply no prospects back home.

This journey took place many years before the era that saw Emmett Till murdered, Rosa Parks taking a front seat on the bus, and the 16th Street Baptist Church explode –killing four little girls simply because they were black. So every step north was taken with the utmost caution, enduring spitting, name calling, and bottles or bricks being thrown from moving vehicles as he plowed forward. When they chased him, he ran. He knew what would happen if they caught him. But they weren't going to catch him. "Not today," he'd said over his shoulder a dozen times along the way. Overall he'd picked his paths well though, so most of the time he'd just have to walk fast and keep quiet. Trying to be invisible. Leaning on his Christian teachings of forgiveness and love, he did his best to stay focused on what he knew would be a better life, just on the other side of those mountains. Deep in the vengeful places of his heart, however, he wanted to punch every one of those ignorant evil folks until they stopped breathing.

Even with all the determination in the world, there were still plenty of lonely nights in desolate, scary places. Strange noises pricking his ears. Sleeping with one eye open became second nature.

It was during one such night that a persistent grinding woke him. It wasn't a harsh sound, more like something being dragged along the ground, in short spurts, over and over. He finally had to go see what it was, even though he might be half-sleepwalking into very real danger.

Ardy pushed through thick brush, rubbing his eyes, and took a couple knocks on the noggin from low-hanging tree branches as he crept towards the sound. The wind was swirling when he climbed out of a gully and into a small clearing. Still ducking and holding his hands up in front of him as the crescent moon was sneaking in and out of the clouds, he hit something soft just above his head. It startled him enough to jerk back and to the side. At first, he thought it was a sack of seed, or a tarp slung over a branch. He fished around in his pockets for a precious match and struck it against a stone at his feet, only to look up and see two ghastly, mangled feet staring him right in the eyes. He backed away and held the match up to reveal the dangling body.

The boy wasn't much older than him, from what he could tell. His face had two big holes in it, one in the cheek and the other in his temple. One of his eyes had been gouged out, maybe by a crow, maybe not, and his left arm appeared to be pointing in three different directions. That's what was making the sound. The cuff of the young man's flannel shirt was rubbing against a big piece of half-peeled tree-bark as his lifeless corpse swayed in the mountain breeze.

Wasn't the worst he had seen, but this guy had suffered plenty before the big brave men strung him up on this old cottonwood tree; they were probably too stupid and lazy to display the body in a more prominent area, as was more typical in the grand tradition of such noble, patriotic citizens.

He thanked the boy silently for quite possibly taking his place, and stood there until the match burned his fingers.

By the time winter swooped in, Ardy had made his way into the biggest city he'd ever seen. There were people of every color and stripe. A newspaper article on the Chinatown area caught his eye, and he eventually ended up falling in love with that vibrant neighborhood. So many traditions and festivities. And Little Italy was right next door. Sometimes a friendly vendor would toss him a piece of fruit or a nub of sausage. They could easily see he was a street kid. But once he got his bearings, he spent most of his time loitering around boxing gyms that were scattered along the fringes of the main drags.

He managed to get a job at one of the out-of-the-way places, emptying spit buckets and taking out the trash. To him, it was all glorious: the sweat, the grit, the fights. Very quickly, he got moved up to laundry duties and equipment wrangling, until one day the owner gave him a key to the place. And then his life changed –working all day, training most nights after the gym was closed. No one ever caught on that he was sleeping there, too.

Studying everything he could, and trying to replicate it, became his world. Now he was determined to get in the ring.

Unfortunately, his boxing career was brief. At twenty years old, in his fifth amateur bout, he got a thumb in his eye and almost lost it for good. And though the doctors had managed to save the eye, his vision was never quite the same. If you can't see a right hook comin', you can't see shit. So, after all that diligence, he hung up the gloves and started to train and coach; taking what he had so meticulously studied and channeling it into his fighters.

By the age of twenty-two, he had saved enough money to bring his mother and sister to the city, and soon after was promoted to assistant trainer for heavy-weight Ted Collins. Ardy's rapidly expanding knowledge of the sport and his insatiable hunger would ultimately give him the opportunity to be Ted's full-time trainer. And it was under Ardy's sober but tenacious guidance that Collins would eventually win the heavy-weight title.

With all of the rewards and connections that the championship brought into Ardy's world, he opened a youth center and boxing gym, and purchased the small bar above it as insurance against tough times. At one point, he had a bid in on buying the whole building but backed out at the last minute. One of his only regrets. He had no idea at the time what 114th and Main would turn into over the years. Still, not too shabby for a guy with an eighth-grade education and no connections or resources to speak of when he had shown up in this quite intimidating metropolis all those years ago.

The kids in his boxing program are his heart. The boxing ring, his soul. But the bar? The bar is his church. The pulpit from which he can tell all the old stories, sing all the old songs, and flirt with every girl in sight. Maybe he's going at it a little hard and heavy these days, but at seventy-four years old he doesn't seem overly concerned about much of anything really.

Ardy was born to reminisce, and he'll answer any question you have:
Greatest fighter of all time?
Joe Louis and Rocky Marciano –Tie.
Best fighter he ever trained?
Ted Collins.
Most dangerous fighter he'd ever seen?
Ted Collins.
Most underrated fighter of all time?
Guess!

Favorite ringside technique?
The Silver Sting.

Implemented to stop excessive bleeding and seal cuts, the Silver Sting is efficient and, in an odd way, kind of stylish. Drop a handful of silver dollars into a bucket and fill it with ice. Leave it ringside, and if the fight goes long and ugly, you'll be prepared.

Let's say your fighter comes to the corner with a big gash on their cheek, and it's freely gushing blood. Quickly wipe it clean, sanitize, get a fresh towel on it, then reach deep down in that bucket and fish out one of those frozen silver dollars. As you move the towel out of the way, slap that coin right on the cut –*tsss*. It's more of a scalding feeling than cold. Press it firmly, but evenly. Hold it there for twenty seconds, then voilà– your boy is numb. No blood, no nothing. Clip on a butterfly, smear a gob of Vaseline, then send him back into battle. Alchemy and wonder. They won't allow it in the States anymore, health department regulations. But Ardy did some fights in Eastern Europe and Central America last year and, according to him, he'd pulled out the silver more than once.

Ardy's chiseled old pub is a locals' favorite; it doesn't get many tourists. A long bar dominates the narrow room. Tight, dark-ish. That would be "dark-ish" as in "dark", as in it's not lit up like a grocery store or an operating room –because it's a fucking bar. Christmas lights are hung up year-round, decoupage of boxing pics on the tables, boxing posters and artwork on every wall, a "Rocky" pinball machine. A classic jukebox with rainbow neon glass sits in the far corner, and there's always a crazy mix of people drifting in and out.

As time marches on, and on, Abby now prefers day-trips. She couldn't always trust herself to completely behave at night, but screw it. She is beat up. "Torn and Frayed", as Mick and the boys would say. Time for a drink. Or two.

Walking into this roadside temple, she sees Ardy carrying a case of beer back behind the bar, not his usual game. It is fairly packed tonight, so maybe he's having mercy on the bartender and throwing him a bone.

As he gracefully stocks the bottles in the front cooler, he peppers one of the older customers with questions. Rolling a toothpick around on his lips with a kind of chewing motion, "And what time did *you* leave last night, Joe?"

"Oh, um… i was outta here around…eight-thirty, I think."

"C'mon. That's bullshit. I left here around eleven, and you were still sittin' there drinkin'. What time did you really leave?"

"Oh? Mm, right... uh... five after eleven?..."

"Okay, buddy. Hey! Abby!"

Abby shakes her arms and stomps her feet, taking in the warmth. "Ardy, how's the world treatin' ya? Long time, yeah?"

"Christ girl, I thought someone was holdin' you for ransom."

"Which you'd volunteer to cough right up."

"Hell no. But I'd find some unwitting noodle-brain to pay the piper for ya." He comes around the bar, reeking of whiskey, and gives her a bear-hug and a kiss on the cheek. "First one's on me."

Zoe is holding court at the far end of the room, and Abby heads off in that general direction, but gradually snakes towards the bathroom.

The door is locked. Fuck. Have to wait. Hope they're not leaving me any presents in there.

She spies a new picture on the wall. It's a 1950s scene of a family sitting around a small TV watching a boxing match. Hanging right above it is a painting of butterflies, possibly forming a mosaic of Muhammad Ali? The door pops open and a mighty drunk college girl wobbles around her, eyes looking two different directions. "All yours, sexy face lady girl..."

25

As the evening winds down, Abby is one of a half-dozen late-nighters under Zoe's spell, listening to her tell voodoo stories.

Zoe leans against the bar as she preaches, blatantly hitting on the young men in the crowd along the way, slurring a bit. "People who do witchy shit; can't help themselves. If they understand that it is a craft, and if they are trained properly, they will come to know that assisting and healing others is the only true path. The path of light. But there are a million other avenues just waiting to be embraced. Some of them oozin' through the dark forest, cold and wet on the ground, trickling up the legs and around the heart. These affects bring clouds. And sometimes those clouds bring storms. Most folks, however, once immersed in the art, do follow the good, and the true. So, it would make logical sense that with so many standing in the light –darkness wouldn't have a chance. Right? It would be overpowered by the sheer number of positive forces in the world. But the impulse to practice, regardless of intent, can be irresistible. And in the end, there is no logic, no reason, only the path one chooses. We hold out hope that the benevolent wind blows fair and free, far and wide. And," holding up a finger, "is strong enough to withstand the tokens of ill will. The impure spirits, that are only ever cast aside, but never completely banished for good…"

From the other end of the bar, a tipsy Ardy chimes in. "Hey, Zo, when you gonna sing me a song?"

"When it's not punchy-the-drunk time, that's when."

"C'mon, beautiful, one for the owner."

"Just mind your little harem girls, Mister Ardy. You just mind your own." She turns back to her captivated audience. "Now, to fight, your resolve must be iron-clad. But you don't have to completely annihilate the curse to shake loose from whatever rears its ugly head. In fact, most of the time you shouldn't even try. It will always be there, waiting with infinite patience for you to overreach in just that way, z'matter of fact. Sometimes all you need to do is let the darkness know that you are willing to stand up to it, and most of your problems should be solved.

"You may need to eviscerate its earthly source though, or what you perceive as 'the source', but remember that what you encounter in this world is just a tool. A puppet doing the master's bidding. And the master, unfortunately, is omnipresent. That spirit will be ever watchful, looking for an opening. So don't give it one. It only needs an inch to sneak in and unleash God-knows-what. But, still, for day-to-day combat in this realm, keep in mind that people who manipulate are cowards. They don't really want to get down and tussle. It's all a pose. Be bold in that moment, and you will surely win that particular battle. Just don't fool yourself into believing that you can win a war. Gods win wars. Soldiers just try to survive to stay alive and thrive, knowing perfection is the biggest lie ever sold…"

Ardy points Zoe's way. "Stick and move! Rocky! Carl Weathers! Damn straight!"

"Ugh! It was Tony Burton tellin' that *to* Carl Weathers in the corner! Apollo Creed didn't tell himself to 'stick and move!' Old fool."

"Wait, but, did I say that?" Ardy looks to the ceiling as if he's trying to remember.

Abby straightens up on the barstool, and the urge strikes. Weaving through the crowd, she spins not so gracefully and almost bumps her nose on the bathroom door. Locked again. "Shit." Someone taps her on the shoulder. "Yeah, I'm waiting too, it's occup—" But as she turns around, there's no one anywhere near her. "Ha! Pranksters."

The Muhammad Ali painting with the butterflies is cooler than she'd first thought. Looking more closely at it while she's waiting, all of the little wings morph into arrows pointing down. Following their lead, she again sees the old black-and-white picture hanging just below it of the family gathered round the TV. But now, instead of a boxing match, the TV screen in the photo is filled with sparks and rolling static. She shakes her head and tries to refocus.

Wow, wow, wow, I need some sleep.

After a hypnotic hand-wash, she meanders back up to the bar, wondering which seat is hers.

"Abigale, let me buy you a drink." Zoe is in her element.

"No, I got it!" Ardy yells from the other end of the bar.

"If you don't shush, I'll shush you for you. I got this."

"Thanks, guys, but I really have to boogie." Abby struggles to get her coat on. "Work tomorrow n' all."

"Nonsense, one drink. We'll do a quick shot, and then you go, fair?"

"No, not fair, but… I'll play."

"Me too!" Ardy eases down the bar. As he tries to put his hand on Abby's shoulder, she slides away to order the shots.

"Three pumpkin pies, please."

Zoe leans back, arms folded, sleepy. "Maybe I don't want no pumpkin pup puppy."

"You started this; I'll finish it. Pumpkin Pies are relatively harmless, and I need harmless. I gotta go."

"I know, I know, I know. You gotta go, gotta go. Damn. Like a talking doll with a pull-string that only says one thing. 'Yyyaaa –I gotta go, Yyyaaa– I gotta go'."

The pale skinny bartender sets up the drinks, lights a match, delicately sets the top of each shot glass aflame, then blows them out. A bit concerned, "Give it a second before you drink those, K, guys?"

"Got it. Thanks." Abby holds out some money.

"No, no. On the house." Ardy picks up his shot.

"'Bout time, 'on the house', cheap ass." Zoe, abandoning her former objections. She raises her shot glass high, "To Abigale, may she always be, well… always be. How's that?"

"Killer. I'll take it. Nice job, Zoe. Cheers!"

Abby walks out of the bar into an obnoxious wind. Head down, she slips a little on a coin, or a beer cap, maybe. When she takes her next step, she inexplicably slides four feet across the sidewalk, as if someone gently pushed her on ice skates. Spinning around, she comes to a wiggly stop. "Whoa."

After a couple false starts, she manages to move on down the block.

Gotta crash. Stayed too long. Fun though. Alright. Crap, I never ate any dinner. Damn it. Just get home. Please, just get me home.

It's almost midnight, and she certainly isn't up for any chit-chat. She hustles along with the occasional not-so-graceful moment but makes it cleanly to her apartment door.

Water. Cookies. Bed.

As her head hits the pillow, she snaps back upright.

Holy shit, I never checked the messages.

She has five.

The first one is from Annalise: "Just calling to say hi, hon. Got back from New Orleans earlier than expected. I'll catch up with you soon. Love you so much, Ab." Mom sounds terrible.

Next is JT: "See you in the morning, kitty-kat. Thanks for jumpin' in today. I have some stuff to chase down early tomorrow, so I'll be starting a little late…"

Jesus, go away JT.

The third and fourth are just hang-ups. Alright, one more: "Hi, Abby is it? I don't believe we've met, but I'm Betty Morton, in 304? And I think our heater is broken…"

"Son of a fuck." Abby octopus-arms it all over the apartment, changing her shirt, grabbing her tool belt, boots, cold water to the face, a lick of toothpaste, spit. She hangs onto the sink as the water drips off her hair.

"I hate to bother you with this, but JT's message said to call you and, well, we actually have ice on the inside of our windows, and, isn't that crazy? So, if you could stop down when you get this…"

Abby navigates her way through the stairwell, one hand gliding along the dirty wall as she descends. Her chest starts to feel warm.

She gets to 304. Dizzy. The blue light of the TV is flashing off the transom, and she can hear laughter inside. Deep breath. She knocks.

"Mrs Morton?"

A moment later, the door slowly opens, and the angelic figurine of a woman standing before her may as well be holding a slice of apple pie and waving the flag. Rosy cheeks –probably from the cold– friendly eyes, pleasantly plump, wearing an oversized parka hood at half-moon. "Abby?"

"Yes. I am so sorry. I missed your message earlier."

"Oh, that's okay, dear. We're just riding the storm out in here. This is my husband, William." He's in a wheelchair that's parked next to the couch in front of the TV.

My incompetence is harming the handicapped. Stellar.

Abby makes her way over to the steam radiator near the, yes, icy windows.

"Hello, Mr Morton, nice to meet you. I'm very sorry about all of this."

"No problem, young lady. Life is a tricky piggy sometimes, isn't she?"

"Oh, Bill. Stop it...Can I get you anything, Abby? A glass of water?"

Abby's voice cracks. "No, no, I'm fine, thank you."

The radiator is cold to the touch. She runs her fingers down the far side to a flat metal knob near the floor. It has decades of paint on it, but there are some embossed letters around the edge. "Open" with an arrow to the left, "Close" with an arrow to the right. Okay. She can handle that much. Pressing her hand down, she tries to turn it, but it won't budge. Maybe it's all the way open and just not getting any water for the heat.

She pulls a wrench out of her tool belt and gets a good grip. It moves a little. Palming the knob again, she slowly manages to ease it open. There is a low hissing sound. The room spins hard, causing her to sway a bit.

"Are you okay, dear?"

"Ah, yeah. Lost my balance for a second. Let's give this a minute. I think we have some action over here." They both look at her, smiling, no animosity whatsoever. Abby knows if the situation were reversed, she'd be pissed off out of her mind. Thank God they're not angry. Well, yet.

After a couple of minutes, she can feel the heat pumping through the radiator; the hiss fades, and it seems to be functioning.

"Okay, I think that valve was just stuck. I'll make sure JT catches up with you guys tomorrow, er, later today, because she's really the expert with these things. But I think you're cooking now."

"Oh, thank you so much. It feels warmer in here already. I apologize for the late hour."

"No bother at all, truly. I'm so sorry that I missed the call. Please let me know if you need anything else, guys. It was nice meeting you."

"You too, sweetheart. Be careful out there."

So, how do you know you're wasted? Because you're taking the elevator to go up exactly one floor –that's how you know you're wasted. Idiot. I go out for a beer, and now I'm in hell.

As the elevator jolts and rocks, she thinks she's going to hurl. Hustling inside her apartment, she peels off her boots, throws the tool belt, and climbs into bed. Face down, fully clothed, lights on, comatose.

26

Abby wakes to a thunderous pounding on the door. She barely pushes herself up, rolls over, and hits the floor with a thump. "Coming!"

Ugh, how is it so bright in here?

Swinging the door open, rubbing her face. "Give me a minute, JT, I'm…"

Batts glares at her with piercing, electric eyes. "Nope, just me. Gee, I hope I'm not disturbing you. Mind if I come in?" He's wringing his gloved hands like a mad scientist.

Abby is wide-eyed, backing away, slow and steady.

"Well, I can see you've been busy in here," looking up at the radio/straw project hanging from the window. "No animal sacrifices, I hope. You know, when I was on my way over today, I wasn't exactly sure what I was going to run into. I mean, don't get me wrong now, I knew it was gonna suck out loud, but, well… You better have a seat, sweetie."

She frumps down on the bed, assessing her completely wrinkled clothes, then just stares at the floor. Getting lost in the grooves of the hardwood. Her temples are pounding and her mind starts to race. What the hell is this about?

"I got a call from the Mortons this morning. They said you were there last night regarding their heater?"

She's trying to pull her hair back or down, something. "Yes, I was…"

"Shut up. They said when they woke up today, their apartment was flooded, and it seemed to be coming from the knob on the radiator. They tried to shut it off, but they couldn't stop the flow."

"Oh, God."

"Now, I get there as fast as I can, and just when I manage to stem the tide, the college kids in the apartment below come up and tell me that there's water dripping from their ceiling. So I quickly go down and clean that up and inspect the damage. Damage that will cost a shit-ton of money to fix." Sniff, sniff.

Holy fuck. I blew it. I'm done.

"Then, when I'm finishing up in the kids' unit, I notice that their transom is all bent to hell. I mean fucked up, twisted like a pretzel. The frame is so bad that the whole thing looks like it's going to fall out onto the floor. I check the list, and they're on it. Then I think, well, she must not have gotten to this one yet—"

"I meant to—"

"Shut… up. But then the boys tell me that you *had* been there, and tightened up a few things, said that you would get back to them about the frame, but you never did. It was hanging by a thread. I had to yank it out of there because I was afraid it might tumble down and fucking kill someone. We did talk about that, right? Not killing people in the building?

"Now I make my way up to the workroom on ten to grab some putty and paint. Maybe find a piece of plywood, or something, to cover the hole that was oh so recently a transom." Abby can tell he's trying to keep his breathing even so he can get this all out. "I also wanted to calm down for a minute before I kicked the shit out of you two clowns, not that I had a moment to go find you assholes because I was running around putting out fires all over the whole damn building as soon as I walked in. Back to back to back!" Sniff. "So I go into the workroom, and there is garbage, all over the floor. As if someone went into the closets and tossed shit out while they were spinning in a circle. It was like wading through a landfill. JT said you guys were up there yesterday. Havin' a little party, were ya? And I know she didn't leave it like that either."

"I am so sorry—"

"I'm not done with you yet, superstar." He tilts his head back, not taking his eyes off her. "So I sift through the crap piles and take what I need in there. Then JT, I'm sure having heard that I was on the rampage, comes up and, trying to stick up for her new pal, attempts to explain everything away. As you can imagine, I didn't listen much, and in turn, passed on a few of my thoughts and suggestions.

"We made our way to the stairwell and, JT? She was calm, at least on the outside. Me? Not so much. She probably wanted to give you a quick warning, but I told her if she did, I'd fire her on the spot. Y'see, I'm more of a 'hands-on' type.

"Next up. As I'm still relaying my take on the various disasters that are popping up like popcorn, and as JT was eagerly trotting back down the steps, I see clothes hanging over the railings, and mud, and cans, and, again, enough shit piled up in that stairwell to sink a boat."

Abby's head is in her hands; she feels like she's going to puke.

"Back downstairs, I finish up with the Mortons, and the half-wit college kids, and while I was thinking of ways to strangle you bitches and ditch your bodies in the East River, I get an itch and head down to the lobby to take a dump. But before I can catch even that much of a break, Ms Conrad comes up to me, kind of sheepish. Not usually the sheepish type, Ms Conrad, y'understand. And by now, I'm thinking, bring it. What else could possibly be fucked up at the ol' Lex today? And she says, '*Mr Batts...*' —all nice and courteous. And, by the way, she hasn't used the word 'mister', or been nice, or courteous towards me, ever." Flapping his arms now as he squeaks out a high-pitched imitation of Ms C: "*I don't want to get anyone in trouble, but when Abby finished up in my apartment yesterday, she left the door unlocked...*'"

I'm going to kill myself with toothpicks.

"*And, well, I just want to make sure that, it doesn't happen again...*'" She went on and on.

Look, I'm not sure why, but she actually likes you. So does JT. We wouldn't be having this much of a chat right now if either of those things weren't true. You understand that, right, honey?" Quickly holding up his hands: "Ah... just nod."

Abby nods, getting lost in the grooves of the floor again. Imagining that she is on a tiny ship sailing through them, out from a port and into the open sea, where she can freely power-vomit.

"Great. I feel like we're reaching some kind of understanding now. Clean yourself up, get some coffee —I could smell the booze before you opened the door— and get the fuck to work. Don't touch the heaters until you talk to JT. They're not flippin' toys. I got the transom and the Mortons, so just stay far, far away from both of those. Hit the workroom and the stairwell, then find that he-she bitch-bag, and between the two of you, I want this place running like a clock. If I have to come back out here this week for anything, anything at all, you're both gone. Comprende, chiquita?"

On the edge of tears, Abby nods.

He daintily steps into the hall and eases the door shut. Shaking his head, he checks out every transom as he makes his way to the elevator.

27

Mid-morning steamers are always high on Batts's list of priorities. And the crapbox in the lobby at the Lex is one of his favorite haunts. Roomy, echo-y, big mirror, and it's hidden behind the elevators at the far end of the building. Half of the tenants don't even know it's there. Reg is the only other frequent flyer, and he's usually a crack-of-dawn and/or late-afternoon guy. More often than not, that would be an "and", as in "also", as in "who could possibly shit that much?" Old bastard's probably sleeping in there half the time. Good trick, actually –getting paid to poop.

Grabbing a newspaper from a table in the entranceway, he wanders back to have a well-earned moment. When he elbows the door open, the lights come on. Motion sensors. Finally.

Also looks like JT cleaned up in here, and changed the bulbs, too. At least somebody's doing one blessed thing I asked them to do, even though it was over a month ago.

Gloves off and folded thin, he tucks them in his shirt pocket, then washes his face with vigor, an all-out assault. He has some floaters in his eyes. Blinking hard a couple of times, Batts tries to focus on a swirl of fuzz in the corner of the room. Something sitting on top of it. Shiny. Lucky penny? He couldn't tell.

After the fourth power-washing ceremony is complete, he shuffles around the sink and, hands on his knees, bends over slightly, to the position he will momentarily take in the captain's chair, and takes a closer look.

Broken earring or something mixed in with the muck on the floor. Christ, she can't even properly sweep up a bathroom. Looks like ya missed a spot here, rat-face. "Slut."

With his command post now firmly established, he lights a cigar butt and opens the newspaper. Glancing over the sports, he sees no wrestling news.

Floor. Op-Ed. Floor. He checks the weather. Forecasting snow right before Christmas, are they? That's a bold prediction. We've hardly had any snow at all so far this year. Odds in Vegas would be three to one that something's coming soon. They all suck. All of them. Weather forecasters. Referees. Politicians. To the floor. He glances through the other front sheets. Fah-loor. Ah, at last – Comics.

The lights go out. "Goddamnit!" What the hell. "Oh!" He waves his arms around, and then –poof– light.

Good Lord. This day. So the motion sensors definitely work. Maybe she can tweak the timer. I'd love to give that little toad some credit for this, but she always seems to find new ways to fuck up my life.

They're both kind of hot, I guess. JT is the clear winner in my book, though. Nice ta-tas on tessie toolbelt, but JT's ass? Wowza. Don't know why I always go for the bitchy ones. Now if I can just keep the rest of the building from collapsing before New Year's.

The lights go out again. "Goddamnit!"

The Glock 43 is Nick's friend. Though he admittedly loves the weight of his .357 Magnum, and the last time out at the range, that barrel was certainly hummin'. The Glock, however, is the only practical choice for potential real-life confrontation, in his esteemed estimation. It can easily be carried in one's pocket, in case push ratchets up to gunfight, and the package comes with two extra magazines. The six-plus-one capacity of the older Glocks has been debated, which is why the newer models have ten-plus-one, giving you eleven lightning-quick shots if you need them. But Nick will stick with his original. Other than a few tactical upgrades, mostly for a quicker trigger reset, she is pretty much standard issue. Raw, and beautiful.

Always assume a gun is loaded and handle it as such. If the magazine is empty, there could always be one lurking in the chamber. They'd drilled this stuff into his head in the army, and at subsequent NRA trainings over the years. Always point the gun down range. Always keep it clean. Only take off the safety when you're ready to shoot.

And, if your friends and family convince you to jettison most of your arsenal –keep a couple favorites handy, along with enough ammo to fight off a SWAT team, or at least give them some pause. Then go ahead and display one of said pieces in plain sight, for some reverse psychology.

With the gun pointed right between his eyes, he disengages the safety and slides the barrel down around his nose and into his mouth. But the dank metallic taste gags him. Making catfish lips, he eases it back out and spits. "Mother Mary, please, God…" Cleaning solvents. "Blaghhhk".

His eye sockets are clammy with sweat and tears, the real solvents that are corroding his soul, and reflecting his ever-present fears.

Why did she have to die?

I can't breathe.

At least Adam is toughing it out. My boy. I am going to miss him so.

After a reset, he slides the gun back in again, letting some of the weight rest on his bottom lip and teeth. With the barrel angled upward, he pulls the trigger hard.

Click. Click. Click, click, click, click, click…

Setting the piece down on the coffee table, he bows his head. Through the layers of fabric hanging over his windows, he can barely hear children far off, maybe in the park, playing and causing trouble.

Kids. Good for them. Sincere.

The bare trees that line the street moan in the wind. He imagines row upon row of oaks and maples doing their sullen hula dance.

There's absolutely nothing keeping today from being his last. All he needs is one, tiny bullet. Just one. And he has thousands.

Liam rounds the corner and makes his way toward the Lex. Reg looks stiff as he approaches. "What'd I miss?"

"Oh, I'm not sure. I do believe the new girl got her first taste of the buzz-saw here. I think."

"What happened?"

"Don't quite rightly know, specifically, but it's causing quite the buzz. Whatever it was, Batts apparently gave her an earful."

"Ah. Shit."

"'Shit' for her, or 'shit' for you?"

"Just 'shit', Reg."

Up on the roof, Abby keeps going over and over the sequence of events, and all of the various points where she'd gone brain-dead. But beyond that train wreck, she's increasingly worried about the situation with Batts. Even if she is suddenly the fuck-up master of the year, she isn't going to take that kind of abuse.

Maybe I'm being a martyr. I don't know. Got to figure this out, though. Son of an onion pit. I fought so hard to get here.

No JT yet. I have zero desire for that right now anyway.

The huge metallic wings of the TV antenna loom against the grey sky and seem to be mocking her plight. Someone had gathered a pile of gravel around the base of the thick metal pole. Certainly isn't adding any support. A plastic six-pack holder is tangled in on one of its rusty prongs, too high to reach. Waving bye-bye in the wind.

Liam appears at the stairwell door, and seems surprised by the little greenhouses. "I had no idea any of this stuff was up here."

"Yeah, the Lex's best-kept secret."

With slightly tentative steps, he makes his way toward her. "Nice day, huh?"

"Careful. Kind of bouncy."

"I heard… heard some. You okay?"

"No. But I will be. Just spent the last few hours cleaning up the mess."

"He seems like a real prick, Abby. Well. I'm going to be crazed at work for the next few days, so I'm glad I found you."

"Oh."

"Yeah." He produces a white fabric bundle from behind his back. Sheer white lace with sequence.

"Fancy handkerchief you got there, Mister."

Dropping it in her hands, "Open it."

"I'm afraid."

"Understood. Summon your inner strength. I think you'll like it." Sweet baby Jesus, please like it.

Abby gently unfolds the delicate cloth, flips it over, and pulls out the postcard.

"I left the back blank, I—"

She breaks down and cries.

"Abby? What? You hate postcards?"

Hugging him softly, "Thanks."

"Sure, sure. I mean, sure."

She runs her fingertips across the lace. "Where did you find this material?"

"In the garbage. Nothing but the best, y'know."

"Bullshit."

"Perks of working in a linen mill. It's called 'Winter Shimmer'. They really were going to pitch it."

She lunges at his mouth and kisses him deep, and long. Liam is stunned but manages to reciprocate. Pushing him back, she sets down the bundle. Her arm twists through some contortions as she reaches under her coat and sweater, unfastens her bra, and pulls it out through her sleeve. Tossing it aside as if it were in the way. Not as smoothly as she would've liked under such circumstances, but today the universe could just lick her ginger.

Pulling his hands up under her layers, she shakes a little. Her tongue is in his warm mouth, lightly tickling its way around. They devour each other as her fingers gently map his neck and face. And now, in spite of every tumultuous calamity that has washed ashore this morningtide, her day is suddenly looking way, way up.

28

in spite of herself, she decided to climb
even though her limbs get softer

in spite of the day that judges so cold
in pure spite
with angry markers

it may be worse that way
striding the indifferent waves
yet all the better to rise
fully spanned
just shy of the walls in a cave

and isn't that how you fly?
direction be damned
to the dregs
to the roots, if you must
for they will eventually touch the sky
through the trembling naked hulls of this haunting arbor

Abby's journal: "Climbing in spite of me" Thee?

29

"You little right bastard!" Reg stomps after a pair of fluffy white earmuffs as they roll down the sidewalk. Each time he gets close, the wind picks up and yanks them just beyond his desperate reach. Snorting out a grunt, he pins them against a large garbage can with the side of his foot, just as a gust blows up in his face, and his hat spirals into the sky for one, beautiful moment, then bounces away on down the block. Fists to the wind, "Scalawags! The lot of ya!"

He was hoping the muffs would be rabbit fur, fox, richity-rich stuff. But on closer inspection, they look to be synthetic and plastic. Good knock-off, but a knock-off nonetheless.

Ah, well, y'ain't that pretty, but we're not going to be oh so selective today.

As his breath fog billows into the sky, he's suddenly too embarrassed to look around and see if anyone saw his bumbling ear-muff dance. Eventually, he manages to bear down on his hat and brushes it off with brisk, determined strokes. He never allowed his uniform to deviate from wax-museum tight.

Something near a drainpipe catches his eye. Looks like someone lost a necklace? Gently easing through the grass so the mud doesn't come up over his shoes, he gradually works the chain out of some debris. His Gram had one of these when he was a kid. "Charm-bracelets" or "charm-necklaces", they used to call them. Maybe. They had a series of little hanging pendants, usually marking various travel destinations. Or, sometimes, family-related events: birthdays, wedding anniversaries, etc. This one is mighty corroded and pretty banged up. "Too bad."

The trunk of his Chevy Impala pops open with a whack from the side of his fist. It's stuffed full of sidewalk prizes: cowboy hat, snakeskin cowboy boots, coats, gloves, a toy telescope, sneakers, shopping bags, a police taser whose metal prongs seem to be coated with dried pork-chop dust, dog leashes, cat collar, two empty (he had very much checked to make sure) backpacks, bottle opener, and a pair of overalls with one and a half straps. His own little thrift store. Reg can't remember exactly where he'd gotten everything; the overalls just generally confuse him these days. Why would he ever grab those? They're not exactly flea-market material.

Giving the earmuffs the sign of the cross, he drops them into the heaving mound of orphaned goods. "Welcome to the party," lifting his flask, which today is filled with the Mother's Milk –aka Jameson's Irish whiskey.

Hunched over against the cold now, he meanders to the alley behind the Lex and flips the battered charm necklace into a dumpster. "No love left for you, I'm afraid."

While Lisa's breasts don't have the sponge they had ten years ago, they still have a delicious shape, in her opinion. Maybe even better. Fuller in all the right ways.

And the electrical tape is so friendly. As long as you tear in perpendicular directions, you can slice it up however you see fit. The trick here is to get pieces big enough to cover the nipple completely, while making sure that they clearly read as crosses, even from a distance. After all, this isn't a mission of petty conquest. We are now part of a mystical force, relentlessly pushing the headers on a combine, harvesting crops from the land of promise. Joyously carving massive arroyos in his big, stupid face by means of uninhibited extraction alone. Leaving not a single plant alive to stand against the sun.

"Stay with me now…" Finishing up the tape job and getting dressed; she decides it's time for dinner.

Let's go over and eat at the Lex today, yes?

No food so far but, digging around the front edge of the dumpster, she's hoping to come across some mittens. The rats had gotten to her fingertips the other night. Lisa can picture those mad vermin, back on their haunches, as if they were placing a bowling ball on the middle shelf. Teeth out. Head tilted up. And silently, steadily gnawing. Sexy, gentle tickles, so one doesn't even notice them feasting unabated.

When it finally woke her up, they didn't move. The largest of them sporting nubs of her flesh in between his front choppers. A stand-off ensued that took the form of a laser-locked stare-down. When she finally lurched and screamed and banged on a drainpipe she could still hear them running away when she stopped. Three of her fingertips and a thumb had been reduced to jelly larvae, a bottle of straight bleach her only remedy...

Alright, I'm starving. Gonna have to jump into the belly of this tin beastie.

She bounds over the side with a smooth, graceful motion. The dumpster is brand new and fairly sturdy, so she isn't worried about breaking through the bottom while separating the wheat from the chaff.

There's a high-pitched squeak that an amateur may mistake for a mouse. Or a rat. (One that's aggressively flossing my fingertips out of its teeth, maybe?) But the pros know the sound of Styrofoam, because Styrofoam feeds the world, folks. "Ha!" She cracks open the dirty white container. Fettuccini Alfredo! Or...could be cottage cheese on flatworms. Either way, shit is bulletproof. Could eat it frozen. Perfect.

Wait. What? She picks up a funky, knotted-up gold chain. "Hello, new favorite thing ever."

Each little charm dangling from the bracelet is from a different city. The San Francisco piece has a streetcar on it. So clever. There's one for New York, Chicago, Dallas. Ah, here we go –Ft Lauderdale, Florida. A marlin with an exaggerated dorsal fin stares back at her through a jeweled eye. And it's jumping... over?... a palm tree in the background. Or maybe right into it. Tough perspective to pull off on an embossed design. And yes, this thing has been beat to hell and back.

The sounds of seagulls and laughter swirl through the alley. The beach was a thoroughly enchanting refuge for Lisa when she was a child. It provided endless theater for what were otherwise painfully dull vacations. She sat right by the edge the shore most of the time, usually alone. And yet was surrounded by a million forms of life and natural energy. The breeze so gentle. The water so warm. Of all the surrogate parents she had growing up, the ocean was her ultimate protector. Made her feel safe. As if she really belonged. So, unlike most of the other kids, she was never afraid to swim far from shore, and dive deep into its loving arms.

The battered chain is way too big for her wrist. No clasp. And it doesn't quite fit over her head. A quick double-up on the forearm, then. Good. "We'll make room for you, partner." It's freezing cold against her skin, a frosty-edged burn spreading underneath the sleeve of her gnarled wool sweater. What a delightful score.

The seagulls are ardently swooping all around her now, but just out of sight, as usual.

Okay, dizzy birdies, you can go fuck off. It's way past time to chow down.

30

On her hands and knees in the middle of the bedroom, Annalise is filling a cardboard box with random items: a hairbrush in need of cleaning, silk handkerchief, pair of sneakers, a thin nightie. There are two small perfume bottles —one for every day, the Gucci Flora, and one for special occasions, Chanel Coco Mademoiselle. She stops and smells them both. Small pain in her chest. And, in they go. Some underwear, a bad bra with teeth for edges, a meager throw blanket, giant fringed hat —she has to stuff that monster in there. And that ring that was buried on Chrystal's dresser. Dirty. Tacky. The tasseled brims on the impossibly broad lids had been a challenge to their relationship from the start, always felt like she was trying to kiss her underneath an umbrella. But Chrystal had impeccable taste in jewelry. Not, however, in the case of this nasty, frumpy—*oh, how I wish I was a proper ring*—ring.

Just add it to all the things I missed that were right under my nose the whole time. No need to keep any of these useless baubles of perpetual pain around. Jetsam, flotsam, out with ye old devils.

All wrapped up against the weather, she squishes through the front door, hugging the overflowing box to her chest. The sun blasts her eyes. "Jesus!" She immediately heads back inside for her midnight-dark Mulberrys. Most sunglasses are a waste of time. But these formidable frames turn day into night. Magic.

The crisp air feels refreshing as she heads down the street, but her whole life is now relentless distraction. Annalise knew that Chrystal was always into something, or someone. It was impossible for that lady to sit still, or truly relax.

I'm sure she's moved on already. Why do I feel jealous? Why do I fall for the ones who are pure trouble? Why is it always such a big splash out of the gate, that then slowly fades into looking for an escape hatch? What's wrong with me? I've had the best of all possible worlds. Nurturing men, stunning women, and I either push them away, or we slowly reveal our layers of insanity to each other to the point of –"Check, please!" Damn it all to hell.

Baggage. Always, and all the way around, baggage.

She had determined that a new relationship had the feel of moving to a new city, getting a new job, new house, new car, a fresh start. And on balance, most of us tend to believe that as a result of these machinations, we can simply shake off our past and walk away from the cloud of tainted dust that hangs in the air; a grinning, lurking phantom, just waiting for another poor fool to stroll through it and carry on the curse. Only to discover that the fool is you, and curses tend to linger far longer than anyone could have foreseen at the onset. Those ornery spells pop straight out of the ground every odd season, as if they'd never been buried in the first place.

Agh. There's not enough make-up in the city to camouflage all the old wounds. I just have to keep reminding myself that there are old victories, too. And they do count. They really do. I wonder how Abby is holding up…

She finally makes it to the end of the block and the pea-green-colored City-Park receptacle, but the old cardboard box is too big to cram in there. Dropping it on the sidewalk, there is a palpable realization of just how light it is. The final pieces of what was her partner occupy a container that feels almost empty. Annalise stands there transfixed for several minutes, lost in mourning.

Snapping out of it, she unpacks the items and pushes them down into the overflowing trash, folds up the box, and shoves it into a slot on the side, under a sticker that reads "Do not put anything in this slot". One finger at a time, she pulls off her stitched leather gloves. And even though they've harmed no one, they get tossed in, too. There is no wind, just the sun and her final salutation. The shadows from a few clouds gradually darken the sidewalk.

JT sits on the basement floor, tinkering with the bottom of one of the furnaces. "Jesus, Abracadabra, I thought you were going to make our jobs disappear."

She always has the one-liners handy. Abby wonders how many times she'd rehearsed that one. "I am so sorry. It was like the perfect storm. I almost threw up on his shoes while he was barking at me."

JT's clearly a little disappointed and bruised. "It's okay, yo. Really. I gave you a ton right out of the gate, and he's a fucking spaz. What else does he have to do but walk around these places and bitch? The stairwell wasn't that bad, the workroom… He was just piling on."

"Well, I deserved it."

"Not the way he doles it out. And the transom, that one's on me. You tried to tell me. I should have at least taken a look at her. And I *did* convey all that to him, twice. But he was already flyin' off the handle. Perfect storm, I guess, like you said."

"No, no. I should have doubled back on that, too. But I think I have all my bases covered here for a minute anyway. I did take one quick break this afternoon…" So if you see my panties lying around… "but the stairwell is spotless, and the workroom is on the edge of organized. Pitched some stuff that just seemed like unusable scrap."

"Cool. Good. The Furnaces and I have been keepin' each other company, as you can see." JT looks as if she's been tarred and feathered with grease and dust, but only on oddly shaped sections of her body. As if she allowed a four-year-old to do a glitter-glue project all over her person with soot. At least it isn't cold down here with those industrial monsters churning out the heat.

Next to the two furnaces sits a beefy incinerator that's straight out of a horror movie –pot-bellied, blood-orange crust, with a huge door on the side that looks like the headgear of a giant. Some wretched knight sent to the dungeon as punishment, to oversee the underworld… Every now and again, there's a small puff-back of black smoke that sneaks out between the bars, but then almost immediately gets sucked right back in and straight up the exhaust pipe. An old-time movie running backwards. The whole setup feels a bit shaky. One more reason to get out of here in the spring.

"I'm going to start my weekend off tomorrow afternoon, but I'll be checking my messages. The Mortons…"

"Oh fuck, the Mortons."

"Yeah, well, their place wasn't 'flooded'. I talked to 'em, and it was just a long puddle, nothing more. And only a few drips got down into the boys' place below. He was just trying to make you squirm. Anyfuckinway, they're tight as a drum. I admire your willingness to jump in, honestly. But if anything like that comes up again, just hit the pause button and reach out. K?"

"I absolutely will." God, I miss his face so much already. I'm screwed. "Any big plans this weekend? C'mon, give me a hint."

"Gonna hit that church again."

"The same one? No way."

"Yep. On it like a bonnet at the Sunday picnic, babe. Not going inside, though. Probably just a lingering troll on the crowd."

"Ah. All weekend?"

"I'll figure it out. Better for me if I just keep things loose."

"And no family for the holidays, right? You said…"

"No, I wasn't shittin' ya. Nothing at all that way, and I couldn't be happier about it. The holidays never really meant all that much. But I don't mind popping into churches, admiring seasonal uniforms, and snatching up everything but the limo when I see a red-and-green-themed bachelorette party in progress."

Abby, carefully, "So, you grew up on your own, or did you have…"

"Fervently finger-fucked by a ferociously unforgiving, phony fairy-tale of a foster system."

"Oh, man, I'm so sorry."

"One of the pricks who couldn't keep his hands off me did manage to pass on some wisdom in the ways of tools and repairs. And a few minor construction skills. He was a foreman of some… something, and in between gulping whiskey and grabbing my bum, he would show me stuff." JT lights a joint and puts her work gloves back on. Widening her eyes at Abby, she carefully hands her the spliff.

Abby spins all the way around, looking for Batts. "Is he gone?"

"He won't be back for a day or two. I know his ways. He wants you paranoid. Disappearing act is a good way to implement that weapon. Go for it. One ain't gonna kill ya."

"Thanks. I really am sorry to hear all of that. So grim."

"It was. There's no way to butter it. But, self-reliance I got. More than most. And while I hate being lonely, I do prefer to be alone. Two different things, y'know?"

"Girlfriends?"

"They come and go."

"You love that vaudeville stuff!"

Wan smile: "How are your radios? Batts says you have a science experiment brewing up in your place."

"I love them like fambly. And, yes, they are in service of an art project as we speak. Well, all except Pearl." Abby taps her shirt pocket. "Need some more batteries, though."

"Good to know. I'll get you some."

Picturing JT bounding down the street with a Santa sack overflowing with batteries, Abby shakes her head. "No…that's okay. I'm due for a supply run. Need to stock up all the way around."

"You alright?" Head down, slapping a rag across the base of one of the furnaces with exaggerated strokes. As if she's putting the finishing touches on a shoeshine. "You're not going to leave me right before Christmas, are ya?"

"I wouldn't do that." We both know I would. "But, I can't say what will happen in the spring. He's not right."

"I know. I've learned how to keep him at arms-length. And that's no excuse, or, whatever. But… well… please, as a favor, just let me know if you're going to bail. I'm hoping maybe after the holidays, either you change your mind or there's something out there for both of us. Is that crazy talk?"

"Not at all. And thanks. I'm here for the moment."

No eye contact. "Until Liam moves out anyway, huh?"

"Fuck you, JT."

31

Floaties? No. Incorrect. Floaties are vessels utilized by children while they swim so they don't plummet to the nether regions of the pool and asphyxiate on chlorinated piss water. Floaters? Floaters. That's it. Had them years ago. Technically –vitreous fibers that bunch up and cause shadows on the retina.

And while "floaters" does foment an exquisite vision of half-dressed, bloated corpses being hauled out of the Bay, Paul has to admit that the eloquence of "vitreous fibers" is holding him hostage.

This is my life. Internal debates on linguistics, semantics, word history, depth of meaning. Technically all aspects of Orthography. "Orthography". Because people use that word all the time. And I live alone because...

It did seem that the vitreous fibers had come and gone quickly way back when. This is pointedly different, though. The world seems darker, his vision more frantic to focus, more volatile. Maybe too much late-night TV.

He is making quick progress plucking the thorns from the rose bushes across the street though, at the far more sophisticated Algonquin Lofts. Their grounds are adorned with rose bushes, while the Lex's are strewn with tumbleweeds.

Maybe instead of the Lexington Arms, a more appropriate moniker for our nonpareil homestead would be something along the lines of–The Rat's Ass, or Suck a Dirty Fork Lodge.

He's surprised that he hasn't pricked himself on all these thorns. Not even once.

The pillowcase is approaching full capacity, and it's a bit heavier than he'd imagined. Freeloaders. "You're supposed to be popcorn for the movie. Mostly air, yet dangerous. But instead –you weigh me down. Inscrutable beasts."

Easing into the tub, it feels like the room is sinking around him. A mild humming sound persists, even when the TVs are off.

So much dirt in here now. So much dirt on me. Maybe ablutions are in order at some point. I can't recall the last time I bothered to bathe.

Jabbing into his feet as he kicks, some of the thorns tickle his heals. Not too much blood. There are barely enough in there to cover the bottom of the tub, but Paul did feel more than a few dig into his posterior as he settled in. Overall, they're mostly soothing.

"Not a total waste of a day. I managed to perambulate with some success, and now a kind of bath here, no?" Who needs water hook-ups anyway? Pachyderms don't need water to bathe. And what recall on those behemoths! I wonder, though… All of those memorial reconstructions of theirs, are they essentially innocent and innocuous? Or do some have fangs?

He picks up a thorn the size of a shark's tooth and gently places it on his tongue. Rolling it around, he wedges it snugly in the roof of his mouth. Biting down fast and hard, it pierces his gums deeper than he'd expected. The pain causes flashes of colored light. But the taste of his own blood is nothing short of glorious.

Quick shadows roll across the ceiling. A lightning storm inside the building? Leaning out over the edge of the tub, he slowly surmises that there are barely perceptible rivers of static limping across the floor. Rubbing his eyes, he looks again. Still there. Maybe he's already a yūrei, a mere ghost, adrift in a black harbor, desperately seeking a merciful vessel to gather him up in its boney hands and carry him the rest of the way home.

There's a rumbling knock at the door. "Hello, Sir? Mr Ito? I'm from Social Services…"

Ah! Ito. Why does that sound familiar? Italy. Yes. Always considered myself quite the cognoscente on a variety of topics. Indeed. Italian word – cognoscente. I love the way it propagates. It engenders such a fine air of dignity. Don't think there's a reasonably functional substitute in Japanese.

Now, I just have to be very still, and very quiet. Apparently, there is a third-generation inbred loose in the building, and she's attempting to gain entry to my domicile. And, things being what they are these days, she's probably a lesbian to boot! Delusional cur.

"Mr Ito? Are you in there?"

156

Abby sweeps up in the hallway and feels as if she's swimming into an increasingly bad vibe. The transoms are singing sad songs today. Cigarette smoke billowing out of one, like the place is on fire. And the nursing-home-volume TV is just blaring static, it seems. The light is usually so pretty from the combined glow of the apartments. Not right now, though. Seems red. Feels dark. She does her work quietly, taking her time, as the new-baby couple, the Jensens, go full-tilt tea kettle on each other.

"I tell you what, I'll go to the office every frikken day, and pay the bills, *and* take care of the baby when I get home, while you just sit around all rump-ass and complain. Deal? I mean, oh-oh, wait, that's what we're already doin' here, right, babe?"

"Sounds just like the plan you drew up, hamster dick!"

And with that, Baby Angelica begins to scream like a hellhound.

Easy, kids, easy! Damn.

Making her way towards the large window at the end of the hall, Abby sees Stewart perched up on his transom. "Hiii. How you doin', poppa?" He hisses at her and jumps back into the apartment as the door opens. Ms Conrad looks a little gaunt, twisting her hands.

"Abby! Oh dear, I'm so glad to see you. I am absolutely mortified that I got you into such terrible trouble. I should have just kept my big mouth shut."

"Hi, Ms C. No, trust me, it wasn't you at all. I messed up… just about everything someone could mess up in one day. Lucky I'm still here, as a matter of fact."

"Well, I certainly didn't mean to add to your pain. He's such a jack-hole, ass-hat of a man. Forgive the blue language."

"Only if I can use it myself? Honestly. It's all good now. Stewart okay? Seems a little twitchy."

Ms Conrad looks over her shoulder into the apartment. "Not himself lately. I don't think anyone is. Animals feel holiday stress too, you know?"

"Ah. True true."

"Well. I will… let you get to it… out here." Fumbling around in the purse again. What is she doing, mixing pancake batter? "As long as you and I are okay?"

"A thousand percent. Thanks for the good words."

"Least I can do. Oh, you missed a spot." She points to a small pile of dirt in the corner. Abby twists to look, then back at Ms Conrad. "Gotchya."

Leaving the hardware store, Batts heaves a giant bag over his shoulder and heads towards the park. Sun racing down again. Earlier and earlier. Huffing along on the sidewalk, oblivious to the world, he almost jettisons a day-tripper into the street with his load.

"Hey, watch it, tubby! You hear me? Get back here! I'll kick the shit out of you! Lumpy-ass bitch!"

Batts neither looks back nor breaks stride. "Oooh. I'm shiverin' with fright over here, twinkles. Hope I can sleep okay tonight!"

The pigeons climb all over the bench, and all over Batts, eating the seeds out of his open hands and nipping at his clothes. Motionless, he stares out into the park. Eyelids fluttering.

Scout is worried. He paces the ground in front of his friend, pecking, but not eating. Just observing.

guy - big - tough - floor - fight - peck - fuck - food - bad - peck - strut - who - what

Batts abruptly wet-trumpet sneezes, and all the birds scatter except for Scout. The two of them make eye contact, and Batts's head rolls down into his chest a bit. He slowly manages to stand up and brushes the leftover seeds from his clothes, leaving a substantial piss stain on the bench. Wiping his nose with his bare hand and well onto his forearm, he blindly picks up his white sack and shuffles out of the park.

She's got to do a quick clean of her bathroom before Liam shows up. His place was mostly together, for a guy's apartment. Don't want to be outdone on day number two. And what was with all those tattered books he has lying around? Is he pulling them out of the garbage? Ah, but those fingers, so… Oof, I don't know, man. Double-jointed mavens of mystery and madness. How was he doing all that?

Abby finishes up and jumps in the shower, grabbing the razor as if she'd like to chuck it out the window. Pearl is amplifying the soul station, and Marvin Gaye is up next –"Mercy, mercy me".

In her robe, toweling off her hair, Abby stares at the nest of radios dangling in the window. She'd found some old nail polish last night and put a little sparkle on the straw sticking out of the speakers. That only took forever.

There's a gentle knock on the door. Damn. "Just a minute!" Throwing clothes in the closet and lighting a candle, Abby takes a breath and looks in the mirror.

Yikes. Okay, here we go.

She's greeted with a flower. "Hi. Nice flower. Are they out of fabric at the shop?"

"Well, they're out of the good stuff. Caaan I come in?"

"Entré. You'll have to keep Pearl company. I gotta finish getting ready."

"Do you? I mean, I like the robe."

"I'll be out in a sec."

Liam sits on the bed and stares at the hanging radios that are strung together in the shape of a quite imposing cross. And while he considers himself reasonably good at remembering crucial details, even if only at that last possible moment before utter embarrassment, he has absolutely no idea who Pearl is.

32

Abby feels bad that Liam's sort of wedged against the wall, but not bad enough to move; for at the moment all she can do is lie flat on her back and starfish out under the sheet on her tiny bed.

His fingers are so beautiful, rolling that little pin joint. He doesn't seem too uncomfortable. "I'll give you some more room in a minute, I swear."

"Oh, I'm fine." He holds up the happy stick. "Yes?"

"Sure, um…" She leans over to grab her lighter off the desk, and Liam is completely focused, watching her stretch. "Here."

He burns off a little extra paper and lightly takes a hit.

Everything he does is so fucking smooth, well, other than trying to knock me over. Safer to keep him in bed. Damn, if he doesn't look like he could go again right now. I think my parts would break. Can't believe that I had enough left in me to hand him the lighter.

Gently gliding her fingertips around his hand, arm, shoulder, she pauses at the massive, nasty-looking scar. "So, what the hell happened?"

"Oh yeah, that."

"Wait, wait, why do you walk through the alleys?"

"Old habit, I guess. I like the scenery. The grit. It's certainly not for the aroma."

"Got it. You don't do that at night, though, right?"

"Not… usually."

"Hm. Well, there are some crazies and dumpster divers around out there for sure… "

Liam holds his breath.

"… So, keep your head up. Alright now –arm. Or shoulder, whatever. Spearfishing, were we?"

"I'm a counselor, social worker, for the county."

"Explains everything."

"And… right… well… One of my consults was in bad shape. And he was getting worse. I didn't realize how much worse, but… He had severe PTSD, and was becoming increasingly agoraphobic. Mostly wouldn't leave his house."

"Thought that was a female thing, generally. Like, being a shut-in."

"Not necessarily, but statistically, you're right. Or so some study says. But PTSD can be a heavy trigger for men. I think this guy had stopped taking his meds, which was an ongoing battle, and one day he snapped. Hard. Zero to a thousand. Took over a restaurant, hostages. It was like *Dog Day Afternoon* on shrooms."

"I love that movie!"

"Yeah, sorry, old references."

"No, no. Totally cool. So, you were a hostage? I think I'm missing something." Why is it a slight turn-on that he might have been a hostage?

"He already had hostages. When I got there, the cops asked me to go in and talk to him."

"Whoa! Bullshit!" She bolts upright. "That is ridiculous!"

"Some of my exact words. They were spread thin. I was his counselor…"

"Still. Man. I'm sorry. I never would have done it."

"I certainly replay the whole thing in my head on occasion, or, well, every day."

"Alright. You went in, and he shot you?"

"No. He didn't shoot me. I was 'moved out of the way' by a sniper when we walked out together. So they could gun him down." Liam sounds lost.

"I am so, so sorry, Liam. Really. Terrible."

"He was armed, taunting them… It was insane. There are big chunks that I don't remember."

"Honestly, though, why did you go in there?" She gently touches his scar.

"I guess because something told me it was time to do what I ask my consults to do on a daily basis –face their fears, head-on, no excuses, just go."

"Okay, sure, but there are stages, right? You don't shove them out into traffic on day one." God, he smells so good. She pulls him down into the bed and puts her head on his chest.

"True, but it all happened so fast. And the worst part wasn't getting shot, although that did suck pretty hard, or that he died, which you think would be somewhere near the top of the list. But the worst thing was that… I didn't feel anything. I mean, after it all sunk in, and I convinced myself that it was real, it didn't really affect me that much –that he was gone. Bait a hook with a worm. Step on a bug. Nothing."

Under her breath, dreamy, "Poor worm. Poor bug."

"Right. I worked so hard to try to help him. Seemed like a good soul deep down, in there somewhere. Then he dies right in front of me and, on some level, I think I was actually relieved."

"Because subconsciously, you were protecting yourself. Have you seen someone about this? Talked with another counselor? Anything?"

"That's mandatory where I work, if there's an 'incident'. So for a few weeks afterwards, yeah, I was on the couch. And she was cool…"

"But not pretty, right? Just cool."

"Yes. Just cool. And I was grateful, but I feel fine. I mean, I've been in some tense situations before. Attempted suicides, self-harm, physical abuse, but that was my first SWAT-sniper-hostage event. Can't say that I wasn't a little uneven for a while when I got out of the hospital. Things move on. With or without us, I suppose," clearly choked up.

"What was his name?"

"Mark. I was hoping he'd eventually come around. At least be another Etch-A-Sketch friend."

"Etch-A-Sketch friend?"

"Yeah. You know –draw a picture, then shake it up, and poof, it's gone. But those were the rules when you started the sketch. You knew one day it could just disappear like smoke. Happens all the time. Mostly, hopefully, because the consult makes such great progress that they don't really need you as much, and they just move on, which is fine. That's the goal. But sometimes you get attached."

"And you were attached to Mark, yes?"

"I thought so. For a minute."

"Well, I know we're all new and everything, but if you ever need to vent or talk through something or whatever." She pulls a bottle of lotion off the chair and starts to apply it to her hands, elbows.

"Thanks. What are you up to there?"

"Ashen. Happens." She could tell by the look on his face. "Dry skin. Look, you need some too."

"Whoa, whoa! I'm gonna smell like a fuckin' flower, man."

"Shhh. Look at your elbows. They're shriveled-up prunes, yo."

"I can't really see."

"Trust, Liam, trust." She quickly does his hands, too, mostly because she wants to stroke them. "Beer?"

"Hell yes, please." He vigorously wipes his hands off on the blanket when she's not looking. "No TV in here?"

Abby puts on his white button-down shirt; it falls just below her waist. The sleeves are a little long, covering her hands. "I don't allow myself the luxury of the boob-tube. Trying to minimize distractions as I figure out, um, everything."

Watching her scoot back with the beer, he is in awe again, but tries to maintain.

Between the one mostly blocked window, the transom, and an undersized lamp, her apartment has a soft, even glow. No harsh light. Reminds him of his childhood bedroom… He would keep it mighty dark in there when he was a kid, pretending that he was in a battlefield bunker. Ever fighting the good fight. Which meant killing bad guys by the dozens, of course, letting them have it with his Thompson sub-machine gun. *Rat-at-at-at-at, rat-at-at.* But more important than all of that –he was always saving the good guys. *"C'mon, buddy, I'll get you outta here. Don't worry. Before ya know it, we'll both be home, safe and sound."*

And his parents, never shy about vocalizing their support for their children, were whole-heartedly on board with these hugely righteous, violently heroic endeavors…

"Liam! Cut the crap! Son of a bitch, I can't hear myself think."

"Aw, Mom! Just ten more minutes. I'm just about to win the war!"

"You'll win a smack on your ass that you'll never forget, Sergeant Dipshit. Cool it!"

33

The hanging radios draw attention to themselves by rhythmically tapping the glass in the ever-present breeze creeping through the mostly unsealed window frame. Their glittery strands of straw throw off a faint shimmer in the meager light.

Liam points up at the cross-radio dealio. "So…?"

"Yes. The fambly. Introductions are in order." Abby reaches over and turns on Pearl again. Otis Redding's "Try a Little Tenderness" gently weaves its way into the conversation.

"This is Pearl. One of the newest members, and absolutely the most spoiled."

"Hi… uh… Pearl?"

"She's shy. Then these guys, well, they got recruited for a project."

"Reluctantly, or…"

"They'll do as I say. You'll get used to that, too."

"I hope so." He tries to kiss her and she lightly bites his lip.

"Okay. So: Blue Lou, Pinky, Lemon Head, Rocky, Soda Popp –with two Ps, Dogg– two Gs, Sparkle, Ebony, and last, but far from least, Cherry. She was a gift."

"She's a beauty. Two Rs?"

"Shhh. And yes, she is gorgeous."

"Okay. Got it. Cool. And… what…"

"Well, you're not the only one with two jobs. In addition to my – apparently not so awesome– maintenance skills, I'm an artist. Puzzle solver. Art is one big puzzle that never gets solved, though. It's like pushing a gob of jelly across the floor with a stick."

"Quite a resumé."

"It's torture sometimes, but way better than what I used to do." Liam's eyes are wide. "Accounting."

"Holy shit! Hefty leap, man."

"It all came to me in a snowstorm."

"Of course it did."

"Well, bottom line is, I feel freer."

"That counts." He slowly stretches out on the small bed, and they settle into the peace of the moment. Both hoping deep down that these rendezvous aren't just temporary distractions. Both too paranoid to say it out loud.

"Alright now, what, specifically, is with the …?"

"Ode to a cactus cross over here?"

He shrugs.

"In general –I'd rather hear a shitty little radio station trying to hang onto a weak signal in the middle of nowhere than go to a concert or… sit in front of a shiny new TV. Music was an escape hatch for me when I was a kid. Helped me navigate my 'mixed' world."

"Mixed."

"Got called that a lot, behind my back by my cousins, and to my face at school. I thought they meant 'mixed up'. Like, when I was real young, I overheard someone say 'half-breed' once. I thought they meant 'half-wit'. And don't get me wrong, that alone was enough to start a fight, which I did. Often. I have a rock-solid one-two."

"No doubt."

"Right. So don't fuck with me." Quick smile. "But when I was about eight or so, I finally figured it out. I didn't mind growing up 'white', but it put me in a strange place. Never black enough for the black folk, and nothing's ever white enough for the whites."

"Is that where the creativity came from? Some of those social stressors?"

"Well, professor stressor… Ah, not really. I don't think so. Probably had more to do with the fact that when I was in high school, I munched enough acid to burn a hole through the hull of a battleship."

"Serious."

"Am I serious, or…"

"No, I mean, never mind. Go on."

"So, yeah, and my mom is somewhat artsy, too. But psychedelics and upbringing aside, I was never satisfied with the world as it presents itself. I mean, look around, man. If this is 'God's plan', can we try someone else's? Please? Over the years I've learned that, regardless of the parameters, I need make time for my own projects, or I'll go berserk. When I was in my teens, the older folks would always say shit like, 'Don't get too far inside your own head, young lady.' Mostly because I spent inordinate amounts of time, way too far inside my own head... as a young lady."

"And the cactus radio thing is?"

"Excellent question, that I keep ducking. Sorry. I'm not completely, quite, sure yet. But I love it so far. It could be an installation project, I guess, if I had the connections. Sometimes I put on a couple radios, set to different stations. Or the same station. Depends. Straw does some strange shit to the audio. Some of them buzz randomly. There's a literal manifestation of the sound wave with those brittle pieces sticking out, if you want to look at it that way. There was also a 'floating coffin' vision kind of thing that set it in motion."

"Floating coffins? I never would have thought of that. Wild."

"Got that part of the idea from a late-night call-in show I was listening to."

"Full circle, then. *The Wheel of Time.*"

"God damn right!" She smacks his chest, and he grimaces. "*Wheel of Time!* You know shamans!"

"Not personally. Read a bunch of stuff years ago."

"Ah. Explains some of the books."

"Sort of. I'd have a lot more to fill the shelves if I hadn't given away so many."

"A social worker who gives his books away. Jesus, Liam, do you ever just tell anyone to fuck off?"

"Oh yeah. I just pick my moments these days. But with the books, it's evolved into a Johnny Appleseed scenario. What you sow, versus what you reap. I've probably handed out a dozen copies of *On the Road* over the years, and now I don't have one for myself and... that bums me out now that I think about it." His voice drifts.

"Jack Kerouac. *On the Road.* Yes. Amazing. So fluid." She relights the spliff, rubs his legs with her feet, and swaps the joint for the beer. "What else? C'mon."

"Okay. Well, I love your radio voodoo cross."

"Thanks. Now, cough it up. You were going to say something else about the books, or something."

"Uh, I don't know where I was going with all that... I drove around the country a lot when I was a pup..."

"One sec, sorry. Where's your family?"

"Mostly out west. I'm the only East Coast boy."

"Never see 'em?"

"It's rare. I'll probably go out there this summer. Been awhile."

"Okay. Back to it. Driving around the country as a pup. Aimlessly?"

"Yeah. Looking for what? I don't know. Loved that freedom, but had some breakdowns along the way. When I first read Kerouac, I was in New Mexico, at a gas station. Ended up sitting at a picnic table on a hill behind the bathrooms and finishing the book while the sun went down."

"Which book?"

"*Dharma Bums.*"

"Nice. Probably my fave."

"At some point, I looked up and there was a guy standing about twenty yards away, pretending not to notice me, just watching the sunset. I packed up a bowl and offered him a toke. He took a quick hit, thanked me, and I went back and sat down again to give him his space. We were two peaceful sentries at the gate.

When the last bits of daylight had vanished, the gas station lights randomly flickered on. The air still had that really warm feel, like the sun hadn't quite made a complete exit yet, but we both knew the situation was fluid. Desert wind comes on quick and cool out there.

I walked down to my barely-held-together, barely car, and before I drove off, he half-waved in my general direction, still looking at the sky. The buzz of the neon, the clunky sound of my engine, smell of gasoline mixed in with the night and the dust. I don't know. Felt mystical. I… think I have to use the little boys' room."

"Oh! Me first. Sorry." She hops off towards the impossibly small, half-frozen bathroom.

Trying to straighten up in there as she goes, ticking through what they were just b-s-ing about: *On the Road*, guarding the gates. Yes. Though all she could really concentrate on for more than two seconds were his hands.

34

JT walks out of Beanie's, stops dead, and looks at her broken pocket-watch. Mocking perplexity, she retrieves a giant coffee scoop from her work boot and gently taps the glass on the watch's face. Holding it up to her ear now. Hmm. Okay. Time to go confess my sins.

The first wave of parishioners exiting the church are younger and faster than most of the slow-moving, chatty crowd behind them. They squeeze out into the night ahead of the logjam, determined to find the chaos and random happenstance that they've been daydreaming about for the last hour or so. But in short order, the doors are clogged with the elderly and fake friends, so those who hadn't escaped within the first two minutes are doomed to have their stay extended –which in the stalled sweat and bad breath of those moments is surely just a small taste of the eternal damnation that the preachers endlessly hurl from high atop the feel-good pulpits of gold and glory.

Watching from the other side of the street, JT assesses the shuffling crowd.

Okay, okay. Nope. Nope. Yikes, not her. Ho! There she is! I knew she'd be here. Knew it. What a body. And that outfit! Dior and Givenchy rolled into one, fighting it out all over again, right on the sidewalk. Stilettos could fuckin' kill somebody. Guessing she's sixty? ish? Looks kind of mean. Not sure if this can get any better.

JT zigzags across the road through traffic to get a closer look, and quickly maneuvers into a good stalking distance.

What should I say to her? Doesn't matter. Get up there.

Gradually increasing her pace, they both get stuck waiting for a signal to change at a crosswalk. A cab races by in a blur, inches from the curb, and they reflexively step back in unison.

"Slow down, dick-bag!" Crap. Not exactly the first impression I had envisioned. But now that I'm in range, it looks like this tasty treat is more sad than angry. "Sorry. Those guys are a little too much sometimes."

"Indeed. Meandering around in this city has become a high-risk activity." Seems far away in her thoughts somewhere.

The light changes, and JT walks half a step behind her and a few feet away. This one obviously has some mighty savage miles under her belt. Bitter, tall, blonde… God is great. God is good.

Liam comes back from the bathroom like he's walking on Legos. Abby leans towards the wall so he can have more of the bed.

"Creakin' there, old man?"

"No doubt about it. I've reached the age where every new injury seems to have found a long-lost home."

"I know what you mean. I used to go to the gym and hit the bag for hours. But these days, I spend more time deciding what to wear."

"Where do you go?"

"Ardy's. 114th and Main."

"I know Ardy's. Love the bar."

"Me too! I never see you there."

"Been a while."

"Yeah, that's another thing I don't do as much myself. Miss those days, though. Used to close that shit down. Zoe is a frequent flyer."

"Really? She doesn't seem the type."

"Oh, if you get caught in there round midnight, she'll put a spell on you. She can hold court like no one I've ever seen. Ardy chats up the girls and works the room, but Zo is the belle of the ball."

"Interesting character, for sure."

"I really appreciate her. She does her own thing, in her own time."

"Maybe she can help me get a new body?" He arches his back.

"I was singing the blues to her about my shoulders last week. New job, tool belt, using different muscle groups. And she said something like, 'The mind dwarfs our viscera, for the flesh is merely cake-mix, waiting on an audience.'"

"Wow."

"She's got a thousand of 'em. You hungry?"

"Always."

"Excellent. I have cookies." She jumps up and grabs a box of fudge-covered Oreos from the top of the fridge, and what's left of Grumpy falls to the floor. She gently places him back up, facing toward the window. Satisfied, she slides back into bed. "Cookie? Take a bunch. I always have back-ups."

"Is that little ripped-up-broom-guy there… another art project?"

"Not yet. Not sure that he will be. Sometimes we just have to make sacrifices to the Gods, y'know?"

"This is true." He lightly touches her neck. "Well, Batts aside, you like it here so far?"

"Mostly. Yeah. What about you?"

"I guess. It's cool around the edges. I'm not around enough to have the best grip, but it seems as if something has everyone a little twisted lately. Random tension."

"I've been busting my ass so hard trying to avoid another giant fuck up, that it hasn't completely registered with me, but yeah, something in the air. People barking at each other a little more? Holidays always suck."

"Aye. 'Tis the season."

35

He's having food visions again. Nothing complicated. Just the basic go-to's: butter cookies, pignoli, anisette. Simple. Sweet. And let's not forget the bread: friseddhre, piadina, panettone. Now he's on a sacred mission.

Sliding the Glock to the corner of the coffee table, Nick hauls himself up with a groan, belly-first. A tiny shaft of sunlight, that has managed to find its way through all the fabric, illuminates dust swirls in the air and zaps his eyes. "Fuck. You."

Halfway to the kitchen, the phone rings. "What?"

"Pop?"

"Adam! My God!" He collapses back down on the couch, rubbing his forehead. "Everything okay? You… you alright?"

There's laughter through a noisy connection. "Yes, sir. We're on evac tomorrow. Just resting up before we head out again. Did I interrupt a mad cooking session?"

"No, no. I, uh… Whoa, wait a minute. Why are you calling out of the blue? You never call."

"Hey, I call."

"You call, my ass. You call like I diet."

"Well, you've been on my mind. You hangin' in there?"

"Sure. I guess. Liam says I'm making progress. What else do those assholes ever say, though?"

"Alright, c'mon."

"I know, I know. Liam's alright, I guess. I'm the one who's fucked up."

"You're not fucked up."

"Eh, maybe slightly touched."

"I wanted to tell you… that I love you, Dad."

"Ho-leee crap! What in God's name is going on, Adam? Is someone pregnant?"

"I'm still gay, Pop."

"Right. Yeah. Well, what then? What gives? You been talkin' to Liam?"

"Nope. Just wanted to tell you that. You're a great father. Always were. And I love you."

Nick decompresses. "I love you too, kid. Still scarin' the life out of me, though. Jesus."

"I'm going to get kicked off the phone here soon."

"K. Give 'em hell on the new deploy. And, Adam?"

"Yeah?"

"Stop bein' such a freaky-ass fuckin' weirdo all the time, please? For the love of God, I told ya, you're never gonna make any friends that way. Jussayin'."

"Okay, think I got all that. I'll give you a shout. Take care of yourself."

"Alright. Sure. You too. And be careful. No prisoners."

"No prisoners, Dad. Copy."

Nick eases back up again and drops the magazine out of the gun, setting the empty piece on the mantel. As he wanders into the spotless kitchen, he nonchalantly tosses the bullet-clip up on top of the cabinets. It lands in what sounds like a sandbox filled with loose ammo.

I really should organize all that, someday.

Rubbing his hands together, eyeing up the spice rack. "Okay, okay, who do I have to blow to get some grrrub cookin' in this joint?"

Reg moves aside to let her pass, but Ms Conrad saddles right up to him.

He tips his cap. "Love your look today, Ms Conrad."

"Thank you, Reginald. Very kind."

"Weather's holding out. And… where might ya be headed?"

"Oh, I just came out here to check in. Wanted to see if you need anything."

"I could use a new back." Reg stretches out his arms. "Aaand, a new front, I'm afraid. Thanks, though."

She presents a chocolate cupcake from behind her back.

"Ah! Now *that* I always need. Bless ya. Looks scrumptious." He examines the tiny gold pendant dangling from the thin red ribbon on the side of the wrapper. It's a little four-leaf clover. Old, but still hanging on. "Oh… what's this?"

"Found it. Cleaned her up as best as I could. Some good luck on a cold day?"

"Lovely. Really. Thank you."

Eloise Conrad is a cranky old bitch, and she knows it. The youthful patience she thought she'd always have left the station long ago, waving a-bye-byes, real good now, via con Dios. But she can be soft if she wants to. Reg will know what to do.

She leans in close enough to smell his cologne. "You know, you can put your slippers under my bed, any time. Anytime at all. You do know that, don't you?"

Twisting, contorted: "Oh, Ms Conrad you're pullin' me…"

She gazes teasingly, unbroken. "What else are we doing today, you and I? No offense, Reginald, but we —are furniture. Why not have a dance, or two?"

Reginald Seamus Stafford is a succubus magnet, and he knows it. Never blames the ladies in the end, though. For he has come to realize —based on the exuberant reactions— that the nomenclature left in his wake often spells out an acute lack of awareness, however unintentional. He's a great companion, but a lousy mate.

Lowering his voice, he treads lightly. "How would that be? Somethin' goes wrong down the line n'…"

She matches his gentle tone. "I'm speaking of carnal knowledge, my friend, not plans. It's been me and one cat or another in there for a hundred years. My plants can fend for themselves most days. The pantry's got some dust. Bedroom window leaks some."

"Uh… I'll let JT know."

"Now, where was I going with all of that… the bedroom!"

The most awkward of silences fill the air with sadistic electricity.

Slowly making her way back up the walk, smooth and sunny, "Standing offer, Mister."

36

The small, frail alcove sits just an inch off the floor in the far corner of the workroom. And Abby doesn't know why, exactly, but by all appearances, it strikes her as the perfect shelter.

It's a tasty little spot, isn't it? I think the bucket needs to live in there.

She pulls out the postcard, and uses the sparkly white cloth wrapping as a hanging tapestry to cover the entrance of the miniature cave. After she finishes tacking it up, she slides in the old majestic bucket behind it.

"Majestic" in the sense of being polished and ready for warfare, aren't you. Despite his apparent age, he's quite a dignified gent. Well, at least he has some privacy now.

As she carefully eases the postcard back into her purse, it hits her that the bucket never got a name. Oh, to hell with all that. He doesn't need a name.

Pearl chimes in:

"And that was the Beastie Boys with 'Cookie Puss', and Sonic Youth's 'Death Valley 69', on Q-MAX 108…"

Sure. Fine. Max. "We'll call you Max."

Liam compulsively cranes his neck all over the large window, peering up and down the alley. "Man, I shouldn't have to live like this."

Sprawling across the bed, he zones out. The "dumpster diving" comment from Abby was a nasty jolt.

Please don't let me screw this up. 'Cause, wow, Abby. My God. Heavenly. What a woman. I'll never recover. But I've got to put a lid on this Lisa sitch.

Pulling the tiny shutters open on the next miniature window in his advent set, right under the pine and holly-filled marker that reads "December 20th", Liam feels a bit of long-lost nostalgia for Christmas. Inside is a little painting of a golden harp, with children dancing around it in a circle. Solstice coming up on the twenty-second. Finally. Then the sun will slowly come back.

Now, how much beer do I have in the fridge, total? There're the two odd Genny Cream Ales in the door, two Bud pounders... Okay... maybe... one and a half Bud pounders.

Paul eases his apartment door open a few inches. There is a faint burning smell in the air. Rubber, dust maybe. Liam is surprised to see him looking so vibrant.

"Poggio Badiola! I take back almost every derogatory thing I've said about you this morning. This is wonderful." Paul snatches the bottle of red wine like a greedy child.

"It's a pretty good Tuscan for the price. I believe 'nothing American' was the direction."

"Impressive. Truly. On your way to the sweatshop?"

"Yeah. Last-minute Christmas orders. It's a zoo."

"Petting zoo. Religion and holidays are for sheep."

"Not gonna get much flak from me on that. How've you been? You seem amped-up today."

Paul brushes at the lint on the arm of his shirt, then gives up and picks off the little fuzzy. "Well, I'm much better at night, and while I'm afraid to surmise what 'amped-up' means in your truncated world of insatiable fetish, I do thank you for what might be considered a compliment around the edges of a not-so-subtle backhand. I would let you in, but as luck would have it I'm tending to the endless needs of the castle: draining the moat, scrubbing the parapets. I wouldn't want you tripping around in here while I'm attempting to extricate the funk."

"Scrooge does his holiday cleaning, now with vino!"

"Has nothing to do with the holidays. I'm on my own clock."

"No shit." There is something strange about the floor, the ceiling. Liam can't quite process it. The light looks reddish, sharp. "We were supposed to go over a few things today."

"I know, I know, and I had every intention—"

He has to get this out: "Paul, be straight with me. Are you cutting again?"

"Leave it to you to fuck this up. Leave it to you!" He sets down the wine and rips off his burgundy turtleneck. The site of more than twenty nasty scars is overwhelming. Some long and mean, others tightly grouped in tiny slashed strokes, zigzags, loops. A warped Cartesian puzzle of pain.

Liam takes an awkward step back. Paul holds up his arms high and slowly spins around as if he's surrendering to everybody. Chest, arms, back – how did he reach?– shoulders, all hacked up. It's as if he'd been flogged and dipped in candle wax, then flogged again.

"Jesus Christ, Paul."

"Look! All of these are a million years old. Look!" Most of the marks are white to tan-ish in color. Nothing fresh as far as he could see, but there were ugly bruises and scrapes on both of his hands.

"Alright, alright. What about your hands?"

"I punched a wall the other day. Stupid and juvenile. But I kicked the tub and stubbed my toe and stumbled and got mad and just swung, and... I was annoyed. Much like now. Anything else, Mother?" His chest is heaving. Eyes doing a defiant dance, sizzling.

"Look, I don't mean to be so abrupt—"

"Hah!" He wrangles his shirt back on in a huff.

"But I have to ask. It's my job, I—"

"Don't. Don't do that, Liam. Using your job as an excuse to treat human beings like sociological experiments. It's beneath you."

"Just promise me that we can sit down and have a coffee, or a good, non-American beer the next time I come over. And talk some. Okay?"

"If you promise to be a little more deft, and a lot less daft."

"Um, I may have to look up both of those before I commit."

"Less of a douche-canoe."

"Got it. Promise. I'm glad you're doin' okay. Really. And I am sorry that I just blurted that out. Guess I'll just go to work early. And we'll talk soon."

Paul exhales. "Right. Well, I do very much appreciate your efforts with the wine. And there will be some peace here soon, somehow. I can sense it. Just let me get there. Allow me to realize at least some of that ever elusive tranquility, young Galahad. Please."

"I'll try, Paul."

Paul locks the door and waits to hear Liam's footsteps fade down the hallway. But he's standing just a few feet away, listening. Each man waiting for the other to blink. Eventually, Liam moves on, and Paul slithers to the floor.

Leaning all the way over, he smashes the top of the bottle off the edge of the tub, sending a fine spray of wine misting into the air, and leaving jagged glass teeth around the opening that sparkle and seduce. "Bella." He puts it to his lips and takes a deep, splashing swig. The spill-over that runs around his jaw and down his neck feels wonderful. Sucking at the bits of glass stuck in various parts of his mouth, he spits out a few little chunks. "Mm. Dee-lish. Nice, velvety texture." Smacks his bloody lips. "A hint of plum. Meaty finish. Exceptional job on the wine, kid." He tilts back the bottle again, slowly twisting it and making fresh cuts in his gums as he drinks. Looking up at the sparks racing across the ceiling in the menacing daylight, he wonders when the full weight of the tempest will finally arrive.

37

Normally he would be zipping through the alleys at full speed, but today Liam's pace is more measured, straining his peripheral vision for any signs of Lisa.

There were moments, even recently, when the memories of ridiculous laughing and ease of intimacy just came rolling in out of nowhere and washed away some of the silt. A time of adventure. The days when their happiness overlapped, the world was an enchanting place, and all of her hopes swam around him like bait. But now he's grown hostile, feels cornered. Deep down, he's beginning to boil.

Approaching Lofty Linens, he rifles through his backpack for anything that may be edible. Passing by a recessed, battle-scarred doorway, he fails to notice two watchful eyes, rippling with green lightning, sparkling in the shadows.

The layers of ice on the high windows in the warehouse seem to mock him as he tries to stretch out his back one more time before finishing up. Long ass day.

When Liam drags himself onto the elevator, blind Steven is in his usual corner. He's probably just been riding up and down again, spreading his particular brand of love. One of his fan-club, Julie, gets on two floors down.

Matter of fact: "Hi, Liam."

"Hey, Julie."

She turns her body, silky. "Hi, Steven."

"Hello." Completely flat.

"Colder today."

He just gives her a half-smile and nods.

Where did this guy go? Julie usually had everyone's undivided attention, let alone Steven's.

She gets off on the fourth floor. "Goodnight, Steven?"

"Night." Stoic. Maybe even he can't keep up the effusive flirting twenty-four/seven.

They get down to the garage level, and as Liam squeezes through the rows of parked cars, he hears something over his shoulder.

"Careful."

Slowly walking backwards now, "Did you say something, Steven?" No reaction. "Okay then, g'night bud."

Not much wind this evening. Still crisp. Stars unusually visible. All the vents in the alleys seem to be cranking out steam in tandem.

Walking under a long awning in the back of an all-night deli, Liam gets plopped in the eye with a giant water droplet that's rolled off the edge of the tarp. He turns the corner and Lisa plows into his shoulder, with follow-through, and keeps walking on by.

"Holy hell, Lisa, you are not supposed to be anywhere near me."

"I'm not going to reiterate the whole 'public throughway' clause again, little boy. Why don't you watch where the fuck you're goin', you fuckin' pussy. By the way, how are things over there at the ol' Lex these days? Y'know, we never talk anymore."

Her normally to-the-minute, just-done hair has devolved into a wiry fire bush. She is topless. No bra, veins popping out of her breasts from the cold, and is that electrical tape on her nips? And she's got... sparkled contact lenses? She turns to face him fully, jiggling her boobs with her hands. There's a charm bracelet wrapped around her forearm, glowing under a security light. A demonic Wonder Woman.

"What is your problem?"

"You don't get off that light." She lets out a bird whistle.

"Get off what, Lis', what? 'Light' like a prison sentence? Punishment? Parole?"

"Purgatory."

"Pathetic." He walks away.

"Paprikash!" *Whistle, click, click, whistle.* Slapping her boobs together.

"Poison."

Spewing acid: "You know, dickless wonder, for all of your overblown talents, it's simply amazing to me that you couldn't find my joy buzzer if it was hitched to a cowbell!"

He just keeps moving, disappearing around the next corner.

She drops to a playful whisper: "And you know something else, lover?" *Whistle whistle whistle whistle.* "I'm not even really that mad yet."

38

The air in the house feels so different. So still. Annalise keeps thinking at any minute, she'll hear Chrystal call to her from the bedroom, or yell from the kitchen with that bellowing voice. The strange sharp echoes of which never totally fade. Every room is now a frigid cavern of failure, a chamber of mocking defeat.

Maybe she was cheating on me after all. Some of the items she'd left behind seemed quite random, but the one thing that really felt funky was that shitty ring. What if it wasn't hers? Then someone probably gave it to her, but who? I'm driving myself crazy for nothing. Again. Good riddance. There is always some semblance of freedom in loss; I'll just have to find it. Alright, evening meditation time.

She turns on a box-fan on the other side of the room for some white noise, which does manage to knock down a good chunk of the more ambitious city sounds. Sitting on her yoga matt –sukhasana, back propped up against a giant silk pillow, candles, incense. She begins.

Her breathing is steady, but her mind is scrambled. Chrystal had come to her when she was so low. At a time when Annalise was broken and meandering, only going through the motions of her life. And she'd lifted her up so high. Cutting sense of humor, delicious in bed, patient, supportive. Hyper-critical at times, but that was fun, too. In retrospect, there was always underlying tension, though. Chrystal rarely gave Abby any credence, and vice-versa. Each of them convinced that the other was doing Annalise harm, holding her back.

She wonders if that's where Chrystal's ever-increasing expectations came from towards the end. All of those demands that just got to be too much. Too heavy to lift. Too petty to bear.

Deeper inside now. Long inhale. Longer exhale. Floating… Birds frolic in a field, picking off bugs in mid-air that are rising with the heat. A steady breeze rolls along the top of the tall grass. Glare from the sun begins to take over the scene. She looks around, and suddenly there is a faint hum. Shadows cut across the valley. A Monarch butterfly settles on a fallen bird and begins to drink its blood, surgically, and with mean purpose.

An abrupt blast of wind whisks everything away, and the sky dims. The electricity in the air is palpable. It pulses. *Fum fum fum fum.* She's startled to see a giant red nimbus in a pitch-black sky, looping from horizon to horizon. No sun to be found. *Fum fum fum fum. Fum fum fum fum…*

Annalise slowly opens her heavy eyes, and her face is right next to the fan. Somehow she'd unknowingly moved all the way across the room. Hunched over on her hands and knees, drooling on the floor. Feeling like she weighs a thousand pounds, she hauls herself up, shaking.

What in hell? This is no help! "Kiss my keister." Maybe I just need some food.

The phone rings. "Yes. Hello."

"Mom! Jeez, it's good to hear your voice. I meant to hit you back sooner. Things have been, well, up and down here. How are you? Why are you guys home so soon?"

"Abby, Chrystal and I are through."

"What? Oh boy. Wow, I am… so sorry."

"No, you're not."

"Mom, I—"

"It's okay. I know where you get it from." She's still wiping slobber off her chin, pouring some wine. "Always trying to be the caretaker. Looking out for me. I try to look out for you, too, but you're so stubborn, Ab. One of the most important questions in life, that no one ever bothers to ask, is: Who takes care of the caretakers? Y'know…"

"Mom, I am sorry. I didn't hate her or anything."

"But you never gave her a chance."

"And she gave me a chance?"

"I know, I know. The two of you, like cats in a bag. She and I were getting bumpy long before New Orleans, anyway. The trip was supposed to be a rekindling of sorts. But," taking a quick hit of wine, pacing, "if you have to frame something that tightly, I suppose you're looking for trouble anyway."

"Are you okay?"

"Sure. A little lost, but I've been here before."

"Alright. Well, I'm, stunned. Um, sooo, I'm going to be on call a lot during the holidays. But since you're back in town, we can get together for Christmas, yes?"

Flat, "That would be nice, Ab."

"For sure. When Mum? What's good for you?"

"Oh, I have a couple of brunches with the girls here and there, but other than that, I'm free."

"Okay. I'm off Christmas Eve?"

"And you work on Christmas Day? What the hell kind of a deal is that?"

"A deal that keeps me employed and in motion. There are only two of us here to cover this whole building. There are perks, though…"

"Working on Christmas Day. My goodness, I just can't…"

"You're not even religious!"

"It's the principal of the thing. But, right, Christmas Eve. Sold. We'll figure it out. You sound tired. Are you eating?"

"Cookies."

"Well, at least I know I'm not speaking with an imposter."

"Get some rest, okay? We'll firm up plans soon."

She empties the wine glass. "Mm, wait, how is the Lex, really?"

"Pluses and minuses, like I said. I'm fighting my way through it. Met some cool people. Boss is a dick."

"All bosses are difficult."

"I guess so."

"Do you need anything? Please, be honest. Do you?"

"Nope. Solid right now. Have one of my own projects humming along, too. I'm good."

"The last time you told me you were 'good', you ended up urinating on a mountain top and quitting your job."

"That was so two years ago."

"Oh my. Two years…" Annalise's thoughts navigate right back to Chrystal.

"Give yourself a hug. Mine soon. I love you."

"Love you too, hon."

Who the fuck keeps bouncing that ball out there?

Liam presses his nose to the frozen window but can't see anyone. Sounds like it's getting closer. He chugs his last beer and, for no apparent reason other than sporting a heavy buzz, tosses his coat around his shoulders like a cape, knocking half of the notebooks off the table.

Once he's out in the alley, he hears nothing but a very light snowfall hitting the ground.

Almost three in the goddamn morning and I have to deal with this shit. Fuck. Well, while I'm here, I should go see who's still open and wants to sell me a traveler. None of the bars in this neighborhood close at two am. That's a joke. Somebody's still serving.

A half hour later, Liam walks back up the hall with a six-pack and sees that he'd left the apartment door wide open. Perfect.

Wrangling the notebooks up off the floor, he heaves them back on the table. First beer quickly down, he digs into his work.

He doesn't normally have dreams if he's been drinking or smoking. And if he does, he can't remember them. He'd read somewhere that the body can't transition into REM sleep or a dream-state if it's processing toxins. And he'd had more than a few brews this evening, but Liam still manages to fall into a deep slumber as soon as he hits the pillow…

He's hanging on to a very rough rope that's chafing his hands, swinging through the air like Tarzan in pitch-black space. It's less of a swooping arc and more like he's being pulled. The wind whips his face as he looks all around for any sort of reference point. Nothing above, nothing below. He wants to let go, but something keeps telling him to hold on tight.

Little balls of white light appear in the distance and soon come whizzing on by him. He can hear a slight electrical pulse as they pass. And maybe… fading conversations? But he can't make out the words. Other than these small orbs, it's still completely dark as he's being helplessly dragged along.

The glowing globes are becoming successively larger as his speed increases. Certain that he's going to hit a wall, he begins to turn away and brace himself, clinging to the now-humming rope.

Many jumbled voices in the air become one, and the conversations meld into single words as each glowing sphere passes…

Angel… Devil… Savior… Asshole…

39

Peeling awake, with a slicing headache that he can't seem to make go away by denying its existence, Liam checks the tiny clock by the bed –eight-forty-four am. A little later than he'd wanted, but it's all fine. There's just enough time to give Anderson a quick call.

"This is Sergeant Anderson. What can I do you for?" The precinct is smoke-filled, like a garbage can is smoldering somewhere in the vast room, and no one cares. Sex workers spew trash talk with zeal, the drunk tank is unusually raucous, and somebody brought in their kid who's running around screaming at the top of his lungs.

Hearing these bellows through the other end of the line, Liam again mulls over how ruthless children usually get a pass these days on what would otherwise be nothing more than a simple, attention-getting crack on the bottom. Not belt-buckles and hot sauce, just an establishment of the chain of command.

Once, his mother had grabbed him and his brother by the hair and smacked their heads together, but only after they had repeatedly ignored her pleas to stop using their beds as trampolines. Of course, in the moment, they couldn't help themselves. They had been getting some good height, too, screaming inanities with every glorious bounce –

"*Whaaanga!*"

"*Ssseenkum!*"

"*Hoonanda!*"

"*Ho!*"

When she'd summoned them to the bottom of the stairs, they'd each held onto an opposing railing, both hands, and took very tentative steps down towards her, slowing as they approached. And as soon as they were in range–

wham! Stars, shaking, stumbling back up the steps, hands out, two Frankensteins feeling their way to their bedrooms to cry themselves to sleep, with only slightly cracked skulls. That's about as bad as it ever got.

Where are you when I need ya, Mum?

He exhales into the phone. "Officer, it's Liam."

"Liam? Liam! Not gonna sue me, are ya?"

"I'm only asking the city to cover my medical bills and lost work. I could ask for a whole lot more, y'know?"

"Me too. It's funny. I was just telling my captain that it is truly amazing how very little is asked of us lowly men-in-blue on a daily basis. And, let me guess, you want to ask me for something now. Am I right?"

"It's regarding a restraining order against my last girlfriend. She's…"

Anderson laughs so loud that Liam pulls the phone away from his ear. "Girl problems? We don't run a dating service, Liam. Go back to your shrink."

"She is defying the order on a hundred levels. I don't know what to do. C'mon, like I haven't helped you out?"

The feral child-savage runs by Anderson's desk and smacks one of the sex-workers on the ass of her leather micro-mini, generating a sound not unlike a bullwhip cracking a porcelain plate in half. Or a gunshot. She reflexively swings her purse and catches the runt squarely on top of his head, and he goes down hard, face-planting into the dingy tile floor. After a long, silent breath, he lets out an earth-shattering scream that only reluctantly tails off momentarily, leaving him just enough room to suck in four or five quick huffs of snot-filled air before repeating the cycle. Thus achieving a threshold of volume worthy of some type of record in the annals of lung capacity versus raw impact.

"Liam, get a lawyer, and leave me out of it. This isn't how you call in a favor."

"Well, what exactly is the protocol supposed to be then? C'mon, man, this is serious."

"Protocol? Not quite sure myself –let me go find out and I'll get right back with you."

Click.

Scout is hoping for more snow soon. Easier to spot fresh food from the air that way. When all those tasty treats are scattered over the top of a big white blanket, it's tougher for them to hide in the dirt and the muck. Not that those aren't good spice.

peck - food - strut - peck - cold - yes - food - no - food - no - no - yes - peck

Either way, he loves to explore with his pals. He's been in charge for moons and moons, and he knows his days are numbered. It would break his heart to be shunned after all these years, as is the fate of many that have led the way for so long. These guys and girls are his friends, and family —well, he's pretty sure. Protective of them all. And no doubt about it, he still feels strong. But at his age, he doesn't know how many seasons he has left.

love - peck - food - shake - peck - peck - no - yes - friends - strut - love - sleep - food

Scout is crazy tired. No signs of the big bench guy today. Time to lead the troops home.

In the tiny ravine just over the hill from the walking trail, Chrystal sits on a forgotten bench that's encircled by high shrubs and fallen trees. Completely hidden from the rest of the world, it's been her refuge ever since the break-up. Leaning back so she can feel the fading light on her face, the tassels on her hat sway and jiggle in the wind. She holds her fingers up in front of her eyes and wiggles them to add to the strobe effect. Easing her lids shut, she goes into a deep state of calm, red streaks flashing and pulsing in every direction.

I told you not to leave me alone out here. So damn sunny all the time. Nothing is sunny all the time! You never turn it off. Never. But your fuel is spent. I told you. Such a seductive voice, so sweet, then everything fizzles into a whimper. Less than nothing.

I could have saved us, but you wouldn't let me. I could have *saved* us, but you wouldn't even let me try. I told you…

Prying open her eyes, she sees a baby raccoon scurrying over a mound of random happenstance directly across from her. She flies off the bench, and the little guy zips out of there in a flash.

Straddling the large dune he was standing on only a moment ago, she shifts her skirt, pulls her panties aside, and urinates. Long and steady.

40

The sex was stilted. He's not himself.

"I love this model house, or... what is this?"

Liam barely cracks a smile. "It's an Advent Window set. You're supposed to open one window every day, as a countdown to Christmas."

"Are you religious?"

"I'd go as far as 'spiritual', maybe. My brother sent it to me, from Germany."

"Thought you said they're all out west?"

"Well, if you keep going west, eventually you hit Germany. He's in the military –army– stationed in Berlin."

"Are you guys close?"

"Apparently close enough that he can send me a fancy dollhouse without getting punched the next time I see him."

Abby examines the miniature pictures in the opened windows. "It really is a beautiful piece. The stain on this wood is so tasty. Dark." She runs her fingers along the top edge; it feels electric. Maybe she's having after-sex after-effects, or feeling that beer from last night. Something's rumbling.

Liam gets up and slowly starts to get ready.

Man, he even looks good when his belly sticks out a little bit. Not fair.

Without looking up at her, "Want some orange juice? I did some shopping for a change."

"Sure, small glass. Thanks. You okay?"

"Yeah. I have a lot to do all the sudden, before the actual holidays hit. Usually a tough time of year for my consults. They're getting invited to all kinds of events that they can't attend, or won't. I have some puzzles to solve."

"Anything you want to talk about? I'm a frikken puzzle master. Well, with other people's puzzles anyway."

"Nah. I appreciate it, though."

"Alright. Well, I better get started myself. JT is being cranky with me, and at some point, I should at least prep some paint jobs… Nnnothin' on your mind, though? At all?"

"Nah. I'm good. Really." Half-smile.

"Cool." She takes in the place with open eyes. Books, notebooks, countdown doll house thing, TV, good view of the alley. Getting closer to the window, she gets up on her toes and looks down at the dumpsters and swirling trash below.

Liam freezes.

"Seen any crazies out here?"

A laugh jumps out of him. "Not lately, thankfully."

"Well, I wanted to tell you, I'm having a great time. Selfish Betty, though, to the bone. I don't know if I can share you. And, I mean, I don't want to get all heavy or anything…"

"You've got no worries there. Zero. And I'm the one who's selfish."

"Please! You help so many people."

"And I fuck it up on the regular."

"You'd have to define 'regular'. We're all just human, y'know. We fuck up. We succeed. We eat pizza."

"But at the end of the day, I always take care of myself first."

"There's nothing wrong with that, Liam. I mean, what's the alternative?" I don't think he's sleeping much.

"I don't know. Almost don't care anymore."

"That is so not true. You were just mulling over the fact that the holidays will be tough for some of your patients."

"Consults. I'm only part of a team. And you're the one who's generous. I hear you hashing with the tenants around the building. Never phony, always warm —even when I can tell by the rasp in your voice that you're fatigued, whooped. You should inspire me, but right now, I don't know…"

"You don't know what?" Gently: "Tell me."

"It all tortures me."

"I torture you?"

"No, no, not you. I just… better get ready for work."

"Sure. Hit me when it makes sense. Okay?"

He's shuffling socks around in a drawer. "Yes, definitely. I will. Busy around the edges at the shop, but yes, for sure."

"Understood. I'll be jammin' myself."

Standing in the doorway thinking, "kiss", she leans back against the frame. He looks up and snaps out of it, bounces over, and gives her a quick peck.

"Have a good day, Ab." Right back to the sock-drawer.

After assessing the immaculately clean stairwell, Abby stops off on a couple of floors that she knows will need some attention whenever she can get to them, and keeps adding to the endless lists in her little notebook. Almost down to the lobby, she hears something behind her.

Straightening the black plastic brim on his pristine felt cap, and not so smoothly slithering out of Ms C's apartment.

"Hi, Reg."

"Abby." Hand-combing his beard as he passes her in the hallway, glowing.

Damn! Everybody gettin' some button today. You go, Ms Conrad.

Her hair is fighting with her, going completely psycho-wire, getting in her eyes, when through the mesh of her bangs, Abby sees one of the college kids from the infamous transom apartment. His face is freshly bruised, dragging a bag behind him.

"Luke? Hi. How's your world? Laundry day today?"

"I don't know. Don't give a shit. Those guys are fucking assholes."

"Yikes. Living with people is tough, man. Maybe you all just need a breather."

"Nope. It's soured. Everything is a fight."

What the hell is this now? They were like peas in a pod when I was there. I thought they were gonna start a fuckin' band or some shit. "Well, somebody has to be the adult. You guys were all getting along so well... maybe..."

"You can kiss that crap goodbye. I gotta go." And he's quickly on his way.

Abby weaves up to their unit. The new transom looks perfect. She can hear static on the TV, but not another sound. There's some gunk on the floor by the doorjamb, and a beer tab? Picking it up, it's an earring with a smiley face dangling from it. Something hits her deep, a pulse. She flashes on her sweeping duties and remembers grabbing something out of a pile of dirt in the stairwell. A cheap toe-ring, maybe? Had a separated band so you could adjust the size. At the time, she'd pitched it without a thought, though. Pocketing the earring, she heads to the basement.

Smells like JT and funk down here. It was getting late yesterday when I finished the endless stairwell maintenance. Ring should still be in the trash, somewhere.

When Abby pulls out the garbage bag, it rips wide open, half of the refuse falling back into the can, while the rest spills out all over her boots. There's not even a candy wrapper left in the strips of plastic that she holds in her hands. "Thanks for that."

She's forgotten her work gloves, so her winter leathers are getting pretty roughed up in this mess. Finally, she hears a *ping*. There it is. Maybe it's just a kid's ring and not a toe ring. Setting it aside for safe keeping, she keeps digging.

Springing out of the building, Liam sees Batts and JT in the alley, horns locked.

"All I get from you, little elf, is grief. You want new thermostats, and exhaust pipes, and regulators, and switches. And hedge clippers, and buckets, and conduit and blah and blah and blah. Like this shit don't cost nothin'." He shakes a flubbery, hairy fist at her.

Leaning right in his face, "Tell ya what, I'll just sit back and let the pipes fuckin' freeze. Then we'll see how much that costs ya, boss-man."

Liam shouts, "Hi guys!", startling the pair as he approaches. "Probably gonna get some weather soon, huh? Man, it's cold out here."

Batts glares at him out of eye sockets that look more like shriveled birds' nests. JT seems exhausted but takes advantage of the opening to stomp away. Batts slowly cocks his head at Liam, sniffs hard, spits sloppy, and brushes on by him.

There's a three-foot strip near the base of the wall that's sporting a pile of branches and plastic. As if it all got swept up against the building from a windstorm, or water drainage. But it's way too cold for running water. Everything is ice. Something shiny catches his eye. Before he even bends down to pick it up, he knows –it's a charm from a bracelet.

41

big bloody love claws
sink in deep
whose blood?
whose life juice?
whose love?

open arms
i sing
you climb walls inside you
dance around me
no music
no touch

only a few days
fall open warmer
so bright
just feel me
cold

a wave and a flash
snake through a tall room
i don't see it
your eyes
only down

Abby's journal: "big bloody love claws/marshmallow marshmallow" ...a detour and a snack...

42

Zoe watches her soul scamper all around the shop. The spirit made manifest is slapping her hands on the floor in front of the talisman altars, kicking off the walls, and occasionally stopping mid-scramble to sing frightening arpeggios at the precious stone displays.

This phantasm is a much younger version of Zoe, donning thick black fabric from turban to toe. The crazy dark kohl around her eyes spirals out into thin lines, forming delicate crosses and stars that spill across her face.

Not sure what all the bugaboo is about, but damn if I don't look great! Of course, I was never actually quite that svelte. Granted. But, 'tis my vision n' such. Slight embellishments are nothin' but accents; they hardly dilute the message.

The last time I let her out on the bus I gave her far too much leash though; she almost flew right out the window! Need to keep this brief.

The increasingly sad-looking soul pauses to smell the air around her, then goes right back to smacking the floor and unleashing off-key melodies.

Seeing the whole room, Zoe concentrates. "Alright now, easy girl. Slow it down to a gallop, darlin'. Where you goin' with all this?"

A few hours later, in a rare moment of solidarity, Ardy and Zoe are sitting at the end of the bar, talking quietly. Perfect winter light casts a comforting warmth over the room.

From his semi-permanent seat near the door, Joe —having long ago become thoroughly numb to society's petty derision with regards to the untoward— suddenly grumbles as if waking from a coma. "Thhhis guy here would like one!"

Ardy and Zoe swing their heads in unison. "Shut up, Joe."

Good ol' Joe makes the effort to bite his tongue, but his rocking body-language, and slight scowl, say that in some manufactured parallel universe, he is in fact the victim here.

Ardy points his chin at Zoe's drink. "Vodka-tonic there, lady?" He swirls the ice in his Manhattan, toothpick working overtime.

"Just tonic and lime today."

"What's goin' on? Zoe?" Delicately: "How about a song?"

"No music in me right now, I'm afraid."

The TV is cutting in and out; there are only a few customers at the bar, spaced evenly so they don't have to acknowledge one another. The pale skinny bartender does inventory as if he's being put upon. And Steven, parked in his usual spot, is just a robot in a cheap seat.

Zoe is dressed in black. Ardy can't recall ever seeing her in something that wasn't more vibrant. No jewelry. No make-up. Not that she ever wears much of either, but he could tell. She's lost her glow. Whatever the hell is going on in here today, he doesn't like it. But he also knows well enough not to push Zoe. "Seems to me… singing used to be contagious, like laughter."

Zero animation: "Amen. My ma used to belt out a few on the front porch at night, and sometimes half the neighborhood would join in." Poking her lime with the cocktail-straw.

"Yeah, well, here's to Ma'." Ardy takes a nice long gulp.

"Been thinkin' about barriers lately. All kinds of barriers. They're essentially false, right? Like borders. Lines on a map. Who draws them? Who decides? And to what end? They sell it to us as freedom, indeed. Each territory operates under its own set of rules. But ultimately, if we acquiesce, are we not then allowing ourselves to be penned in? What are we anyway, cattle? I prefer to address the universe as a whole, not in predetermined bits and pieces."

"Agreed. Yes. For certain sure. Give me one second." He walks to the jukebox and puts on "Ooh child" by The Five Stairsteps.

Zoe picks up her head. "Well, now, if that isn't the best thing you've done in weeks."

"Don't start on me, girl. Just lookin' for some rope-a-dope in here."

"Thai Chi." She almost smiles.

"Pre-cisely. Take this funk, and spin it 'round, and… shoot it back where it came from! 'Cause we are in world-famous Ardy's Ringside tonight! Round for the bar!"

Joe sneezes. "Hallelujah!"

Ardy takes Zoe's hands and tenderly spins her on the barstool. She sloths off it like a sleepy child in a trance. Soon they are both dancing, a couple feet apart, subtle movements. As their shoulders and hips remember their oft-forgotten purposes, Zoe finally lets go and laughs. "You better get some new shoes there, golden gloves. Don't trip over yourself out here now."

He just sings back at her, goofy grin cemented on his puss.

Even Steven momentarily picks up his head, weakly smiles, and raises his mug to the heavens.

Stewart's water bowl is bone dry, and his litter box is overflowing. Every dish and teacup and piece of silverware is scattered about the apartment, some of them resting atop piles of clothes. All the cupboards are open and empty – minus a few canned goods, stacked in random patterns.

"The cans go here." A completely naked Ms Conrad reaches up and taps each can of beans, then quickly shuffles over to the next cupboard. Her hair is matted down with three different kinds of toothpaste, while her radiant eyes vibrate as if she's trying to look at everything at once. As if the smallest detail might escape her and ruin all of her plans. "The cans go here." *Tap tap tap, tap tap* tap.

Nestled in the transom, Stewart trains a wary eye, occasionally jerking his sleepy head from fatigue.

43

It's one of those diners that looks as if they'd tiled the place with what was left over from the bathrooms –lotta white. Good mix of folks in here, though. It's clearly no Beanie's; more of a glass and plate clinkin', large and small folk all shoutin' with equal voice, loud as shit, maw-huncher kinda vibe. But Abby can hide in here. Sometimes she likes buzz. And beyond that, she can't quite summon the strength for JT yet this morning, so this will have to do.

She grabs the last stool at the counter, which she'd always preferred over tables anyway. And as the waiter wrangles the paper placemat that's soaked with soda –soda at eight am?– he flops down a wet menu that reads "Tom's Diner". But the half-lit neon sign in the front window clearly spells out "Jack's Place". And while she's pretty sure the regulars could give her volumes on this particular discrepancy; she doesn't have the energy for them either.

And let's not dismiss the wet menu. Wet because it's been wiped off oh-so-very recently, if not right in front of you, with the same grimy rag that he's been sloshing around on everything else in his path since two hours before you woke up.

Not really looking at her: "Coffee? Orange juice?"

"Both, thanks."

Parked right in front of the omelette station, she's in for a free show. Lovely. A young man with cannon-arms is working it hard and smooth, in constant motion. Back-lit by a sun that has reluctantly decided to go ahead and rise above the skyline, sneak-peepin' through a tiny window on the far side of the room. Soon everything is glistening: his muscles, the eggs, butter, pans, a giant glass of water that he occasionally chugs.

He is a machine, this young Matthew. She gathers it's "Matthew" from the "Ho! Big Matt!" he's getting from the staff passing by his station. The whole scene is somewhat silhouetted.

Don't think my eyes are totally awake yet, but still –have I mentioned muscles?– nice form, my friend.

There are three to five bowls of eggs ready to go at all times. As he empties one into a pan, he reflexively grabs more for the next round. Crack, plop, whisk, set aside. Constantly ducking and reaching for random containers filled with gorgeous chopped veggies, properly wrapped meats, salty cheeses.

Whatever's lacking in bedside manner and sanitation in the front of the house is put to shame by the cleanliness and professionalism in the back. There's an invisible wall between the servers, slinging full water glasses as if they're empty, and the slick if not feisty hash jockeys on the line –preppin', cleanin', husslin'. Don't get me wrong, everybody's husslin', it's just that the troops engaged in direct combat with the grease-hungry mob at the tables take more shrapnel, that's all.

The only monologue coming from the omelette station is "order's up" chatter –"Four twenty-two, meaty-meats, extra cheese, all day!" Or, when he's out of something: "Spinach! Mush… no… yeah… mushrooms! Got a hole in my shroom-boat that needs some love, people!" Wiping the sweat from his brow with a clean towel, he washes his hands every two minutes –lightning fast.

Separating the whites from four eggs, he sets the yolks aside. Hand-wash. A massive splash of liquid butter goes in the pan, blue flames from the hollowed-out gas lines licking up around the edges. Abby's guessing he has no hair left on his forearms. All long ago sacrificed in the pursuit of orgasmic breakfast perfection.

Egg whites –in. Flipping the other omelette on the right burner well up into the air, it's nothing short of radiant in its flight. Then he pivots back to the white omelet and drops in almost all the vegetables at his disposal. "Desperate for greens over here!" Taking a long drink of water, he reads the next few order-slips.

First omelette is done. "Four forty-four, green onion swiss, up!" Fresh eggs are quickly on for a new order that gets ham and chorizo and… meat stuffs. Sweat towel, hand wash. Season meat omelette. Now back to the veggie. Flip. Plates it. "Four-sixty-four now folks, alabaster-veggie flyer, flyin' in!" He is a madman with a food-plan. A true artist.

I wonder if he ever needs any help with that towel, or anything…

She had forgotten all about the trinkets she'd found in the garbage, and in every random crevice of the Lex; it was as if someone were leaving breadcrumbs. Her hip pocket suddenly felt heavy with their weight.

After breakfast, I'll see if Max wants to hang onto them while I figure out what's going on. Maybe I'm being paranoid, but if someone is messing with that place —shit is fucking unacceptable. It's still my building, for now.

Okay, let's go ahead and ride the elevator after inhaling three pounds of meat and eggs, shall we? Chorizo should be illegal.

Sashaying into the workroom, Abby had to admit it was looking a little better these days organization-wise, but it's always a bit gloomy regardless. And the windows are humming a faintly jarring refrain, just to round out that Boris Karloff/Peter Lorre chamber music feel.

She bends down to pull Max the mighty bucket out of his little cave, but she doesn't immediately see him. "You hidin' in there, buddy?" Reaching into the ice-cold space —nothing. Slapping her hand around like a flopping fish, he's gone.

Abby rockets out of the elevator towards JTs apartment, or what's known around the building as *the foggy grotto*. As she stomps down the hallway, she can just make out JTs reflection in the transom window. "JT? JT!" Silence.

Pulling out her skeleton key just as JT tries to bolt the door, Abby beats her to the punch and pushes it open with some force.

"What the fuck! You can't just charge in here—"

"Bucket. Now. I'm not messin' with you. Don't test me."

JT shrugs. Abby brushes by her and opens the closet. Max is sitting on the floor, no worse for wear.

"It was just a joke, Jesus."

"I told you to keep your hands off my stuff."

"Who says that's your stuff?"

"Who says it isn't? You?"

"If you wanna go there, Abby-centric, I'll dance."

"Whatever." As she turns to leave, she sees a few small pendants and some refuse on JT's dresser. "Where did you get those?"

"Well, I didn't fuckin' buy 'em, Ab. What is up with you?" She sparks a spliff.

"Look, I'm sorry, but I really need to know where you got them, there's…"

JT blows a huge hit of thick smoke right in Abby's face, emptying her lungs.

She spins away towards the elevators, on the verge of tears. Over her shoulder: "Fuck you with your fuckin' shit, you fuck!"

"Articulate, Abrovsky!"

The furnaces are a pain in the ass to work on, but at least it's usually warm down here. Not at the frikken moment, though.

Stuffing some combustibles into the incinerator, JT leaves the door open and just lets the heat wash over her.

After making a quick list, she gets to work on the hinges of Ol' Betsy – the nastier of the two sister furnaces. Evil twins. Masks and gloves are usually bullshit, but she protects herself for this amount of airborne poison. Plumes of rust ascend into the air as she slaps a steel brush in both directions.

Good, that went quicker than I thought. It ain't pretty, but the little door opens wide enough to get the pilots re-lit if they go out; no more lilt in the swing, seals up reasonably well. S'all we need from you today, babies. We'll jack up those pilot lights to full-height mañana. As in –not right now.

Sauntering back over to the incinerator, she tosses in the mask and gloves. Her face is a funky swamp of sweat and grime, so she tries to wipe it off with her shirt. But that's also covered in layers of muck, and just adds to the scum-on-a-pond effect. "Fuck." She spits and pulls out another joint.

Frikken shoe-scrapin' rat-weed. Takes three whole tubes just to catch a wee buzz n' shit. Long morning. Almost had a fight… Abracadabra. Better watch her ass.

A wave of fatigue hits her. Wobbling backwards, she lets her butt hit the wall, tilts her head up, eyes shut, puffing away. A rare moment of tranquility.

After a couple minutes, she looks out to see Batts lunging at her with a gargantuan pair of hedge clippers. The open blades slam into the wall on either side of her neck, sending chunks of plaster flying. They're not cutting her, but she's pinned. His black eyes emit silver sparks. Before JT can scream or react, he punches her in the face with enough force to put a head-shaped dent in the drywall behind her. Everything goes black, and there's a loud ringing in her ears. She feels the blades tickling her skin as she starts to sink. He's leaning on her kind of sideways, barely holding her up. Trying to claw and kick him with everything she has, there's just no way to get any purchase as his girth has most of her body smothered, and every movement allows the edge of the blades to cleave into her neck. Her mouth is open, but only a small squeak escapes as warm tears snake their way down through the grit on her face and mix in with the blood flowing from her nose.

She twists and reaches for the knife in her boot, barely getting her fingertips under the notch in the handle. But just as she tries to flip it up into the palm of her hand, Batts shifts his weight, and the weapon falls to the floor with a clang. Ignoring the futility, she continues to stretch out her fingers towards her only hope, as Batts bears down and punches her again.

This time she's just about out cold. The ringing fades. His body is still pressed against hers as the shears let go and fall away on their own. The harrowing decay of his breath consumes her. Her vision comes back momentarily, and as she makes one final attempt to scream, he puts a tingly cloth over her face. She manages to get her hands up to his wrist, but that's it. Only the menacing drone of the furnaces now. His weight is crushing her.

Far out, from across the universe, she hears Batts's voice as she fades. It's small, but unearthly sinister: "I just want a sniff..."

44

The rattling windows in the workroom graciously accept Max as a guest. Layers of clouds outside are jockeying for disparate positions. With almost no insulation in here, Abby can smell the snow coming. Yanking a knotted bunch of spent jewelry from her pocket, she drops it in the pewter vessel. Shiny pasta in a rolling boil. They seem to flutter and space out as they swirl. Her fingertips vibrate as she slowly runs them around the top edge of the bucket. "Stay cool, buddy. I gotta go grab some stuff and get to work in here."

Hustling to the stairwell, Abby swings around the first landing and is overwhelmed by the sheer volume of garbage and clothes strewn everywhere. Peering over the edge, down through the maze of floors, the trail goes all the way to the basement. It's a helter-skelter hodgepodge of shoes, paper bags, bottles and cans, but mostly clothes.

"I just cleaned in here!" Okay. Now I'm officially my mother. Well, I don't have time to wrestle with this particular flavor of "what?" at the moment.

Kicking things out of the way as she descends, her pace slows, and she starts looking more closely at the garments. So familiar. Impeccable, tight wool. Thin.

Stopping off on Ms Conrad's floor, the transoms yield neither light nor sound, nothing. Everything is dark. Her door is propped open. "Ms Conrad? Hello?" Abby walks into a labyrinth of chaos. Tablecloths and curtains in piles, furniture overturned, candles melted to the quick, yielding puddles of hardened wax on the floor. The apartment smells of urine. Stewart hisses behind her, perched on top of the coat rack. "Hey there, okay, easy…" Gently taking him down, he doesn't resist, but is mighty shaky and stiff.

She sets him up with water and food. "I'll be back, promise."

"Reg?" He's sitting out on the curb, wringing his hat in his hands. "Reg? Where is Ms Conrad."

"Abby. Abby, I swear, I didn't… I had no idea, I—"

"Reg, Reg, c'mon, c'mere, I gotchya." She helps ease him up and walks him into the lobby, parking him on a bench by the elevators. "Stay here for a second, soldier. I'll be back in a minute, OK?"

Lifeless: "OK."

She jogs back down to Ms Conrad's and pours a glass of water. Stewart is back up on the coatrack, but the bowls are empty. Filling his water bowl again, she sees the patterns of cans in the cupboards for the first time. Pyramids, intricately curved walls, single vertical rows ascending according to size. Each labored creation set in its own cave. Stewart meows extra-long and loud. "I know, big guy, I know. Stay cool. We'll get this."

Reg is gazing around at the sculpted patterns on the ceiling in the lobby as if he's psychically coaxing a gravity-defying gnome through a maze.

"Here, drink, please." He blindly takes the glass and sips some water, wincing as sips turn to gulps. It slows him down; his breathing calms.

"Thank you."

"What happened?"

"She was screaming. Ranting, running around. It was so sudden, I… She seemed fine yesterday. I swear…"

"Where is she, Reg?"

"They took her. I had to. She wasn't making sense. I thought she might hurt herself."

Abby forces eye contact. "No one is blaming you. Where is she?"

"St Margaret's."

The smells of feces in the hallway, mixed with traces of bleach, tell Abby where she is. The rehabilitation ward at St Margaret's Center is nationally known for its contemporary and compassionate care for seniors, as they specialize in treating dementia and Alzheimer's disorders, only charging a minimum of fortunes.

She schmoozes them hard at the nurses' station and gathers that Ms C most likely has late-onset dementia, with severe mania and delusions. The nurses and aides take turns rolling their eyes, as if to imply that "severe" doesn't quite cover it.

Bunched upright in the corner of a railed bed, Ms Conrad looks a thousand years old. Tiny and frail. The tangled plastic tubing that's piping oxygen into her nose is coiled like a boa-constrictor strangling her delicate face.

Her head snaps. "Did Batts send you to fix the TV?"

"Hi, Ms C. How are you feeling?"

"Like someone stepped on me on their way to the grocery store. Do you have any food? They keep trying to feed me porridge."

A nurse comes in who could be Zoe's doppelganger. Militant and fatigued, she makes her way through checking vitals and resetting monitors. Speaking far too loudly out of habit: "You didn't eat your lunch, Ms Conrad. Aren't you hungry?"

"Do *you* have any food? They keep trying to feed me porridge."

"I'll leave it here in case you want it later, alright?" She puts the blanket back up over her legs and tucks it in. "And who are you, Miss?"

"Her niece."

Not buying it, "Well, visiting hours are over. You need to go soon." Much louder: "I'll be back in a minute, Ms Conrad. How about some Italian Ice?"

"Yes! Yes! Grape? Please? Oh, God. Thank you."

"Okay." Then, to Abby: "You've got five minutes, love."

"Thanks."

Ms Conrad mashes the remote control, and the TV is going wild. It's mostly running static with occasional station audio leaking in, as if it's some bootleg signal from across the border.

"Traffic... out of town... crime rate... storm warning... underwritten..."

"Ms C? What happened?"

"What do you mean? What are you babbling about?"

"What's been going on? How did you end up in here, hon?"

"Ambulance, I think." She lets out a breath, exasperated. Her hands momentarily surrender and stop torturing the remote.

"Well, I hate to see you like this. They're going to take good care of you, though. I have to go now, but I'll check on you tomorrow, okay? Oh, and I fed Stewart. He's fine."

"Stewart Granger? He died years ago. Maybe they should have a bed in here for you."

"They probably should. Try to get some rest, lady." She backs away and knocks Ms C's purse onto the floor, upside down, full dump.

"Clumsy fool!"

"Jeez, damn, I'm sorry." Abby bends down, touching the powdery dirt. She lifts the purse and reveals a nest of tortured jewelry: earrings and bracelets, necklaces, rings, charms, crosses. "Ms Conrad?"

Her eyes are dancing and radiant. They possess a deep internal glow. Disgusted: "You have no idea. None. Loneliness doesn't follow you around, like some infernal cloud… conjured from hell. You'll never know what it's like to be completely and utterly on your own. No one to talk to. No celebrations. No grieving. No one gives a hoot. Nobody. Ever. You will always smell of companionship, and lately –prurient mists... Ah? We can hear you through the walls, little harlot. Banshee. Traipsing around all pokey-breasted and head-long in heat. You think we don't know? Well, you're not the only one. I have a paramour myself, not that you have any real concern for my welfare, but he's good. Damn good. Rings the bell every time, he does. So I don't need you now. Never really did." She points at the pile of junk on the floor as if she's flicking crumbs off a table with her index finger. "And take all that crap with you. No more magpie messenger girl for me. Oh no. I'm a new woman these days, you see. I –am going to be young again."

"Where did you get all this stuff, Ms C? Please tell me what's going on."

"What? What's not making its way through all that hair into your feeble brain? Every room is silent. Every space, empty, except the mirror... that demon. No quarter there. No mercy… and, all this junk," slapping at the IVs. "I've been dying for years! Dying for your pleasure. Can't you see that?"

"I guess I better go, hon. I…"

"Oh no, you don't. You are going to stay right here and fix this infernal television set, or I am going to call the police!"

45

The Guns-&-Ammo calendar has been exceptional this year, hanging in a place of honor in the kitchen. The December photo is a Smith & Wesson .500 snub-nose revolver. Hardcore gun-porn. A 325 and 700-grain shell, both fifty caliber, are shown side by side in the bottom corner for comparison. Looking as if they both could leave quite the mark, make a nice dent.

Okay, I was right. It is today. *December 22nd, 3:30 p.m. —Liam.* And it's a quarter-to-four already. Where is that snake? Well, I guess that's that. Too bad. I was all ready and waiting.

Maybe I'll go get the mail, so I don't have to hear about that if he does show up. He could stroll in here any minute now, right?

Out of breath and sweating, Nick dumps the stash of envelopes on the table, pulling some from the depths of his army jacket. "There… that wasn't so bad."

Almost four o'clock. Goddamnit, Liam. And how the hell is it that I've become so completely dependent on someone else to simply walk out the front door? I'll go down and sit on the bench by myself. How about that? Right. Sure. Sure, I will. Why not?

Nick eases down the walkway and notices that it's quiet in the neighborhood overall. Distant voices. Light traffic.

Good. Fine. I'm fine.

Taking two steps out onto the sidewalk, he barely sees a skateboarder who buzzes around him from behind, out onto the street, then back up on the walk. "Hi, Mr Nick!"

"What… David? Oh. Hi, there."

Back inside the house, staring at the ceiling with prayer hands over his mouth and pacing. Five past four. Crap. Nick pulls the calendar down off the wall and starts leafing through the dramatically lit photographs of glorious weapons, each one meaner looking than the next, and it soothes him. Flipping it over, he'd never noticed the illustrations on the back. It was some kind of re-creation, or a reprint, maybe, of an old-time ad for a Father & Son trail camp in the mountains. Little sketches of them doing various activities –hiking, fishing, canoeing, and, of course, shooting out on the rifle range. The last frame is a rough sketch of the two men looking very serious in a duck blind, waiting for their chance.

And I'm never going to do any of this again, right? This is it. Me and the darkest house on Dumbo Street. Never going shooting with my boy. Never getting out to the market. Never gonna piss on my neighbor's car in the middle of the night. Christ, I can barely get the mail. Bullshit. "Fuck all of you."

He again steps outside, locking the door behind him. Here we go.

When he gets to the mailbox, he leans on it a little. His feet keep moving, but his upper body stays with the post until he jerks himself away.

Easing down the sidewalk, each step is like goo. He may as well be slow-motion log-joggin' over Niagara Falls. A couple on the other side of the street is walking a little ball of white fluff, that may or may not be a dog. When they wave at him, his eyes reflexively roll.

Doesn't anybody just mind their own business anymore? Go walk your cotton-ball coyote snack, and piss awfff.

By the time he gets to the bench, he knows in his heart that he won't make it back to the house. He sits in a casual pose, but on an ass of marble. Giving the ground at his feet a good once over, he doesn't dare check to see how far away he is from his front door. Because, if he does, he'll explode.

As he starts to settle in, a dump truck sticks its nose out onto the street. What now? It pulls out a block away, but heads in the opposite direction, engine fading as the driver works his way through the gears, like no one had ever told him there is this thing called a "clutch". The sound of gnashing metal makes Nick's teeth tingle, but it quickly dissipates until the only noise he hears is the reassuring echo of his thundering heart trying to punch straight through his chest.

The clouds are racing. Dark, grey, threatening. It smells awesome, though. The unmistakable air of unstable weather. Ions. Storm coming, for sure. Ceiling looks cool today, anyway. Ceiling? Sky. Right. The sky looks cool. Sometimes they call it a ceiling. Sure they do. Pilots n' shit…

The sidewalk gives way to Liam, hurrying down the block. Awkward but in motion. Nick pretends to be chillin'.

I can do this, just sit. Still.

Plopping down on the bench, Liam looks straight out into the park. Nick catches that and joins him. Not a whole lot to see. A couple is strolling along a walking trail way off in the distance. Pigeons. Some papers blowing around.

Without breaking his gaze on the scenery, Liam puts his hand, palm up, on Nick's knee. Nick immediately grabs it, and the two of them sit there in silence, tightly holding hands.

The sun breaks out for a flash, throwing long shadows from the tree line over the bench. Nick rotates his head as he looks up at the increasingly animated clouds, and hangs on for dear life.

46

Zoe's Occult & Mystic is dark. Abby can't even see a cat in there. "C'mon, Zoe?" She scribbles a message in her notebook *—Please call if you can. Something I need to run by you, Abby.* She adds her phone number and slides the note through the mail slot in the door.

Ugh. Maybe she went down to Ardy's.

She mulls over what little she has to sketch with —crusty charms, random debris, JT, Ms Conrad. She'd managed to scoop up most of the jewelry off the hospital floor while Ms C went on and on about the TV.

TVs. Static. Electric. Electric eyes. Right —what the fuck was up with Ms Conrad's eyes? What's up with mine, for that matter? Everything is shadowy. Hazy.

Kerouac wrote about finding a box of children's toys in an abandoned house, and expounded on the theory that kids infuse life into their playthings through the power of love and devotion, unwavering belief. And repetition. Faithfully executing daily ceremony, until they get some form of energy in return. Whatever's brewing at the Lex is no voodoo doll thing. And amulets are for protection, not curses. That's assuming there is a curse, or someone's trying to turn that place upside down.

Maybe I'm doing the whole "self-fulfilling prophecy" thing. Like since I suck at the job so far, I won't let myself believe there isn't something bigger that I can grab onto. Help solve. Ah, bullshit. Somebody's fucking with that old pile of bricks. I think.

She pulls out a few charms and pieces from Ms Conrad's contributions. Could that be all there is to this? A lady gone mad, planting tarnished gold seeds around the building hoping for trees to magically grow? Completely unaware that she may be leaving some dangerous chaos in her wake?

The jewelry is almost hot to the touch, the tips of Abby's fingers are alive with sting. What in hell? What am I chasing?

Ardy's Ringside Bar is fairly empty. No sign of Zoe. "Quick shot of Jameson and a Stella, please."

"Sure, Ab."

TV is off. She points. "Broken?" Skinny-pasty just shrugs. Looking around, she sees Steven at the far end of the bar. "Hi, Steven. Has Zoe been in?"

"Last night."

"Ah. Well, I'm outta here in a sec, but if she swings by…"

"I'll tell her that your wheels are grinding so hard that the birds have stopped chirping."

"Yeah, that works. Thanks." He's kinda cute around the edges, isn't he.

She downs the shot and walks around, beer in tow.

With the Christmas lights up year-round, along with most of the other holiday decorations, the "Giving Season" doesn't really feel much different than any other season in here. Minus the notable addition of the oversized stockings hanging up behind the bar, which the bartenders hate –but Ardy insists on. And only if you've bartended or worked for him in some capacity do you get a stocking. She knows. She's tried. He won't budge. Although, he would let her pick up a shift any time, just so she could get over that hump and claim her space on the wall.

Something to consider. I certainly won't be at the Lex much longer. Man, I don't wanna crap out on that, though. But JT? I don't know. And Liam. Don't get all twitchy on me now, buddy. I've got plans for you. Maybe the same thing is eating away at everyone over there. Where is my peaceful happy life?

She gets to the bathroom door, and the Muhammad Ali/butterfly picture is hanging at an odd angle. The old-time, family-gathered-round-the-TV shot below it is roughed up –glass broken, frame bent, but still holding together.

Finishing up and washing her hands, the room starts to spin.

Damn, from one beer? Okay, and the whiskey. Whoosh. Time to go.

When Abby walks out of the restroom, the whole place is pulsing. Steven is gone; no bartender. Abby lurches and grabs the wall, knocking the butterfly picture to the floor with a crash. "Son of a bitch." I can't be trusted.

On her hands and knees picking up the random shards, she looks up and sees the mini-TV on the retro picture. The family is drifting away, the TV's rolling static; her head spins and spins.

She drops everything and runs outside to the curb. Leaning on a telephone-pole, the world slows down. The cold air feels so good. Then it all hits her again in a rush, and she vomits, some splashing up on her work boots. People steer clear of her or cross the street. With one hand on the pole, she hangs her head.

Finally surrendering to gravity, she sits down a few feet away from the puddle.

Oh, girl. Gotta regroup here.

Leaning back, her hand slips on something. A gold brooch. Maybe it's supposed to be a bird? She has no idea, but blindly adds it to the warm collection in her pocket.

Shit's following me around now. Oof, I hope I don't have to walk the plank. I'll sink like a rock!

Another wave of nausea hits her. She tries to pull her hair back, but at the moment, those stubborn locks are having their own conversation with the wind. "Oh no... hopscotch."

Not sure how much time has gone by here, but, hey —thanks for checkin' on me, guys!

She manages to make her way down the block, but just ends up sitting on the curb again. No more nausea, only the bleak getting bleaker, and tears.

Munching on a piece of gum feels good, spitting randomly for some mouth rinse. Abby pulls out her compact and the tortured face looking back at her, rumpled and sullen, is enough to finish her off.

Good Lord, I've morphed into the butt-side of the plague.

Just when she's seriously thinking about sleeping there for the night, a cab pulls up. "Off Duty" light is on. It takes determination, but she manages to stand up and sees Pearl's original owner behind the wheel, flashing a somewhat familiar sneer. But it drifts into a small smile, and he nods towards the back door.

They ride in silence the whole way to the Lex, meter off. She wants to say thank you, that she loves Pearl, and so many other things, but she just sits there. He checks on her in the rearview mirror as they pull up to the front walk.

Reaching over the seat, he gently pats her knee, like a small child awkwardly tapping on a drum. Putting her hand over his, she squeezes it a little, covering her heart with the other. Easing out, she tentatively scales the curb.

Catching a second wind as she enters the building, she stops in the middle of the lobby, mind rippling. Trinkets, static, buzz. Buzzing. Vibrations…

Ear to the door, lightly knocking: "Liam? Hello-oo? You in there?" Perfect silence. Abby pulls out her keys.

As she enters, the musky scent of his apartment instantly takes her to a warm place. She can't help herself now; she misses him all the time.

Running her fingers along the Advent Window set, it pulsates as if it has its own motor. Opening the next tiny window, nothing. A little dusty, but it's empty. She tries the next. And the next. When she opens December 25th, a flicker of cold air escapes and inside on the tiny ledge is a small rusty cross, clinging to part of a dilapidated chain. Picking it up, the cross dances around in the air.

"Abby, what are you doing?" Liam is standing in the doorway, looking all kinds of furious.

"Liam! I am so sorry, I—"

"Why are you in here?"

"I know this is nuts, but please, hear me for one second. Something is going on in this building. Look." She holds up the cross. "This was in your advent window puzzle."

Heart in his throat. Oh my god. Lisa. Son of a bitch.

"And I don't know what, exactly. I mean, I'm starting to get a picture, but it's shaky. JT, well, I'm not, did you hear about Ms Conrad? I think—"

"You know jack-shit."

She stands up, still a little dizzy, and sticks her finger right in his face. "Don't fuckin' talk to me." Followed with a solid punch to his bad shoulder before she runs down the hall.

"Abby! I'm… sorry…"

She's long gone. He stomps around and debates going after her.

Fuck. Did she puke in here? Damn it all. I can't confess every little thing. I can't. Not now. Every time I open all the way up to someone, I blow it. I'll just have to fix this on my own. Make amends later, eventually, somehow.

I'll find the squawking, naked nut-job out there, get a general location on her lair, and... wrangle a cop, show the protection order, and at least get her good and scared, if not arrested for this shit.

"SHIT!"

47

The workroom sits up high enough to feel like she could reach out and touch some of the low-hanging clouds zipping by. Abby steadies herself at the windows, head in her chest.

Sirens and car horns sneak in randomly, along with an increasingly loud moaning. The window frames have been the subject of much attention over the last few weeks, but along with everything else in her life, in the end, it's essentially a game of whack-a-mole. And as the barometer continues to fall, the glass generates an ever-widening range of call and response.

Max looks as if he has his own little storm brewing. Dropping in Mrs C's contributions, there's now enough junked-up jewelry to more than cover the bottom of the bucket, but none of it ever completely lands.

She places her hands firmly around the pewter base, and all at once, she's flying... high over mountains that dwarf the valleys below. There are hundreds of starlings, making strange patterns in the sky. At one point, they take the shape of a massive cross, then a huge shield.

Now they begin to circle –like they're trying to form an attack group. The wind starts to howl, and the clouds begin to spiral. At first, the birds all descend but then quickly pivot, shooting right by her into the open sky. As she looks up to see where they're going, everything turns black –maybe a few stars that quickly fade, but that's it. She's alone.

Letting go of Max, she snaps out of it and leans back on the windowsill. Dizzy. The trinkets are increasingly animated, swirling around and tapping at the walls of the bucket. Through weathered eyes, it seems as if the room is closing in on her.

I'm hallucinating. Maybe dying. What difference would that really make? Suppose it could be a budding, eager tumor gleefully eating away at my vision? I'm completely losing my mind with this jewelry crap.

So Ms Conrad is cursing her own building? Getting involved with witchy shit –*Ms Conrad?* JT? Oh, and by the way –fuck JT. And fuck Liam too. What is his damn deal? Maybe he just wanted to get laid. Can't say that was totally beyond the scope of where I was, out of the gate anyway, but man, I fell into that quick. Whatever. And, yes. Right. They can both pick a body part and suck it.

I've got to get a grip from somewhere, someone. Zo, where are you? Maybe she called.

"Easy now, Max." Turning to the windows: "Please keep an eye on him for me, okay? And while I'm gone, everybody behave."

Wiping crumbs off her bed, Abby checks her messages. Two are hang-ups. Then there's one that's mostly static and choppy, probably a prank. Nothing from Zoe. She goes back and listens to the last one again, and she can kind of hear Annalise's voice mixed in with the static. Maybe? One more time. Mom –yes! Can't make out what she's saying, but that's her.

The hanging radios lightly bump the glass just often enough to be disturbing. She shuffles through a stack of photos while she waits for Annalise to answer the phone. "Mom? Mom, can you hear me?" The line is breaking up, all kinds of fuzz and squeals. Echoes of Annalise's voice pop in and out, but that may just be her recorded message, hard to tell. "Mom, please, I think, I need your help. Please. Mom!" More noise, and then silence. Not even a dial tone. "Look, if you can hear me, it might be, might be… Mom? Fuck!" She throws the phone at the wall. The room tilts.

Oh please, I can't puke again. My throat is already in shreds.

In a trance, she goes back through the pile of pictures. There are a couple of great ones taken from inside the greenhouses. The light is wild, scattered–as she had hoped. Kind of angelic, too, though. Softer than she'd anticipated. She had high hopes for the huge TV antenna up there as well, but it's half-blacked out in most of the photos. Something went wrong on those. Poop. Would have been keepers.

Then a shot of the radio-cross catches her eye. In it, Cherry is all in shadow. Not just dark, but smudged out completely. Shuffling through, they're all the same –Cherry, at the top of the cross, is too dark to see. From every angle, every depth of field. Impossible.

Up on the chair, she carefully pulls the whole thing down and lays it across the bed, snapping off some straw here and there in the process. As if she's disinfecting a wound for a child–"I know, I know, I'm sorry, all done, okay, you're okay…" With occasional face-squints as more things start to snap, she separates Cherry from the pack.

The chipped nail on her index finger slips into the little grooves on the tiny white wheel as she rolls the power/volume button around. Nothing. Batteries are mighty fresh, but have I ever actually turned her on? I don't think so. Scrolling through the channels now, volume all the way up. Zip. Nada. It's giving off vibes, but no signal.

She shakes it gently and hears a faint rattle. Wedging a screwdriver into the opening on the side, the front plate pops open, revealing all the usual innards: transistor, wires, speaker, tuning, attenuation, antenna compartment –and a little stud earring. Just a gold ball on a bent post with a rusted ornamental backing.

"Holy shit. Chrystal."

48

Chrystal strolls around in front of the mini-TVs, sprinkling a few trinkets and chains on top of the small piles of dirt at the base of each one. Reminds her of Christmas ornaments on little brown trees. "You know, I've been collecting these random pieces ever since I can remember. They seem so desperate to me. Lying in the street, on the sidewalks, attempting to shine, begging to be seen. Impetuous."

"So what exactly is their purpose now, Cee? What's with all the hyperactivity the last few days?" Paul sits on the edge of the tub, mouth sporting multiple cuts, hands black from bruises, shivering a little. He's wearing his very best red turtleneck and dress pants, but his bare feet —sliced up like shredded deli salami— look to him as if they're pleading for some socks and shoes, though more lacerations would probably be less painful at this point. The last few days it's as if he's been walking around on angry, bloody potato chips. His vision has been fading rapidly. Everything is a tunnel. So Chrystal, at best, presents as a soft silhouette to him.

Her voice echoes through the mostly empty apartment as she washes her hands in the kitchen. "Well, at first, this was all just an experiment. But larger purposes have revealed themselves along the way. And, even as concise goals are coming into sharper focus, it does seem to me that some small thing may be amiss. Nothing tragic, but I've lost one of my helpers downstairs, at least temporarily, so now it's up to me and you, and our eager little companions here. And the jewelry, yes, it has many functions. Some of which I'm sure are beyond my grasp, but they're mostly here to... assist us, help us see. Their collective yearning to revive what once was, to relive those days when they'd shone so brightly, is unimaginably powerful. And that endless desire, that heat, will ultimately give us the strength to face any storm."

"How fortuitous."

"It's been mused that television is kind of like church, a congregation of souls. And those TV signals –or radio waves, or X-rays… cosmic rays– they're all around, everywhere. They wash over us, like the blood of a butterfly.

"You know, a butterfly's blood doesn't circulate in isolation. No veins or arteries. It simply splashes around, back and forth, up and down. Giving its internal organs a good soaking. A bath of life. The question is –how do we tap into that essential plasma? No? How do we engage and learn and grow in such a river? In that well-spring." She makes her way back around and turns up the volume on each set. The crackling static on the screens shoots sparks out into the air. Her shoes click out a syncopated rhythm on a floor that's covered in mist. Paint chips on the wall occasionally pop off and flitter about, and the ceiling is completely concealed by a black fog that randomly glows with pulses of light.

"OK. Then the baubles are… a conduit? I'm still not—"

"Sure. A link. It's all about energy. The flickering static is the blood of a butterfly that's come to take us home. Home, Paul. Imagine that. And the charms…"

"They're your puppets? Doing your bidding?"

"Not my bidding –our song comes from the universe. Remember, it's all of us. Together. A communion of spirits, essentially."

He looks at his feet again. "Butterflies are poison. Puppets are pathetic and sad."

She breathes deeply. "Only through a certain lens. You see, this energy, once amassed, will impart amazing visions that… will allow us to soar. Why should it be inevitable that our powers fade, or that our meticulously constructed armor is destined to grow rusty, and vulnerable?" Straightening her coat, checking her nails, "We can fly *above* the heavens, looking down on their paltry offerings and petty seductions, as we glide on our own path, through wondrous gardens, and overflowing fountains that… shower us with gold, washing clean the barnacles from all of these… heinous anchors –whose only real purpose is to keep us tied down in the middle of a malignant ocean, this wretched sea that's perpetually littered with such… grotesque decay…"

As she continues to espouse her cultic vision, Paul drifts back to the days when he'd get so willingly drunk on her exquisite juices that singing for his supper felt effortless. And when they'd crossed paths, he'd always been in good voice. It was as if they possessed the same brain. Everything was enchanting at the beginning.

Running his shaky hand across the edge of the tub, he flashes on a decadent bubble bath from years ago. Visceral dynamism was never an issue. And her eyes, they were completely different then. Sparkling and, without a doubt, ravenous –eternally hungry, but in a way that he'd considered mutually beneficial. Mostly because, at the time, he was the target of said hunger. He would give anything to get that back. To feel her warm hand, ready and willing to save him as he reaches up out of his grave.

There is a radiant wishing wheel deep inside his mind, glorious sunlight bouncing off its fine ornamentation and golden appliqué as it whirls. Paul holds his breath, and wishes so hard.

Chrystal, quite pleased with herself: "It's simple, really. If the gods are hungry –feed them. Yes? And these little gems so desperately want to regain their capacity to shine, to be loved, if only given the chance. The chance not only to reanimate what once was, but to empower, embolden, to… embrace a greater caliber of warmth and devotion than we'd ever thought possible. To fly. To soar!..."

"You keep saying that."

"To be made truly whole again through the sum total of a unified will. And so, you see, in a way, there are little pieces of me everywhere, but at the same time…"

"I'm in pieces over here, Cee. I'm falling apart. Nothing resembling a whole person, not anymore. I was hoping, at the very least, you'd have the faintest glimmer of concern left… for my well-being. And that just, maybe, you'd find the notion of stitching me back together somewhat palatable, if not… worthwhile."

The lights go out, and now the room is mostly lit by the TVs. She raises her arms, and the trinkets and static intensify their spastic dance. "This, everything we've accomplished, will make you feel better. I promise."

"But I feel worse…"

"Give it some time."

"So much worse. And your smile. It was demonstrably different when you wanted me. I still remember, you know? Where did that go?"

"It hasn't gone anywhere, Paul. People move on. We've had this discussion…"

"Did you ever love me?"

"As much as I was able." Twirling around for one last look at her electric church.

"Did you love her?"

Her heart flutters. "As much as she let me."

"Do you still—"

"SHE'S MINE!" Chrystal begins to shake and turn red as she approaches the tub.

He sniffles a couple times. "Can you touch me. Please?"

"Paul, I'm exhausted."

"Please? Hold my hand. Touch my face. I'm so lost."

Standing over him now, eyes crackling with light. "I'll always cherish what we had. You know that. And I'll be back soon. You know that, too. We'll talk more then, okay?"

Like a frightened child, he trembles as he reaches up to her with a withering hand. Tortured short breaths. "Please…" His nose starts bleeding.

She weaves around him, disgusted. "For God's sake, clean yourself up."

The apartment door ghost-shuts behind her as she marches down the hallway with long, brisk strides. Her radiant face beams with the expectant vibrancy of a child on Christmas Eve who's already seen her presents, and still cannot wait to rip the wrapping off every single one.

49

Abby emerges from the rooftop doorway and notices the greenhouse doors are wide open. She sticks her head in the larger of the two to see the pots overturned and soil scattered all over the floor.

Bounding across the roof now towards the looming TV antenna, she kicks at the pile of gravel near the bottom and uncovers a crumpled gold choker, half-inch thick, probably a guy's. Most likely the former property of a modest, humble coke dealer.

She pockets it as something rustles in the alley below. Tip-toeing to the edge she holds her arms out wide to keep her balance. She leans way over and sees Chrystal rushing by the dumpsters, hand over her hat and moving with a purpose.

Bolting back towards the access door, Abby is lifted higher with each step. The bubbling roof finally throws her the last few feet right into the side of the doorframe, which she promptly bounces off and hits the deck. Looking over her shoulder, the black tar-strips continue to vigorously undulate where her footsteps had just made impressions, causing the greenhouses creak and moan.

Ducking inside, she snakes her way around the breathing pipes that randomly seem to reach for her as she maneuvers through the shrinking passageway, snagging her clothes and bonking her on the head along the way. Despite her best slithering and ducking, she incurs one bump and scrape after another until she reaches an opening that's closing fast. She barely squeezes through the last bit of tangled tubes as they pull off her coat and practically spit her out into the hallway.

"What the fuck! Give me back my coat!"

She glowers at them on her hands and knees, while they all retreat back to their normal positions, feigning innocence.

The sound of the elevator bell slices through the air. Someone is stomping her way. Oh, God. Batts.

Abby springs up and runs into the workroom, drops the necklace into Max's bubbling brew, and reflexively hangs the bucket on her arm, slapping at the paint chips on the nearest wall as if they've offended her.

"Where the hell have you been all day?" Static is zipping around his head like insects putting on an air show.

She fake-coughs. "Mr Batts, I've been prepping paint jobs, and—"

"Bullshit. I asked you where you went."

A miracle sneeze escapes her, so she amps it up and turns towards him with the follow-through. It's just enough to make him take a step back into the doorway. "I only went to check on Ms Conrad. I wasn't gone that—"

"How about I'm not fuckin' payin' you for that?" He starts towards her.

"Understood, I'm sorry. I'll work late tonight to make up for it. I've made quite a bit of progress…" Holding up her hand, "Please, I don't feel well, please…"

He stops, sniffs. "And what if I don't give a shit?"

Partially bent over, holding her stomach: "They're awful today. I need to keep working in here." Still kind of coughing, arm straight out –hoping that somehow this will magically keep him at bay.

Growling, he turns and picks up a massive pipe wrench. Abby's knuckles crack audibly as she slowly curls her fists. Their eyes lock. Two time-popsicles in a static dance. The clanging in the bucket momentarily distracts him, an in one swift motion, Batts spins away from her and mashes the imposing tool on the doorframe, sending splinters of wood flying. Pointing the top-heavy hunk of metal her way now, "This room gets painted today, or I'll take it out of your ass, hear me? And use the Goddamned tools! Tools! Tools!" barking in an evil loop. He slams the door hard enough on his way out to make Abby and the windows jump, but it just slowly swings back open, as the frame is now too battered to cradle it.

Sitting on the floor, hunched over Max, watching the paint chips mix in with the dancing trinkets, Abby quietly sobs.

What was with his head? Some aura on that freak. I'm beyond delusional now. And how arrogant am I? Really. How stupid? To think I could just waltz in here and do this job. At the end of the day… I am the fraud I hate.

On the other hand, part of me really does believe that ultimately I-did-the-best-I-could-with-what-I-had. Didn't I? Yyyeah, sure you did. Keep tellin' yourself that shit. And define "best". Not the first time we've heard that one. OK, so you were a master at navigating the intricacies of multi-zillion dollar accounts for multi-zillion dollar companies. For years. You crushed it. Fine. Congratulations. But these days, you can't even pull it together enough to get a room painted? Big splash, then fade away. Splash. Fade. Over and over. And now this gig is toast, too? Already?...

I don't fit in with anyone. I don't belong anywhere. I never did. I've felt more alone in crowded rooms than in my little hovel of an apartment dozens of times, and no one gives a shit. So why should I? Why is it asking so much that just one of my plans works out? Just one...

The bucket's frequencies finger out into the air and intertwine with the howling wind that keeps the windows singing those sad-ass bellows. Creating a gloaming harmony for an even more foreboding song.

Chrystal makes her way through the deserted park towards her cove. Giddy. Though part of her does still feel that the stars haven't quite fallen into anything resembling rigid alignment. Nonetheless, energy levels are percolating.

May need to peel one off here. I'm starting to have mini orgasms just walking around.

Setting her hat down and thus allowing it territorial ownership of the bench, she marvels at the mound of debris and jewelry she's built up in this makeshift cave. It's over two feet high now and crackling with energy. Glowing, vibrant, whimsically pulsing, and nothing short of glorious.

Both hands under her skirt, slow, tickling, tapping. Now her rhythm picks up.

Oh God, please make, make me, you can't make me, no, no, stick meee, yes...

Scout's troops are scattered about, off the beaten path, scrounging for whatever they can come up with before dark. But today is not a good food day in City Park. Nobody around, really. And, as if it's his fault things have been thin lately, some of the younger pigeons are giving him dirty looks. It's certainly not the first time he's felt such push-back, but they're becoming increasingly whiney about these temporary droughts. Little bastards.

Chrystal speed-shines her lips and peaks with a series of huffs. Snapping out of it, she gradually focuses on a young albino pigeon leaving droppings on top of the sacred mud pile. She explodes off the bench, and the bird quickly shuffles through the brush to the other side.

Darting around the exterior of the grove with a hard lean, Chrystal catches the young pigeon just before take-off –impaling her with a four-inch stiletto, full stomp, straight through the breast. "Filthy squab."

The bird's dainty wings buzz with hummingbird urgency, but she is tent-pegged to the ground. A gruesome pop and wheeze escape her, and that's it.

Scout hears the faint distress cry, then nothing. He's quickly up and over in that direction, but immediately spots a giant mean woman standing over his already quite dead friend, wiping blood and guts off her shoe.

With all the fury he's ever felt in his life, he dives toward her but is quickly surrounded by his flock, who not-so-gently steer him away from the scene. Bouncing around in the mass of wings, Scout gets swatted more than once on his blind side as he tries to maneuver out, but it's no use. They're virtually carrying him. Cruising on a trajectory up and out of the park.

Encouraged that, at the very least, they're still somewhat protective of their captain, he flaps his wings harder to make his way to the front of the pack. But once again, they maneuver him back into the thick of it. Are they really that concerned? Then it hits him –he's no longer the leader. Today's the day. They're not his army anymore. He can feel it in his gut, that bottomless swell of hurt and loss. Ten minutes ago, he was in charge. And now it's over.

Sending the wrench clanging into the far wall of the bathroom, Batts takes his seat on the throne. He lightly sniffs the air.

Where's the soap smell? Everything is dry and crisp. And no comics in the paper today. Frikken bullshit. Think I'll go ahead and give newbie another visit later on. What the hell was she moanin' about anyway? Cramps? Wench.

He sees tracers in the air as the lights go out. Flapping his arms, they pop right back on.

Yeah, y'know what? I believe we'll re-address that situation as soon as I wrap this up. Smelly little cow needs some old-time discipline. And if it is rainin' red on main street, then we'll just take the dirt road instead. Pound some ground 'round. Did I say *bitch*? "Bitch."

The lights go out again. "Fuck!" As he reaches for toilet paper, he waves his other hand. Nothing. He throws his arms around in every direction that nature will allow, and still, he sits in complete darkness. "Ah, good Christ." He thinks for a brief moment he can detect the woodchip/paint-solvent aroma of a hardware store.

The fluorescent lights finally flicker back on as JT charges towards him full-bore, plunging the blades of the hedge shears deep into Batts's neck.

Her eyes are pools of glowing red light, surrounded by the blackened and bruised sockets that have swollen up all around her face. Batts helplessly swats at her, wedged in the seat. But she's beyond his reach, so he slaps at the razor-sharp blades, slicing open his hands.

She keeps leaning, trying to stick them all the way through to the wall behind him, but there's just too much neck, and he's too far away.

Damn, I really wanted to return that part of the favor.

Out of frustration, she starts screaming and pumping the blades up and down. Blood is spraying out in every direction and misting in the air, like God's eager thumb depressing the end of a fat garden hose. The points of the massive shears finally manage to poke through the back of his neck.

Hm, can't be too disappointed with that, I suppose. All in all, awfully close to perfect.

He leans forward, convulsing and gurgling. The static flying around his head starts to scatter about the room.

She can't believe all the blood. "Ooh, what big eyes you have!"

His jaw is involuntarily snapping open and shut, making a horrific dull clanking sound as it bounces off the blades.

Giving it one last shove through to the handles, she steps back, soaked. His head rolls to one side and looks as if it may just fall to the floor. Folding her arms, she mimics his head tilt. "Nice job on the clippers, Michael. Really. I approve, for sure. Whole-heartedly, in fact. Whaddya think?" Large chunky blood bubbles ooze out of his severed windpipe and pop. "No, no, no, shhhhhh. It's okay. Eeeasy now. Tell you what —if you completely agree with everything I said, just sit there, and bleed."

50

death wears a mask that looks like life
black smoke gives face to the wind
a steel framed hearse is no match for my teeth
strained clocks strike thunder in the nethers

starlings swirl hard and shape up your lips
your eyes form conical holes
a penny for each
as if I owe you
hot blood punches out of the sky

Abby's pocket notebook: "And still, no snow face."

51

Liam's hawked every side alley he can think of between work and the Lex – no sign of Lisa, or whoever she is today. He picks up empty bottles and random pieces of glass that he finds along the way and gleefully smashes them against dumpsters, brick walls, drain pipes, fire escapes, stop signs, and telephone poles. Leaving trails of glistening dust and potential hazard behind him. He'd always loved that shattering sound, ever since he was a kid. But as refreshing as it feels to wind up and hurl the stuff, the overarching gloom of the day leaves that divine noise of instant destruction to fall quite flat against his ear.

Ten years ago, I wouldn't have been this winded. Christ, I don't even know what "ten years" means anymore. So sick and tired of being tortured. And who's the torturer? Paul is right. My life is an endless loop of self-induced, useless chores. A scramble to nowhere. The dutiful masses in this town are crawling over each other like ants out on a binger; and I myself am playing at what, exactly? In the end, am I really doing anyone any good at all?

Coming to him from far off in the distance, riding on a blustery wind, he can barely hear the protest girl with the megaphone, who's still giving it to the indifferent office building.

"And now, since you don't have the guts to do it yourselves, you let your killer chemicals perform your evil deeds for you! Pesticides instead of guns… COWARDS!"

I wish she would stuff that bullhorn and get a job… but I guess I have to hand it to her –at least she's singularly focused.

A block from home, a big red rubber ball goes bounding past him at a good clip. Liam instinctively starts to run before turning back to see Lisa charging at him in a full wind-sprint, eyes and mouth flaming green, mostly naked. *Whistle whistle click click, whistle whistle click.*

He half-stops as she overtakes him, and they tumble. They're both quickly back up and at it though, as he sheds his pack and coat, growling over his shoulder with venom: "Don't make me hurt you, Lis'."

"I'm gonna chain you to the bottom of the ocean, sweetheart!"

Within spitting distance of the basement door, Liam shifts gears and leaps up to grab the bottom rung of the fire escape. He climbs awkwardly as Lisa wraps her arms around his legs. She claws up a little higher and sinks her teeth all the way through his layers, deep into his calf muscle, thrashing her head around like an angry pit bull rag-dolling a chew toy.

The pain is blinding as he lifts his free leg and gives her a solid kick to the face. Falling back and hitting her head on the pavement with some force, she is out, stone-cold. He almost jumps down to finish her.

My God, who am I now?

Locking the ladder back up in place and out of reach, he begins a painful climb. His shoulder is on fire, his calf a knotty sponge. Up and up, landing after landing, energy fading fast. Making another flight of steps and humping around the rusty railing, Liam's confronted with a window that's pulsing with red light. Hands up over his head to cut the glare. A bathtub. Paul.

In an increasingly animated corner of City Park, the whole tree cove has taken on a hazy glow. And inside it, the twinkling star on top of the muck-jangle Christmas Tree is the pigeon's limp corpse, glimmering in the wind as if she's the keeper of an internal flame that flickers and dances on the edge of extinction. Her lifeblood seeping into the soil, conjuring ancient cycles and seasons.

The trinkets and jewelry act as ornaments, and try to impress by doing their best jumping-bean imitations. Gold popcorn on a mud pile.

"Ann. My true, dearest Ann. Angel. Please. You know. Today's the day. Tonight's the night. The longest night. A darkness utterly complete. Please. Come." Still admiring her handy work, a small trickle of blood escapes Chrystal's nose.

Agh. Well, all the excitement today. "See how I need you, lover…"

Liam heaves up the sash and, getting one leg in, it hits him sideways that there are thin waterspouts of blood twisting up from the floor feeding a black fog that envelops the ceiling. The transom is smashed, TVs all blaring static. "Paul?" There are thorns everywhere, and the tub is filled to the brim with them. "Oh—my—shit." He reaches in and fishes around. Nothing.

Spinning back toward the windows –and there he is. Sitting underneath the far ledge in a massive puddle of blood, legs spread, propped up against the wall. Head lilting as if taking pity on a bug crawling below. Blackened, twisted lips. Blue skin. He's gone.

Liam collapses, bearing the weight of the world, and crawls through a swirling mist. The echoes of helicopter blades whapping in his brain as he trudges along. "You're such a selfish asshole!"

With burning eyes, he reaches Paul's feet. They are ghastly, engraved with a dozen fresh, horrific cuts. But that's not what caused this. There's a thick piece of glass in his swollen left hand. It's from the transom. Inner thigh gashed wide open.

Knew exactly what he was doing. Plenty of leverage with that haughty wedge. Probably bled out in less than ten seconds. Fucker.

Reaching over and gently brushing Paul's cheek with the back of his hand, his heart breaks.

52

The clouds race along and darken by the second. Swaying unsteadily on the workroom floor with her legs firmly wrapped around Max, Abby almost nods off.

So now I have to pack all my shit and move out. Tonight. Or, like, now. Look at what that beefy bastard did to that doorframe? That could have been my head! I've got no choice. Universe on my side—not quite. Not today, anyway.

Zo always said that you need to ask the question. Okay. Please help me? Pretty fuckin' please? I don't even know who I'm supposed to be asking. And Chrystal –she hates me this much? All this madness? I mean, what in God's name… Does she have wee people thrashing through here doing her sorcery? Alright. Not exactly sorcery. Alchemical…Hoodoo. Whatever. No way Ms C cooked this up all by her lonesome. Bullshit. She loves this place. It's Chrystal. That bitch. I can feel it. Like I'm tryin' to fight Mothra herself now.

Her thoughts reach back to a time when Zoe was throwing out stories to a handful of people at the shop: "Earth, Air, Fire, Water, they don't carry empathy. Each of them is… utterly indifferent. And yet the spirits given agency by such means are far from it. They have intent. However opaque and twisted, it's there. Observation and passivity aren't the goals. Impetus will drive action. Still, the conjurer's power is always short-lived. The storm will pass, and so will their window to leach and manipulate. Or dance and sing. Or whatever their purpose was at the start. Most of these creatures are willing marionettes themselves. Glued to the possibility of what their temporary whirlwinds might bear. Hope. Faith. Benevolence. And, unfortunately at times, a most unrelenting darkness. So, when you encounter that particular flavor of enchantment on life's journey, ask for help. Ask out loud. Humble yourself. There is no freedom in a radiant reflection. That's just another string to be pulled…"

Abby reaches over and grabs Pearl for some comfort. She scrolls to 93.9, WXMS –playing holiday music year-round. Nat King Cole sings, "*Have yourself a merry little Christmas*" back at the windows.

Welling up again, and now Max is starting to sound like a pinball machine.

Keep the faith. Intent. Sacrifice. This will not beat me. Liam. Mom. Zoe. "Fuckin' help me." Jesus, please. What in hell is happening? Goddamn white people. I am not going to make it. I know I won't.

Yes you will.

No, I won't.

Nine little TVs in here? And where did all this crap come from?

Out of one of the mini-junk piles that sit in front of each screen, Liam picks up a long razor-thin gold strand.

This thing could be a belt. I think. Lisa? In here with Paul? And Paul running around all May-Day-n'-shit with this garbage? Impossible. No way. Can't be. Abby was right: something bigger, different, maybe…

Opening the closet to grab a dustpan, he's met with the sight of a dozen blades and knives vibrating all over the floor, spilling out of an antique box that's been smashed. They spin around and twist up in the air, bumping into the walls before falling back down. Lethal lightning bugs trying to get out of a jar. "Fuck you," slamming the door.

A vengeful pulse precedes his look, as the TVs stand defiant in their rumblings. One by one, he brushes up the mounds of debris and dumps them in the garbage, spilling half of the refuse all over the floor as he strides back and forth.

The daggers start to bang around harder inside the closet as he circles back to the first TV. He tries to shut off the buzzing set, but the screen just keeps humming and spewing static out into the room. Wrenching the plug out of the wall socket, he awkwardly kicks the mini-Zenith hard enough to tumble over himself. Barely catching his balance, he unplugs the next set, picks it straight up over his head, and lobs it into the kitchen. When it hits the floor, the tube explodes, spraying glass and sparks out into the air.

Nnnext.

Mostly cleaned up, Chrystal steps out onto the crunchy frozen grass and makes her way towards the jogging trail. Then all at once, her nose starts to bleed again, bad. She becomes torn between her own condition and that of her white tweed coat. Another level of blood gush begins, and she looks around for anything to help stem the tide. Tilting her head back, she tucks a small twig up under her cracked top lip. It used to work with a folded hunk of cardboard when she was a young girl. Would stop the flow of blood almost instantly. Not today, however.

Freshly out of the shower, and randomly having seizure-like shakes that cause her to embrace indiscriminate objects in the room as if she's demanding answers, JT gradually tosses everything in her apartment that will fit into large garbage bags. She rifles through a stack of stolen IDs, trying to find one that might remotely look like her, if you squint. Out of the ceiling tumbles a tightly bound wad of cash that gets rammed into her pants.

An obnoxious pounding at the door stops the train.

Whoever it is, has their hand over the peephole. It starts again. Echoes from a deep chasm–*Boom—Boom—Boom*. Getting down on all fours, JT lines up eye-level with the floor just as two large white gloves slide in under the door and start slapping her face, fingers spread, with assertion. Desperately swatting at them, they do a gyrating dance in the air just out of reach. Bowing to each other and performing do-si-does. She swears for a moment she can hear a square-dance caller giving out instructions through heavy static…

> … *bow to your corner*
> *now to your pard'*
> *throw that chicken*
> *back out in the yard…*

just as the pair loop around high overhead and come steaming back down to whack her anywhere they can find an opening. Jamming fingers up her nose, flicking her eyeballs, cracking her bottom hard enough to launch her into the air. "Stop fucking touching me!"

Diving onto the bed, she quickly balls up in a blanket as Batts's disembodied white gloves continue to orbit her frame and find ways to connect solidly with her flesh. "Stop it! Somebody! Help!"

259

53

"Of course, when I need you most... you little shit..." As Abby scrolls through the stations, Pearl just spits out one commercial after another.

"That's Uncle Buskie's Specialty Meats. Over forty-four years of quality and..."
    "After they'd thought about it, long and hard, they agreed it really was the best set of kitchen knives they'd ever..."
    "... had a vacation like that? Then why wait? Be one of the next ten callers and..."

Finally. A little Van Morrison to help me maybe not fucking kill myself. *Into the Mystic.* Frikken lifeline.
    The contents of the bucket swirl hard enough to make the handle rattle and her head throb. Abby pulls out the postcard for one last look and wishes with all her heart she could just live on that street. The one where the snow perpetually falls, and even imperfect souls are allowed to dwell in peace.
    I'm completely lost now. No anchors. Just drift. Chasing shadows. And in such harsh light –brandishing pronouncements one after another in an endless queue. Yeah, you can keep all that petty derision to yourself. I don't need your shit anymore, either.

Every time Liam unplugs one TV, the static hum on the others jumps in volume. The next set shatters into a million pieces when he tosses it across the room.
    "And that would be... five! PRICKS!"
    A pair of scissors makes its way out of the closet, sails through the air, and just misses his head, sticking into the wall right in front of him. "Holy

fuck!" A fine mist of blood rains down from the ceiling as he pulls the next plug –"Sssix…"

Chrystal goes down like a rapidly deflating carnival prop. The blood dripping out of her ears catches her lips, and really doesn't taste all that bad.

My God, I'm having a stroke, aneurysm, I don't… Ann, Ann, why have you abandoned me?

Her wide-brimmed hat kicks off and frisbees out into the park on a trajectory that, on a more temperate day, would have elicited UFO sightings from multiple vantage points.

Standing up militant in the middle of the workroom, Abby's had enough.

Fuck packing. I'm always running away from something. What is it that I'm never running towards? Alright. Here's one –never ran towards that window. Ten stories high?... Looks like a pip.

She embraces Max warmly. "Wanna come with me, buddy?" Tiptoeing over to take a peek, she looks down as best she can, with her nose squashed against the vibrating glass. "Take a little trip? Maybe we can find a way out together, yeah?" Her whole body trembles.

Through a blurry haze she catches her reflection, and the image looking back at her is just a featureless blob of rolling TV static wrapped in electric hair. "Snow face."

This is it. All roads lead here.

Shifting her gaze to the swirling menagerie in the bucket, the jewelry flips and hops like frogs in a maelstrom. Hoop handle firmly grasped, she slowly starts to twirl, holding Max straight out at arm's length.

Almost prone, Chrystal leans on one elbow, trying to yell out over the howling wind, but it's no use. She sees no one.

Please. Not now. I'm so close.

Sparks and blood drip from her eyes and do ball-lighting jiggles on the ground in front of her.

Dragging a dumpster with frozen wheels over to the fire escape, Lisa climbs on top and, stretching up on her tiptoes, just barely grabs the ladder. Determined and focused, she climbs. *"Whistle whistle whistle whistle whistle..."*

Abby spins in circles all around the workroom, leaning way back. The trinkets in Max's shell are glowing bright enough to illuminate her face, and the path he's carving in the air has a vertical dynamic to it —as if she's giving a small child an airplane ride up and down as they fly.

Spiraling towards the windows, she ramps up her speed and screams at the top of her lungs, slinging the bucket and shattering the glass. An updraft momentarily lifts Max and flips him over, just as an avalanche of snow thunders down from the heavens with a magnitude she's never seen, and thrusts the silver vessel earthward, scattering its cursed belongings to the sacred winds.

As he wraps his trembling hand around the last plug on the final television set from hell, the closet door bursts open, and all the various blades thunder across the room towards Liam's face. Following through with a willful yank on the cord, the TV screen explodes, just as a loud crash emanates from high above. He half collapses against the wall.

Maybe that was a bomb. Go ahead. Blow us up. Like I give a shit.

The swarm of flying cutlery falls to the floor, harmlessly sliding up around his feet. He looks outside at the swirling snow as it pours out of the sky like an undulating sea of white locusts. A bucket sails by, tumbling through the air just beyond the fire escape.

Only a few rungs up on her climb, Lisa's shoulder is squarely pommeled by a howling Max, and she once again falls back, bounces off the dumpster, and hits the pavement in the alley on all fours. Hanging her head, she gradually becomes mesmerized by the falling snow.

Chrystal's face smacks the ground as the storm moves into the park.

Somehow, she painfully manages to prop herself back up on her hands.

Then, through a veil of electric noise, she sees her. Up on the path. Not more than ten yards away. She tries to shout, but only whispers can escape her foamy lips. "Ann! Ann! I knew it! I knew you would come for me. Ann! Help mmme! My only lllove."

Zoe walks up next to Annalise. Side by side, and thoroughly unmoved, they simply stare at Chrystal as she pleads for her life.

"Zoe? Is that you?" Still whisper-shouting into the ferocious storm. "Thank God. Zzzoe. Ann. Please…" Chrystal reaches toward them as if to pull, reflexively nodding.

Scout swoops down over the treeline at the edge of the park and is zeroed in, wings pinned back, slashing through the raging blizzard. Auguring slalom-like and cruising low, he barrels ahead with wicked speed. Flying just inches off the ground now, he angles up at the last second and plunges head-first into Chrystal's eye-socket, burrowing into her skull.

Frantically flailing at his furiously flapping wings, she rolls on her back and cackles out wails that sound more like walrus barks. Scout relentlessly twists around the inside edge of her frontal lobe as deep and as hard as he can. She goes limp.

Flopping out onto the snow a few feet away and scraping the gore from his face, Scout rights himself, standing straight as an arrow. Then ducks down into a barrel-shimmy not unlike a wet St Bernard climbing out of a lake.

He takes off and gains altitude to make another run, but there's no need. She is no more, plainly; even as the snow quickly starts to cover her body.

now - dead - what - bitch - hurt - dead - too - tough - bad - break - fight - me - witch

JT cautiously peeks out from underneath the blanket, and the gloves are lying limp on the floor. Her eyes dart around the ceiling to check for any other flying objects before she leaps up and tosses the white devils into one of the heaving trash bags. She forearm-brushes in the remaining contents of her tables and dressers with abandon, then drags everything to the basement.

Coaxing the dumpster back to the wall, Lisa looks through a couple of others and finds a ripped-up T-shirt to cover her freezing chest. She reaches into yet another and throws a large bag over her shoulders, scanning both sides of the alley for more clothes and coverings as she heads towards home, pressing steadily through the snow in bare feet.

Zoe reaches over and gives Annalise's hand a light squeeze, then walks away. Leaving her to stand quite alone in the howling wind to watch her familiar slowly disappear under sheets of white.

Abby and Liam stare out of windows a few floors apart in the old Lexington Arms. Through clear eyes, and with lucid vision, they watch the hundred-year storm come ranging in. Both now inexplicably feeling that the day holds the possibility, however remote or slight, that their demons may finally be cast aside.

54

Reg never got to take his bathroom break. He's checked twice now, and both times the door was locked.

He knocks hard with the side of his fist. "C'mon Batts, stop pissin' around." Nothing. No running water, silence.

Maybe that jackass locked it on his way out or something. "Batts?"

He puts his key in the door.

Resting on the sidewalk by the street are his lobster-red felt coat, folded immaculately, along with his starched hat, sitting neatly on top. Both succumbing to rapidly accumulating snow.

In the distance, Reg walks down the middle of the road in an over-priced dress shirt, watching the trees sway in the violent weather, wondering how many inches they're eventually supposed to get today.

Wearing overalls with one strap, and a cowboy hat over her freshly shaved head, JT moves steadily towards the back of the Greyhound bus as the other passengers file in. She had to put on four pairs of socks to make the snakeskin boots work, but it was worth it in order to complete the outfit.

I can hang with this. Wish I had a bandana or something to cover my nose, though. The pungent bouquet of fake leather, BO, and stale cigarettes are teaming up for quite the nasal assault in this junker.

She tosses her backpack up on an overhead rack and takes a seat next to a little girl in a red-and-white holiday dress, her mother already asleep by the window.

The little princess, way too loud: "What happened to your eyes?"

JT mouths the words *fuck you*, and the little girl yells out, "Hey!"

Her mom jumps as JT tries to hide underneath her massive ten-gallon hat. "What is it, honey?" Sizing up JT.

"Ohhh, nothing. I'm hungry, Mommy."

"Oh, for the love of God, give it a rest Henrietta." She quickly nods back off as the bus pulls out of the station.

JT wonders if she can handle this. "So, how old are you?"

"Seven and three-quarters. I'll be eight in eighty-eight days. Um, yeah, eighty-eight."

"What do you like to do?"

"I play with my friends a lot, and sometimes, when I see my cousins, too. We're going to visit my cousins now. They're in Reno. Reno's hot, but Mommy says it's a dry heat, so that's okay. All I know is we stay in the pool most of the time out there because dry heat is still kinda hot. They have a dog –Teddy. We don't have a dog. My mom is a magic seamstress. She made this dress. Do you like it?"

JT nods, eyeing up other seats she may grab when this kid falls asleep. Henrietta looks bored.

God help me. "Do you like magic?"

"Oh, very much. We saw a magician last year, Fredrick the Phenom. He made a tiger disappear. We—"

"Do you want me to show you a few tricks?"

"Wow! Sure!" JT gives her the "shhh" sign and pulls out a tiny pink clutch from her overalls. "Hey! That's mine!"

Her mom starts to grumble but just shifts in her seat, lightly snoring, head bouncing off the window when the bus hits a bump.

JT hands it back. "Want me to show you how I did it?" Morphing into curiosity, Henrietta nods. JT walks her through the basics of the art. "If you want to distract them, never say 'um' or 'well' or 'so' while you have eye contact. Always make it bigger than that. Make shit up."

"Ah, you used a bad word again."

"Wanna walk off this bus with all of your stuff, little girl?"

"I'm listening."

"If you're in a jam, use a sudden head-turn. They'll follow your gaze." JT whips around to look down the aisle, and Henrietta spontaneously kneels up on her seat to do the same. When she sits back down, JT once again shows her the purse. "See? Want to try some?"

Snatching back her petite bag once again, pouting. "Okay."

JT holds her hand out flat. "Stingray."

Henrietta mimics: "Stingray."

Separating her fingers –two and two: "Lobster."

"Lobster."

Pulling her thumb underneath: "Bird."

"Stingray, lobster, bird. Stingray, lobster, bird..."

"Henrietta, focus." JT reaches across and pulls the zipper on mom's handbag silently, smooth as glass. Henrietta's eyes get huge. "Shhh." Showing Henrietta her hand –flat and into the purse, then opening her fingers, she grips something. Adding her thumb, she slowly pulls out a set of keys –no jingling, held tight, and quickly into her pocket. All while she easily could have been juggling with her other hand and carrying on a conversation with a passenger across the aisle.

Silently returning the keys, she whispers, "Your turn." Henrietta nods. "Now, remember what I told you."

Right. Stingray, lobster. Reaching around gently, she grabs something. Bird. Henrietta pulls out a condom. Whispering, excited: "I did it! I did it! Wwwhat is this thing?"

JT grabs it and drops it back in the purse. "Oh, that's yucky adult medicine. But you get it now, right? If you go into a pocket, your hand should be the shape of where it's heading. Keeping it flat is fine, but you may need to curve it a bit, depending on the situation. Always lead the action. If you can't control your subject's attention, or the conversation, or if it's too risky – you never do the job. Walk away. Hear me? Walk–away. It's all up to you, from beginning to end. That's how you stay in charge. But don't underestimate yourself, either. No one's gonna expect Polly Purebred to be snatchin' up car keys."

"I'm not so pure."

"So I'm learning. But you've got a great cover, kid. I'd use it."

Practicing: "Stingray, lobster, bird... And, I'm in charge? Really?"

"You are now, honey. It's your world." She sweeps her hand as if stardust is falling from her fingertips. "All these people? They thought they were just goin' for a bus ride, but little did they know –they were steppin' straight out into Henrietta town."

Huge smile: "I think I have to go to the bathroom."

"I'll keep an eye on ya, killer." Not such a bad kid.

Detective Anderson walks Abby to her apartment, looking up at the transoms. "You sure you'll be okay here tonight?"

"Yeah, I'll be fine. Thank you, Detective." Sounding like a child who's already asleep before they hit the bed, carrying an equally worn-out Stewart tucked up in her arm.

As they round the corner, she sees something dangling from her apartment doorknob. Snatching it up, she works her key.

Anderson's watching her closely. "Everything okay?"

"Yeah. Just beat up."

"Alright. We'll be keeping an eye on the building for a while, and we'll have a uniform out front most of the time, at least for a few days until we can get a better grip on this." He flips through his notes. "No word at all from… JT… is it?"

"No. Like I said, we aren't close."

"Well, officially, we're going to list her as a 'missing person' case for now. For her own protection."

"Understood."

Handing her his card. "We'll talk again soon. Goodnight, Abby."

"Night, Officer."

She shuts the door and throws the bolt-lock. The sillcock key slips down around her neck –a perfect fit– and Stewart, no amateur by any stretch, immediately starts begging for food.

55

I love the mist steaming up off the river on these cold mornings. And the air smells so clean. Fourteen inches of snow last night! My goodness. And they say we're getting more today. Dangerous, actually. So pretty, though.

The hulking black car pulls up as far as seems reasonable. "Wait here for a minute, please, kind sir." Annalise scooches across the back seat.

"Alright. Be careful out there. You sure…"

"I'm not helpless. I'll be right back."

John doesn't like it but just reaches up and turns on the radio.

"And it's almost nine AM at WNEW, headlines and a traffic update next…"

She plods through the snow towards the riverbank, slowly and deliberately. Picking up decent-sized rocks along the way and dropping them into her tote.

A tiny, brave bird hops along the water's edge, snatching crumbs and bits from the crevices. The river rolls and rumbles, its banks showing beards of white. The entire breadth of this roaring beast will be completely covered with thick ice soon enough.

She removes her gloves and throws them into the huge purse for good measure, zips it up tight, and with one lunging swing, tosses the bulging bag as far as she's able out into the water. It splashes hard, bobs up once, then rushes downstream, sinking out of sight.

"Well thanks, Cindy. Sounds like the holidays aren't so jolly out there in traffic land. And now for some breaking news and a big story out of downtown this morning where a couple of tourists uncovered a gruesome, grizzly find in City Park —an as-of-yet unidentified… headless corpse, frozen solid, and buried in the fresh snow. The police aren't giving out any other—"

Annalise bounces back into the car, shivering but vibrant. "Ahh. Are you hungry?"

"Are my eyes open? Who you talkin' to?"

"Good. Breakfast?" She blows on her cupped hands.

"I was thinking more along the lines of… an Irish Coffee?"

"God, I love when you talk like that. Let's make that happen, shall we?"

.

56

Valentine's Day came and went. Liam had always considered it a weak excuse for a holiday, made up by the greeting card companies to torture everyone just a little bit more. Like Christmas isn't enough? Thank God all this crapolazola is over with for a minute. Why is February the suicide month? Valentine's Day.

The weather hasn't really let up since the Solstice, but at least it's been a little warmer the last few days. And Nick appears to be doing just fine out here so far. Hopefully, the horses keep him level.

As they cross the street, two of the carriages pull out, leaving just one that's hooked up to a massive white steed. These carriage breeds are usually Percheron, but this one is big enough to be a Belgian.

Liam ignores the driver, who's smoking a cigar and reading the paper; he just starts petting the majestic white monster uninvited. "Hi, buddy, you gonna go stompin' around in this crazy snow today?"

Nick tentatively pets the giant horse as well, running his hand down the mane toward the shoulder. The horse jumps a little but is mostly loving the attention. Laughing: "I can't believe the shit you have me doin' out here..." Then his whole demeanor changes. Stepping back, breathing a little heavier. "Gotta go." And he's down the sidewalk in a flash.

"Take good care of her, pal." The driver doesn't acknowledge as Liam scurries after Nick, who's already a good thirty yards away, head-on-a-swivel, and crossing the street toward home.

In the midst of a quiet night, Abby and Liam slowly stroll along the boulevard arm-in-arm. The steady snow is falling thick but gently past the streetlights, making a fresh powdery layer on top of the existing frozen stuff.

Stopping in front of Zoe's Occult & Mystic, she pats his shoulder and runs inside.

Zoe is on her pedestal, preaching to a group of wide-eyed customers. Without breaking stride in her speech, she smiles at Abby who's flashing a peace sign and as she makes her way to the back of the store.

"...Quite often, the tendency and natural impulse is to think that if we look closely, or close enough, that we can see the spirits and the spiritual all around us. But sometimes we need to set our sights much further away, through the trees and out into the distance, to the horizon and beyond. Forgetting about sharp focus and just letting go. And thus - embracing spooky action at a distance. For in those moments there is nothing spooky at all in the knowledge that someone or something seemingly unnamed is staring back at us through the ether. This is when we blossom, when wisdom becomes power. And all at once we cross our manufactured barriers into a world of absolute bliss and revitalizing peace. Falling headlong into the prenatal fluid we'd so long ago abandoned for logic and reason at all costs.

"And for the first time we'll come to grips with the realization that those watchful eyes were in fact always there. We will in the midst of that epiphany know in our hearts that not only were the benevolent guardians standing with us from the beginning, but those same glistening entities who bless us over and over again as they dance a sacred dance out in the atmosphere - they are also us. Every one of us. Not a reflection - but our actual souls. The spirits are in us, and we are, without a doubt, in the spirits. There is no difference. *We* are all around. *We* are protecting ourselves all the time, as much as any entity does. Our omnipresence is eternal, and has nothing to do with our skin and bones. But is instead part and parcel of a glorious and radiant light..."

With some hesitation, Abby retrieves the postcard from her purse and takes off her gloves, smoothly touching the picture. Then into the *give & take* box it goes, immersed once again with the mish-mosh of random photos.

Zoe hardly notices Abby leaving as she continues to charm the flock. "There isn't any love in the universe like spiritual love. It always outlasts the flesh…"

Shuffling up to Liam and shaking some of the snow out of his hair, Abby gives him a quick kiss. They continue on in silence.

All at once, she pulls him down the sidewalk.

Hotdog stand. You bet your sweet ass we're stopping here.

Manning the lop-sided cart is the same fixture of a man Liam had left his linen rack with over the holidays. The guy looks up and does a double-take. "Are you that asshole who left his fuckin' dresses with me?"

Abby's eyes sparkle as Liam cough-laughs. "Yeah, I'm sorry about that. I—"

"Let me give you fair warning here, dickweed –don't ever pull that shit again. I'm not your goddamn babysitter. And another thing…"

"Heyyy, while you two are catching up, can I put in my order, please?" The vendor just stares. "One dog, natural casing, extra onions." Painted smile as she looks over at Liam. "Sorry, man, I'm starving."

The vendor mechanically begins to slap the onions on the wiener. "So right, now watch this. Here's a good example." He hands her the hotdog, and she hands him the money.

Taking a big bite. "Mmm. And whatever he wants."

"Uh, sure, I'll have the same."

"Hey, you payin' attention over here? Money… comes this way. Food… goes that way. Only. Forever, and ever, amen. Got it? You hand me food back again and I'll snap your arm like a Goddamned twig. Twitchy bastard."

Abby is all about the feasting, trying not to laugh.

My god, she is so beautiful, and enjoying every second of this. "Okay, okay, I get it. I apologize. It was such a crazy day…"

The slight vendor starts on Liam's order with a snort, then suddenly waves out his arms, flicking onions into the crisp winter air. "And who the fuck comes out in this weather?"

Epilogue

Summertime in the park.

When you see the same thing every day, it slowly disappears. That's why Lisa travels, likes to stay in motion. It forces her awareness. If you're sedentary, it's all the same. Let's say you grow up in Hawaii, or in the furrows of the Rocky Mountains, or on Santorini Island, and live there your whole life –is it awe-inspiring? Maybe. Doubt it, though. You may love your home, but there's no way it can feel perpetually nascent after you've soaked in that same tub for such long stretches.

So it is with places that basically have the same weather year-round, versus more fluid locales that go through a radical change of seasons. If the shift is dynamic enough –from ice to flame, for instance– it's like traversing a rugged canyon, and in the end, you can't help but grow. Spiritual molting.

The first truly warm day of summer smells so green, so fully alive. Jasmine and sage. Freshly cut grass and hemlock. Her candy-apple red hair is pulled back in a tight bun, blazer of her stretch-wool business suit draped over her shoulder. Strolling along slowly, Lisa is utterly at ease. She had long ago broken free of her zombie orbit to feel the warmth of other suns. And today, she is allowing herself to realize some victory.

Heading off the trail, she plays with a border collie for a few minutes while the owner pathetically tries to hit on her.

Spotting a bench in the shade, she takes a load off, vigorously rubbing her feet.

Still can't get used to these shoes. But the leap-frog promotion to VP of the Design Division, and a new penthouse apartment uptown, certainly do take the sting out of, well, just about everything.

The pigeons come around to gauge her charity. "Sorry, guys, I don't have anything, I don't think…" Shuffling through her bag, Lisa finds a couple packets of restaurant crackers. "Ah. Here ya go. Hey, be nice. Everybody, share."

A straggler tries to join in but is mostly shunned. Every time he tries to get a nibble, two of the larger birds chase him right to the edge of the feeding circle. Poor guy. His coloring is so cool. White and brown patches.

When he turns and comes closer, she tries to scoop him up, gently, but he flitters away. Next time around, he mostly lets her cradle and lift him, still resisting some, yet awkwardly settling into her hands, cooing. "What happened to your eye, little soldier? Jeez." Looks like he's seen better days. She pets his head in a smooth line.

Seems strange to say, but he's giving off a vibe as if he's depressed. Well… that deck back at the apartment is huge, right? "You want to come home with me? I've got a great place for ya. Sound good? Now… What shall we call you… Palomino, yes? Obvious choices are still choices. Pally for short. How's that, huh? How we doin' so far?"

The nice lady holds the oh-so-recently christened Palomino close to her chest and heads back out of the park.

A little freaked, he thinks about trying to wiggle out of her grasp and fly away, but he's so spent. And she's really warm. Smells good. The palms of her hands don't menace.

And these days, it seems like he's lost just about everything. Maybe there's something better waiting for him on the other side of this. Maybe it's a chance worth taking.

About the Author

Batman & baby sis

harlan garrett is member of the transom project art collective and lives in the Midwest USA, along with a fluctuating menagerie of benevolent spirits & magical objects.

Please contact us if you'd like to write a review, enter our random shiny trinket lottery, or for any old reason at all.

@harlanpoprocks

thebloodofabutterly.com

harlanmichaelgarrett@protonmail.com

09e6afbd-52b2-4a45-85b4-7f69aa748c0bR01